# The Farmer's DAUGHTER

## Robbi McCoy

Bella
BOOKS
2014

Bella Books, Inc.
P.O. Box 10543
Tallahassee, FL 32302

First Bella Books Edition 2014

Editor: Katherine V Forrest
Cover Designer: Linda Callaghan

ISBN: 978-1-59493-381-3

## About the Author

Robbi McCoy lives with her partner and cat in the Central Valley of California between the mountains and the sea. She is an avid hiker with a particular fondness for the deserts of the American Southwest. She also enjoys gardening, culinary adventures, travel and the theater. She is recently retired from her career as a software specialist and web designer.

# Dedication

To all the bindle stiffs, blinkies, wingies, gandy dancers, road sisters and boxcar Willies who rode the rails of America, including Dot's grandfather John who lost his leg on the tracks. Theirs is a rich and colorful subculture that is nearly extinct today but played a leading role in shaping the modern United States—its labor force, its railroads, its social programs, its folklore and its folk music. This book is dedicated to the American hobo, an icon of twentieth-century America.

# Acknowledgments

The story of Mutt and Annie is dear to me. It has been percolating in my mind and notebooks for years, and I am so thankful that it is finally ready to take flight. Among those who helped me bring it to the page are the following.

Many thanks to the fabulous editorial duo of Katherine V. Forrest and Cath Walker for your excellent advice and many good saves. To Karin Kallmaker, thank you for suggesting a way to structure this story that made it work exactly the way it should. All of the women of the Bella Books family are talented, experienced and professional, and I am privileged to benefit from their desire to produce quality fiction.

I thank my grandmother Arlie McCoy for stories of what it was like to be a poor Southerner coming to California in the 1930s when vast numbers of Americans were on the move looking for work. I only wish I'd asked her for more.

My heartfelt appreciation goes to my mentor Gladys Andersen for her help with this book and all previous ones, published and unpublished. Thank you for your time, excellent advice and the unwavering support you have given to my writing career throughout the years.

As always, the contribution of my partner Dot has been invaluable. This book was a long time in the making and she was with me all the way, including hopping on and off antique boxcars at the excellent California State Railroad Museum in Old Sacramento so I could get the moves just right in my mind. And a big thank you for helping me write the folk song, "Tumbleweed Jack." It was a breakthrough moment when you actually came up with the music for that one and sang it out loud. Darlin', I'd juble joo with you any day.

# PROLOGUE

She pushed through the screen door onto the wide front porch with its ancient but still functional glider and dozens of wind chimes hanging from every available spot, creating a lively enclosure of shells, metal, glass and ceramic, all of it quivering in the breeze in a mosaic of shape and color, and of course sound. Ringing, dinging, clanging, tinkling bits of detritus collected from city streets, junkyards and beaches, resurrected and reimagined in the minds of many nascent artists, each was a unique and personal gift from someone who had come here and then moved on. These diverse creations were a celebration of those people and a reminder of how they had enriched her life. Singing jubilantly, they surrounded her like a loving embrace.

She reached up to finger a ring of thin metal suspended on a wire, one of eight such rings fashioned from tin cans, arranged strategically so they played against each other's edges. This mobile was rusty with age, but occupied a place of honor between the two columns framing the entrance to the porch. This had been the first. She still loved to hear its melody, a light, tinny clanking that transported her through time and space as certain sounds and odors do. She gave it a jiggle to excite a tune from it.

She placed her cane carefully ahead of her feet as she took each of the three stairs down from the musical haven of the porch into the front yard where a beagle ran up to her, tail wagging. He followed her down the path and through the gate to the road, where she retrieved the day's mail. The mailbox was stuffed with a triumph of pastel-colored envelopes addressed by hand to "Ms. Shirley Hopper" and originating from all over the country. She clutched these covetously close and smiled to herself, aware as she often was these days that her life was and had been full. Young people didn't write letters anymore, but at least some of them still sent birthday cards in the mail.

Thinking about her age, she had trouble comprehending the span of her life. The years just seemed to sneak up while a person wasn't looking, and pretty soon the way forward looks quite a bit shorter, and the way back looks improbably distant, so far away that it fades into a fog and the details blur and mix themselves up. The reason it seems like it went so fast, she had decided long ago, is that one forgets so much. Whole months of one's life, totally forgotten. It was entirely possible that more had been forgotten than remembered, especially in these later years. You can't choose what you remember, but that's okay because in her experience people remembered more good than bad. At least she did. Bad memories were dulled by time until she almost never thought of them anymore and no longer felt a sting from their long-eroded barbs.

On her way back to the house with her birthday booty, she paused beside the peach tree to examine the fruit. This old tree could still put out a crop of the sweetest white peaches in all of Mississippi. They hung heavy on the branches, most of them still holding on to a green tint, but the higher up ones that faced the sun looked close to ripe. When a tree puts out superior fruit like this one did, people naturally want to know what variety it is. Way back when, she could answer that question correctly, but she'd long since forgotten, so now she just said, "Annie's Peach."

She had planted this tree as a tribute to Annie in 1951 when she had returned home from her travels. White peaches had always reminded her of Annie. In her youth, she had spent many a hot summer afternoon in the boughs of a peach tree, day-dreaming and breathing in their delicate and tantalizing perfume and admiring their bashful blushing skin covered with downy hairs sparkling like tiny slivers of glass in the sunshine. A white peach is a tormentingly beautiful fruit, as perfect as anything you could conjure in a dream. The look and smell of it seduces your eyes and nose, and your mouth must follow. As your teeth sink through the skin and into the juicy flesh, a burst of warm honey nectar floods your tongue and runs down your chin. That's when you think, this is just about the best thing in God's creation!

She had seen a lot of peaches in her day. Thousands, maybe millions. In South Carolina, Georgia and California, stacked in crates waiting to be loaded on trucks. Truckloads of peaches. The thing about peaches is that you can't pick them ripe, not commercially. They're too fragile. They bruise as soon as your fingers land on them. So the pickers had to take them underripe. Working those orchards, she had always been sorry to have to do that because there's nothing better than a tree-ripened peach.

*Yes, sir*, she thought, squinting up through the branches at the topmost fruit, meeting Annie had been the pivotal event in her life. It had permeated the spirit of everything that came after. It had changed her world forever, bringing love and hope and the possibility of happiness. If she had never met Annie, she wondered, what would she have been? Who could say? It had been too important to imagine things any differently.

In a long life, a lot of days pass without leaving a mark, but that warm April day in 1942 was something she still remembered intensely, and she knew she'd never forget a speck of it. She reached her hand to her chin involuntarily, running her index finger over the tiny, smooth scar that could still be seen if a person knew to look for it. Life had been plenty rough that year. She shook her head with wonder, contemplating all those decades since, yet the loveliness of Annie's peach-like cheeks were as fresh in her mind as the day she had first set eyes on her, an uncommonly pretty girl on a farm in Nebraska, fully ripe at the age of sixteen and wanting something terrible to be picked off her tree.

With one arm hugging her haul of birthday cards against her chest, she reached up as high as she could into the tree, her eye on a piece of fruit with a full blush on it. She'd lost a couple of inches of height over the years, but she was still taller than most women. Pushing herself up on her toes, she managed to get her fingers around that beauty and pull it free of its branch. She held it in the palm of her hand, admiringly, the first ripe peach of summer.

Just like Annie, she thought, ripe and ready to be plucked. There's not much you can do with a piece of fruit that's ready to be plucked...except pluck it.

*So that's what I did*, she thought with a sly, private smile, and bit into the peach.

# PART ONE

*April, 1942*

# CHAPTER ONE

Fragrant spring grass waved in front of her eyes as Mutt glanced around to make sure no railroad cops were in view. The sun was just about to peek up into a cantaloupe sky and the air still clung to the cool of the night as the highball whistle sounded, one short and one long blast, signaling that the train was about to leave the yard. A few minutes later the locomotive huffed by her hiding place, sending up a furious cloud of black smoke. She sprang to her feet and started running, running like a jackrabbit with a hound on her tail, running in the same direction as the groaning train and just as fast, closing the distance between herself and the open boxcar she had her eye on. The plaintive whistle blew again as the locomotive labored out of the rail yard and the yellow cars of the Union Pacific picked up speed.

Alongside the front of the car, she matched her pace to the train's, her pack smacking against her back. She planned her mount, knowing that one careless mistake could plunge her under the wheels where she'd lose her life or, at the very least, a leg or two. She caught hold of the grab bar and swung herself up. She planted both feet firmly on the stirrup, hugging the ladder rungs close to her chest. She heaved a sigh of relief. She had made it!

She must have done this a hundred times already, but each time it was just as thrilling as the time before. The rush, the danger, the feeling of her muscles pitted against the force and speed of the big machine made her feel alive.

But she wasn't safe yet. Hanging on the side of the car, she could be easily spotted, so she climbed up to the top deck, then crawled to the edge and lowered herself over. She pivoted in through the open door with a practiced routine as smooth and graceful as any ballerina's pirouette. She prided herself on this move. Not everybody could do it. She hopped into a corner and settled down to ride.

On the other side of the car, in the opposite corner, the dark figure of a man crouched in the shadows, motionless. After a momentary stiffening, she sloughed off her bedroll. As her pulse slowed to normal and her eyes adjusted to the dim light in the car, she saw her companion's face more clearly. He wore a dark hat and a dark brown suit over a white shirt, typical hobo attire. His tie was undone, hanging around his neck alongside his open shirt collar. He half sat, half lay against his bedroll looking her over.

"Morning." He spoke in a gravelly voice forced unnaturally loud to reach her over the clatter of the moving train.

"I hope y'all don't mind sharing," she replied in her practiced timbre. It was meant to sound like that of a young man, a tenor voice, not too high and not too low.

"My ride is your ride, friend."

Sometimes she could tell where a person was from by the way he talked. Riding the trains, she had met people from all over, even from foreign countries. She wasn't sure about this man. All she could tell for sure was that he wasn't from the South. He was a Yankee.

The train curved to the north on a wide arcing track and the rising sun flooded into the interior of the car, illuminating its corners. Her companion had big watery eyes and a thick stubble over his face. He looked to be about forty-five or fifty, but it was always hard to tell age on these wandering men. They seemed to age faster than most folks.

"Got a smoke?" he asked.

Mutt shook her head. "Don't smoke."

"What are you called?" He sat up straighter.

"Mutt."

"Mutt? Just Mutt?"

"Just Mutt."

"I'm Frogman." He lifted his hat. "Pleased to make your acquaintance, Mutt."

The faster the train went, the louder it roared, making it impossible to converse from one end of the car to the other, putting an end to their small talk. Mutt linked her hands behind her head and watched the scenery fly by.

After a half hour, Frogman took a chunk of cheddar cheese out of a paper sack and held it up so she could see it. He waved her over. He didn't look crazy or mean, she decided, and she figured she knew how to recognize crazy and mean by now. She moved to his side of the car as he cut a hunk off the cheese with a pocketknife. He handed it to her and she ate it in one bite.

"Why're you called Frogman?" she asked. "You pretty good at gigging frogs?"

He shook his head. "It's because of my eyes. When I open them big, they say I look like a frog." To demonstrate, he opened his eyes as wide as he could.

Mutt fell into a convulsion of laughter, his face was so comical with his bulging googly eyes.

He chuckled at her reaction. "Why do they call you Mutt?"

She shrugged, thinking about her freckled, turned-up nose and stiff, tobacco-colored hair. Even cut short like it was now, it was hard to tame. "Just because I'm kinda funny looking, I guess. It's the name my daddy's always called me. It don't bother me none. I got used to it long since."

"You don't seem funny looking to me."

Mutt kept her thoughts to herself, realizing that she might not look so funny to somebody thinking she was a boy. Nowadays, catching a glimpse of herself in a mirror and seeing the round brown eyes of a handsome young man looking back, she sort of liked the way she looked. Looking like a boy wasn't hard for her with her long-limbed, lanky frame and almost no curves. She'd always been thin, but after more than a year on the iron road, she was even thinner. With the right clothes, the right haircut, a few smudges of ash on her chin, she fooled them most of the time. Just like her daddy had always said.

"You'd make a better boy than a girl," he had complained. "It's a damned shame! Underneath all that grime, there's a real pretty girl in there. I know that's so 'cause you got your mama's eyes. One of these days you're gonna have to change your tune if you're ever gonna get yourself a man. No man's gonna look twice at you with your farm britches and dirty fingernails and the way you hop over fences and never walk through a gate like a lady. If you're fixin' to be an old maid, well, you're going about it all right."

It was fine with Mutt if no man ever looked twice at her. More than fine. *Finer than a frog's hair*, she thought, invoking one of her favorite expressions.

As time went by, she had gotten better and better at her disguise, learning how to walk and talk so nobody'd get an inkling. She imitated the swagger of the young men and the way they sat with their legs stretched out in front of them crossed at the ankles. She even imitated the way they put a hand over their privates while they slept as if protecting themselves from a bogeyman.

She didn't mind being a girl, but she had learned soon after leaving home that it was safer not to be a girl traveling alone, especially among lonely, desperate men, many of whom reminded her of her father…and not in a good way. After only two weeks on the road, she had decided on this disguise, and things had immediately gotten easier for her.

Frogman offered her another slice of cheese and she took it. She had last eaten two hours before at a hobo camp near Des Moines where the menu had consisted of bread and sausages, or, as the hobos termed it, "punk and gut." She wasn't yet hungry, but she'd learned not to turn down food when it was offered. You never knew when you'd get your next meal.

"Where you headed, Mutt?"

"I'm catching the Overland to California."

"I'll be stopping off at Omaha, so you'll have the place to yourself after that. But this freight stops at every jerkwater town.

Let me give you a tip. If you get off at Columbus, Nebraska, a red ball is coming through that yard at five o'clock tomorrow morning. You catch that and you'll be in Cali in the wink of an eye. The name of that train is Big Charlotte, number 4403. Columbus is a hot yard, though, so be extra careful."

"Much obliged!" said Mutt. She knew that a "red ball" was a through train carrying fruit and vegetables, one of the best ways for a hobo to cover long distances fast. Listening to the old-timers was the quickest way to learn how to travel safely, how to get work and where to get food and shelter.

"And watch out for the cinder dicks," Frogman added, referring to railroad police who rode the trains. "They know we favor that freight and they'll be on her too. You might get yourself a comfy reefer to ride in." He smiled to himself. "I know a 'bo named Reefer Charlie. He won't ride anything but a reefer. If he sees an empty reefer sitting in a yard, he'll catch out on it whether he was going that way or not. Just doesn't want to waste them." He chuckled and snapped his knife shut. Then he took a metal flask from his front pants pocket and held it up to Mutt. "Fancy an eye-opener?"

"I never touch it."

"Good for you. You're a good, upright young fella. Just don't go preaching at me and we'll get along fine."

"I ain't no preacher!" objected Mutt.

Frogman raised his flask in a salute and drained it, then tucked it back into his pocket. "Where do you come from, Mutt?"

"Mississippi."

"I would have guessed someplace like that from the sound of you. Alabam, Mississip, Louisiana. Someplace like that. Whereabouts in Mississippi?"

"Jenner Springs."

"Don't know it. What kind of place is that?"

Her mind drifted back to the little town where she'd gone to school, surrounded by miles and miles of corn and cotton fields, clear fishing streams and hickory woods. "It's like any other kind of place," she said. "There's a general store, a school, a post office, three churches and four bars."

"Sounds like any other kind of place, as you say."

"It's farming country," added Mutt.

"Is your daddy a farmer?"

"Used to be. Now he lets out a few acres to sharecroppers. He don't farm no more himself. We used to have chickens. We once had hundreds of them. Layers. Not anymore."

"Why's that?"

"My daddy's a good-for-nothin' drunk. He let it all go to hell."

Frogman raised one eyebrow, revealing a conspicuous amount of white around his eyes, then shook his head. "Seems like a story I've heard before."

She was sure that was true. There were plenty like her. Dirt-poor Southerners. They call it dirt-poor because all you got is dirt. Bare Mississippi dirt and a barn with one cow, a handful of chickens and a sagging farmhouse. A mean and worthless father and no mother. She was gone by the time Mutt was six. By the time she was fourteen, the farm lay fallow and they had nothing. Daddy could barely drag himself out of bed most days. Her older brother Ray said Daddy wasn't always so mean and worthless. He used to be a good worker and a decent man. Even went to church on Sundays. She couldn't picture that. That was before Ma died, and Mutt didn't remember much from then.

After Ray left to join the army, things got a lot worse. So she left too. She hadn't been back and didn't know what had happened to the farm or her father since. Although she had been cold, lonely and hungry plenty of times during the past year, she had never once thought of going home. There was only one thing there she was sorry to leave behind: her dog Tippy, the little beagle mix she'd had from a pup. It nearly broke her heart to leave him and she'd probably stayed longer than she would have because of him. But she couldn't take a dog on the road. She knew her father would feed Tippy. He'd always treated animals better than he treated people. She just hoped he didn't take it out on Tippy that she'd run away. Just thinking about her little dog caused her to choke up, so she shook the thought from her head.

"How long you been hoboing?" she asked Frogman.

"Twenty-three years."

"That's a long time!"

"You're right. It's quite a stretch." He leaned against the wall, letting out a sigh. "I've seen everything. I've done everything. I've been a cattle stiff in Texas, a sea stiff in Maine, a timber stiff in Washington and everything in between. I've seen the inside of every jug and Sallie on the entire N.P., S.P., Pennsy and the Cough and Snort, just to name a few."

"Cough and Snort?"

"Oh, you haven't heard that one, huh? Colorado and Southern Line."

Mutt liked to listen to the old-timers talk. They had a language all their own, and she had made a quick study of it. She knew he was talking about time spent in jails, for vagrancy or trespassing, and Salvation Army shelters. Any hobo who'd been riding for any time at all had seen the inside of a jail cell or two. Mutt had been lucky so far and had avoided being locked up. She'd been arrested once along with a dozen other hobos in a camp near Laramie, Wyoming, but while they were being rounded up to be put in a truck, she'd made a run for it. There had been only two cops, so they couldn't go after her. Being put in a cell with a bunch of men could be a real problem for Mutt, so she had been far more desperate to avoid jail than the rest of them. Some of these men didn't mind a jail cell now and then, depending on the town. Those who had been around a while knew what jails to avoid where the grub was foul and they were forced to work in labor gangs for weeks on end. But that wasn't the case everywhere. Sometimes a few free meals and a dry bed were a welcome respite, especially in winter.

"It used to be easier to get a job when you wanted it," Frogman said. "Ever since all those farms got blown away, everybody's been on the move. Whole families are on the road traveling and looking for work. I met a fella last week who used to be a lawyer in New York. He looked no better than you and me, sitting in the jungle with only a ragged pair of trousers, a dusty hat and a toothbrush to his name. He lost it all in the stock market crash in twenty-nine and lost his business too. He decided to walk away and he's been flipping freights ever since. It's a sight better than suicide, I told him. Some of them jumped out of buildings and killed themselves." Frogman shook his head. "That's what it's like having money and property and things like that. Canopy beds and Chesterfield sofas. You've got a lot to lose. Me, I've got nothing to lose. No home. No family. No Chesterfield. I've got no worries. No, sirree. No worries at all. I've been riding the rails since I was eighteen. About your age."

She did a quick calculation in her head, fixing his age at forty-one, just a touch younger than her father. "I'm seventeen," she said. "I was born in the year of our Lord nineteen twenty-four."

He chuckled. "How long since you left home?"

"It was a year ago March. Thirteen months."

"You should go back home, young fella. You don't want to live like this if you don't have to."

"Can't go home."

"You sure?"

"Sure as shit."

One of the best things about being disguised as a boy, she had decided, was being able to curse. Girls were not allowed to curse. When she had ignored that rule a couple of times back home, she'd suffered the consequences. She'd had her mouth washed out with soap and her behind strap-whipped. Her brother Ray could say what he wanted. He got into his own brand of trouble often enough, but not for cursing. She had pointed out to her father how unfair that was. "Why can Ray say it and I can't?"

He had slapped her face hard, angrier than ever. "I'm gonna be dead and buried before you're ever gonna figure out you're a girl, ain't I? I thank God in Heaven your mama never had to see this, what a foul-mouthed, ornery rascal you turned out to be. I'm gonna tell you this one more time. Ladies do not swear, and believe it or not, Mutt, I'm gonna turn you into a lady yet. If I ever hear that word comin' out of your mouth again, I'm gonna wallop you so hard, you won't be sittin' down for a month of Sundays."

Frogman stretched his legs out straight and asked, "So this is better than home?"

Mutt hesitated, not because she was unsure of the answer, but because she didn't like talking about it. "Yeah."

After a heartbeat or two, she heard his voice, barely audible over the rattle of the car, saying, "That's a shame."

They lapsed into silence for a while and Mutt sat against the side of the car facing the doorway as the morning warmed up. She rested her head on her bedroll and closed her eyes, her body vibrating in tune with the wheels on the rails. The movement of the train must have rocked her to sleep because she woke up with a start to see Frogman standing at the edge of the doorway, facing outward and shooting a yellow stream into the wind where it diffused into a fine spray. After buttoning up his trousers, he stayed where he was, holding fast to the open door and looking ahead.

"Omaha coming up!" he yelled over his shoulder. "Remember what I told you about Columbus."

"Yes, sir," she said, jumping to her feet.

"Good luck to you, Mississippi Mutt." Frogman opened his eyes so wide they looked like two fried eggs, sunny side up, then he laughed and slung his pack over his shoulder. In a few seconds he was gone. Mutt dashed to the open door to see him standing upright beside the tracks. She waved and watched him recede in the distance. Then she ducked back into the shadows as the train rumbled into the rail yard.

# CHAPTER TWO

One of the yard cops strolled by looking for freeloaders, his boots crunching on gravel, his club clanging against metal as he absentmindedly struck it against the rail cars. Mutt huddled in the center of a cattle car surrounded by nervous calves, well hidden by the patchwork of brown, black and white animal hide.

As Frogman had said, there were plenty of refrigerator cars on Big Charlotte, and a few of them were empty, but Mutt didn't dare get in one until the train was moving. The doors of a reefer lock from the outside and some of these railroad cops took a sadistic pleasure in locking hobos inside where they would freeze or suffocate.

There were other places, like the rods under the cars, where a person might go unnoticed, but that was a dangerous place to ride and plenty uncomfortable with all the cinders being thrown up from the tracks.

She noticed that the black calf beside her hadn't taken his placid sable eye off her for a while. His look suggested he couldn't figure out just what kind of bovine she was. A loaded cattle car was one of the best places to be while a train was sitting in the rail yard, but the bad thing about a cattle car was the same as the good thing: cattle. They just go on doing their business wherever they are. She did her best to dodge splashing urine and splattering cow pies, tying a handkerchief over her nose and mouth like a bandit to cut down on the stench. With the flies swarming and the heat mounting, she lifted her face heavenward in a silent plea for departure.

Finally, Big Charlotte began to move and they were on their way. Safe now from the yard bulls, Mutt moved to the side of the car where she could breathe fresh air through the wooden slats. One of the calves shoved his head toward her and nuzzled her with his wet nose. She patted his thick neck companionably. He flung his head up and backed away, startled, causing the entire car full of animals to readjust itself uneasily.

"California," she said with satisfaction, "here I come!"

Everything she knew about California was hearsay. Last fall, she'd been in Washington and Oregon, but hadn't gone any farther south before heading back east. If you were a farm worker, she'd been told, California was a good place to be. There were crops to pick year-round. It was steady, dependable work that sometimes included room and board. A prudent worker who didn't spend money on booze and cigarettes could save enough to rent a room for the winter. She had heard that if you stayed in Cali for the winter, though, you didn't need a room because it didn't rain or snow there. With all that fruit and all those nuts dripping from the trees and no bad weather, she reckoned California must be as much like paradise as any place on earth. She briefly wondered how they could grow all those crops with no rain, then shrugged and decided she'd find out when she got there.

With her nose protruding between the slats of the cattle car, she watched the city of Columbus, Nebraska thin out bit by bit until there were just a few houses here and there. Finally, there were almost no houses at all, just fields of hay and a lone windmill now and then, weathered gray against a pale blue April sky. She'd been through Nebraska several times, viewing its fields in the frame of a boxcar door. When you're riding the rails, Nebraska is smack-dab in the middle of everything, but so far it had not been a destination for Mutt. The only time she'd got off here at all was yesterday at the Columbus station as Frogman had instructed. She'd spent the rest of the day in town, then slept at the Salvation Army until it was time to return to the station to catch Big Charlotte. At the Sallie, she'd met a couple other hobos who had similar plans, but she hadn't seen them this morning.

The train traveled steadily across the plains at a moderate pace, and pretty soon Mutt's stomach started to rumble with the regularity of the clickety-clack of the wheels. She'd had to leave the Sallie too early for their oatmeal breakfast. The previous afternoon, she had gotten a substantial meal of roast chicken and potatoes from a kind housewife, a woman older than her father who had called her a "sweet boy" and taken a maternal interest in her welfare, if just for half an hour. She'd saved a hunk of bread from that meal and had eaten it this morning for breakfast. The woman had given her a shirt too, one of her husband's, almost new and sparkling white. Mutt had folded it neatly and packed it in her bedroll.

She often found that she had an easier time getting handouts through the back doors of houses than some of the more mature fellas, especially from the older women. Her youth garnered sympathy. She enjoyed the attention of these compassionate housewives, as she had spent most of her life motherless and had missed out on the comfort of maternal love.

The closest she had come to it was with her Cousin Opal. Fred Hopper, Opal's husband, was her father's first cousin. They lived near Clarksdale, Mississippi, near the Arkansas border, far enough away from Jenner Springs that Mutt had never been to their place. Fred and Opal hadn't been to visit in so long, Mutt could barely remember them. Ray thought the last time they had come was for their mother's funeral. So the last time they saw Mutt she was just six years old. Ray could remember more about them than she could. He said Cousin Fred and their father didn't get along. But whatever bad blood there was between cousins Fred and Kirby, every year right on time, on June 21, a birthday card addressed to "Miss Shirley Hopper" arrived in the mail from Clarksdale. Inside the card, every time, there was a stiff new five-dollar bill.

Other than school teachers, Cousins Fred and Opal were the

only people who called her Shirley. Opal had hardly ever seen Mutt and wasn't around enough to know she had a nickname. What she knew about Mutt was pretty much limited to the birth announcement that got sent out to everybody even remotely interested in Grace and Kirby Hopper's second born. Mutt had seen the announcement, affixed to a page in the baby book her mother had made. It had said, importantly, as if royalty had descended upon them, "Announcing the arrival of Shirley June Hopper, June 21, 1924, six pounds and four ounces."

Despite being unable to remember anything about Fred and Opal, it had always made Mutt spectacularly happy to get that birthday card, the only thing she ever got in the mail. Cousin Opal had remembered her birthday and had gone to the trouble to buy and mail a card. That was something!

It had been enough to make her consider heading for Clarksdale when she had run away from home. Cousin Opal would take her in, she was sure of it. She had always signed her cards, "Love Fred and Opal," and Mutt had no reason to question the sincerity of those words. With nowhere else to go, she had wanted to go to the one place in the world where somebody cared about her. But there were problems with that plan. She knew that Opal and Fred would call her father and tell him where she was. Then he would ask them to send her back. And they would, of course, because he was her father. Unless she could give them a good reason not to. That's where she always realized the flaw in her plan. She couldn't tell his cousins why she'd run away. She couldn't tell anybody.

A startling awareness of wetness around her left ankle brought Mutt abruptly out of her daydream. The calf crowded up next to her was nonchalantly urinating on her foot. She jerked it away, but too late. She realized it was time to find a more comfortable place to ride. She couldn't stand in a cattle car all the way to California.

She climbed up the front of the car and onto the deck of a reefer, hanging on with both hands as she inched over to the edge so she could look down and out along the length of the train to find an open door. From the top of the train, she had a grand view of the countryside, an endless expanse of farmland planted with wheat and corn. The locomotive was some distance away belching up smoke, and the caboose was about the same distance behind. They were traveling too fast for being outside in the weather. Sometimes she liked to ride on the deck, especially at night when the temperature was mild, and search the sky overhead for shooting stars. But today it was windy and cold, so she needed to get inside.

Seeing an open boxcar six cars ahead, she made her way across the catwalks from car to car, holding tight so the pitching of the train didn't toss her off. Mindful of Frogman's advice, she kept her eye out for cinder dicks. The sooner she got inside that boxcar, the better.

She had spanned three cars without incident when a blue cap suddenly appeared at the edge of a car just ahead. She froze in place on her hands and knees. The cap swung around so the bill faced her, then a face rose up under it to clear the top of the car. It was a roundish face with dark eyes and a thick mustache. A wide nose took up most of the space between the vacant-looking eyes and tightly shut mouth.

Mutt held her breath, but it was too late. He had seen her. The cop climbed up another rung, scowling at her. A car and a half separated them.

"You there!" he hollered, his voice nearly sheared completely off by the wind. "Get off this train!"

The clang of his boots reached her ears as he scaled another couple rungs. Then his arm rose up over the top of the car, revealing a pistol in his hand.

She scuttled sideways like a crab to the edge of the car above the ladder, then heard the distinctive pop of a gun and a sharp zing as a bullet ricocheted off the car behind her. Panicked, she quickly dropped over the side onto the ladder and out of sight. She wondered if that had been a warning shot or if he was one of those sadistic bulls who got a thrill from picking off hobos.

She had heard stories, plenty of them. She had even witnessed the work of these men firsthand. Near a hobo jungle in Little Rock, Arkansas, she had seen the bodies of three men in a ditch at the side of the tracks. They'd been there a couple of days and were bloated and rotting. They'd been tossed off a train after being killed. Some said they'd been left near the popular Little

Rock camp as a warning. The hobos dug graves and buried them right there by the tracks. Nobody knew who they were or where they had come from. The sight was seared into her mind and she wished she hadn't seen it. But having done so made her take the danger seriously. It was the reason her heart pounded so violently now.

Clinging to the ladder with the ground whizzing past, she realized she had done nothing to improve her situation. All he had to do was get on top of the car and look over to have a clear shot at her. Her only hope now was that he would lose his balance and fall off, which wasn't likely. She momentarily considered that she might be able to grab him and pull him off when he showed his jowly mug over the edge of the roof above her. She climbed up one rung to where she could reach the top of the car in anticipation of his arrival. She planted both feet firmly and hung tight to the ladder with one arm.

The scene played out in her mind detail by detail. As soon as he appeared, she'd grab his coat and yank with all her might. She figured if she caught him by surprise, maybe she'd have enough strength to pull him off. He'd come sliding over the top of the car directly over her head, carried by the force of the wind, and be flung to the ground. With no chance to prepare, he'd likely land on his head or back and be killed by the impact.

She'd never killed anybody before and didn't want to. Maybe he wouldn't be killed, she considered. Maybe he'd just break a leg. But he looked like a heavy man. He'd hit the ground hard, and at this speed his chance of survival was slim.

She set her teeth together hard and waited for his face to appear above her. When it did, cheeks flapping in the wind, she locked her eyes on his coat collar, easily within reach. Just grab it and yank hard, she told herself.

But her hand clung instead to the ladder rail, her murderous plan dissolving in the face of reality. She knew she couldn't kill him.

He pointed the pistol directly at her head. "Get off!" he ordered.

"I can't! It's too fast." She heard the high pitch of her voice and realized fear had made her forget her disguise. It didn't matter. There was too much noise with the rumble of the train and the wind whipping past them for anybody to notice.

"Get off now or I'll put a bullet in your head. Your choice!"

Observing the look of loathing in his eyes, she decided he was serious. She would have to "hit the grit," something that hobos all fear and something that had torn many of them to pieces. She recalled meeting a man who had most of the skin of his face ripped off when he'd been tossed off a fast-moving train. He was badly scarred and had only half a nose. Still, it was better than ending up like those three dead men in Little Rock.

She looked behind to see the ground rushing by in a blur. The slope that held the tracks was covered with black cinders. Beyond that was a grass-covered ditch, a potentially softer landing. If she could clear the cinders and roll, maybe she had a chance. If she didn't make it, she might break both her legs or worse. She'd lie there helpless for days until she died. There wasn't a house or structure of any kind to be seen. Just fields and fields of newly-sprouted wheat.

When she turned back to face the bull, there was a sneer on his lips. He didn't care if she made it or not, she realized. He just wanted to watch her try. Whether or not she had the strength to pull him off the car, she had never seriously intended to do it. In the back of her mind, she knew she was the one in the wrong. She was breaking the law. He was doing his job. And enjoying it too much, she reflected. The tinge of guilt she felt for her transgression was just about equivalent to the guilt she felt for leaving her father all alone back on the farm. It wasn't much, but it was there. Which only went to show that she had more human compassion in her than either of them. Okay, she thought, that was the fine sentiment she would take to the grave with her, that she was a better human being than this bastard… and that pathetic drunk back in Mississippi.

He moved the barrel of the gun closer to her head and took careful aim.

"I'm going!" she hollered.

Loosening her fingers from the metal rails seemed impossible, but somehow she coaxed herself to do it, crouching on a rung to give herself as much of a liftoff as possible. She had hopped off moving trains plenty of times, but never going this fast. She mentally aimed for the grass, closed her eyes and hurled herself away from the train, curling up with her head tucked in. She heard the triumphant hoot of the railroad cop fade into the wind.

When she hit solid ground, it knocked the wind out of her and flung her out of her tuck. Flipping and rolling out of control, her body barreled downslope and into the ditch, crashing into the far side of it. Like a billiard ball hitting solid against the side pocket, phlunk, she dropped into the bottom of the ditch and stuck there firm, lying face down in several inches of cool mud.

She turned her head, spat mud from her mouth, and listened to the train passing a few feet away. The ground vibrated around her. She waited, numb and lying on her stomach, bordered by the two walls of the ditch. If she were seriously injured, she thought, she might already be in her grave. The rumble of the train finally faded into the distance, giving way to the reassuring song of a meadowlark somewhere nearby. Then a frog started croaking, recovering from the violent interruption to its day.

Finally she ventured movement. Amid various indistinct pains, she climbed out of the ditch. She pulled her bandana from her pocket and wiped it across her face to get the mud away from her mouth and eyes. As she swiped across her chin, a stinging pain jumped out at her. She reached up to encounter blood. Her chin was cut open. There was a second cut on her left arm. But her legs worked fine and she felt pretty good, considering.

She looked up at the blue sky, noticing how much warmer the day was than it had seemed on the train. She took a deep breath and smiled to herself.

Singing a song she had learned in a hobo camp, she took off along the tracks in the direction the train had gone, thinking that it was turning out to be a fine spring day in the Midwest of America. Yes, indeed, a fine day.

"As fine as a frog's hair!" she said aloud.

*Tumbleweed Jack went on down to the track.*
*He caught himself a freight, bindle on his back.*
*He made a little money cutting hay in old Bonaire,*
*Then he rode back home to Momma,*
*but she couldn't keep him there.*

*For the smokestack is a puffin',*
*The steel rumbles on the track,*
*The train whistle's blowin'*
*Calling Jack back.*

*Drinking boiled coffee from second-day grind,*
*He played a sweet song and passed a little time.*
*He rode the rails from Boston to the San Francisco Bay,*
*Then he met a girl in Natchez,*
*but she couldn't make him stay.*

*For the smokestack is a puffin',*
*The steel rumbles on the track,*
*The train whistle's blowin'*
*Calling Jack back.*

*Fifty years gone by and that 'bo still rides,*
*Though he's got lousy ears and even worse eyes.*
*He can barely reach the stirrup and needs help getting down.*
*But you know he won't stop ridin'*
*Till he's caught the old Westbound.*

*For the smokestack is a puffin',*
*The steel rumbles on the track,*
*The train whistle's blowin'*
*Calling Jack back.*

# CHAPTER THREE

She followed the tracks through lonely farmland, walking sometimes on them and sometimes beside them for over an hour before she sensed the vibration of a train approaching. She couldn't see it yet, but with her hand on the track she could feel it. She heard the sound of a distant whistle, then it came into view. She stepped off the track to level ground and waited for it. The ground trembled under her feet as the mighty locomotive thundered by, its coal cars full of coal, its cattle cars packed with cattle and its open boxcars occupied by the men who rode for free. They flashed by, men in worn coats with weary eyes staring out of haggard faces, all of them headed somewhere, anywhere, headed away from some gloomy story, on the move, always on the move.

In the open door of one of the cars, a young man sat peering out. He wore a brown tweed coat and a newsboy cap, his face fresh and full of excitement, a notable contrast to his companions. He waved enthusiastically at Mutt and she waved back, wishing she could climb aboard his car.

She didn't know how far it was to the next rail yard or grain elevator or whistle-stop town where she might catch another freight. The old-timers could tell you everything about every route. If Frogman were here, he would know how far she had left to walk. She was hungry and hot, and her cut and bruised body was sore and tired. But all she could do was follow the tracks until she got somewhere.

Hobos spent a lot of time telling stories about their adventures on the road, some true and some questionable. Up until now, Mutt had had few stories to tell and nothing that would impress these experienced veterans. But now, she realized, she had a good one. Didn't she just get thrown off a train traveling at forty miles an hour and survive with just a couple of scratches? Happy with the thought of being able to tell her new story, well embellished, she walked with a livelier gait.

It was after noon when she walked across a trestle over a river and decided to stop for a while to wash up. The mud from her earlier tumble had dried and cracked on her clothes and skin, some of it falling off on its own. The river was cool and refreshing. She washed the mud off her clothes as best she could, standing in the river in her undershirt and shorts. She scrubbed herself and rinsed the dirt from her hair and the blood from her face and arm, and emerged feeling better. She had a change of clothes in her pack, including the brilliant new shirt. But she didn't want to pack wet clothes away, so she let them dry in the branches of the trees until they were just damp, then got dressed and went on her way.

The energy she got from the river stop quickly dissipated. Her stomach grumbled in a continuous refrain of dissatisfaction and she felt discouraged. In the hours she'd been walking, she'd hardly seen a building at all. Just fields of grain, a few cows, and the endless iron tracks of the railroad. That mean old cinder dick had put her off in a bare stretch of countryside miles from any town. Maybe she should have walked the other direction. She'd have made it to the outskirts of Columbus by now, but it was too late for that.

She finally came across a country lane that crossed the tracks. A quarter mile down it she spied a big red barn and what looked like a white house just a little farther on. There were a couple horses grazing near the barn and a tractor sitting idle nearby. It was the first homestead she had seen for hours. She decided to take a chance that somebody friendly lived there and detoured down the narrow lane.

The house was two stories high with wood siding and columns framing the double front doors that opened out onto a wide, inviting looking porch. A screen of wisteria vines climbed up the west side, shading a porch swing from the afternoon sun. Stretching out from the wide porch steps to meet her was a sprawling green lawn framed by a split rail fence. From one of the trees in front of the house hung a rope with a tire swing at the end of it. Three red hens pecked at the grass near the porch steps. A stone path from the fence to the porch was laid out like an invitation to come up and drink a cool glass of lemonade.

The place looked comfortable and homey, a farmhouse in the country like Mutt's own home in Mississippi, but nothing like it either. This was more grand than her house and much better kept.

An unseen dog barked as she passed through the gap in the fence. She had taken only four steps when the front door swung open and a girl came out, a girl about Mutt's age wearing a frilly white dress with fitted sleeves down to the elbows and a row of satin buttons down the front. Her honey-blond hair looked like sunshine falling in soft waves around her pale face and over her shoulders.

Mutt was struck dumb, thinking she had never seen such a pretty girl before. She stared and the girl stared back, regarding Mutt with unperturbed curiosity. Her hand was still on the edge of the screen door, holding it ajar.

"Who are you?" she called, her voice gentle and melodious.

Just then a man emerged from the side of the house carrying a shovel and wearing a battered straw hat. He was tanned and thin, a rugged, serious look about the set of his jaw, his legs lost somewhere inside the considerable cloth of his overalls. He looked over at her and squinted.

"Hey, there!" he called, walking toward her.

She removed her hat and pronounced, "Good afternoon."

He stopped in front of her, his face dappled from the sunlight filtering through his hat. He looked her up and down, no doubt taking in her mud-stained clothes and the bedroll over her shoulder.

"Where'd you come from?" he asked.

"I was riding a train and accidentally got off it."

"You one of those hobos?" His tone hinted at disapproval.

"Yes, sir. I've been walking for hours and worked up a powerful big hunger. I can work for a meal. I can do most anything on a farm. Slop pigs or drive a tractor." Out of the corner of her eye she saw the girl on the stoop glide over to the swing and sit down.

"We don't see too many hobos way out here," the man said. "The trains don't stop around here. It's just you, is it?"

"Just me, sir. The name's Mutt."

"How old are you, Mutt?"

"Seventeen."

He looked skeptical. "You look more like fourteen."

"I'm seventeen, sir. Born in the year of our Lord nineteen twenty-four."

The farmer removed his hat momentarily to give the top of his head a scratch, revealing thinning, dust-colored hair. "I suppose you can help me with the fences, but you can't work on an empty stomach. I'll ask the missus to get you something to eat. We've got over three hours till sundown. Still time to string a good stretch of wire. If you work, you can sleep in the barn tonight. Then you can be on your way tomorrow morning. Is that understood? By the way, I'm Callahan. Isaac Callahan."

Mutt shook his hand with hearty gratitude, then followed him across the lawn, unable to take her eyes off the girl on the porch. She sat with her legs crossed at the knee, swinging one foot to and fro and smiling at Mutt with a curious look on her face. Mutt passed close enough by the porch to catch the bright blue force of the girl's eyes. They both craned their necks to get a last glimpse of one another before Mutt rounded the corner of the house.

"Was that your daughter on the front stoop?" she asked.

"Yep. That's Annie."

"She's pretty!" Mutt blurted, less as a comment to Mr. Callahan than as an involuntary expulsion of enthusiasm.

"Whether she is or not, that's no concern of yours."

"Yes, sir."

He stopped walking and turned to face her, his face stern. "If you go anywhere near that girl, I'll blast your ass clear off with my shotgun. You understand?"

"Yes, sir!"

"You can wipe her right out of your mind now." He turned and took long-legged strides away from the house.

*Annie*, Mutt repeated silently, not at all ready to wipe her out of her mind. There was something about that girl, the elegant turn of her body and the teasing curl of her slightly parted lips that had hit Mutt right between the eyes. *Annie Callahan*, she thought again. The name became a refrain in her mind like the songs that got stuck in her head on trains, set to the clickety-clack rhythm of the wheels on the track until the words themselves were like a train traveling in circles around her head.

*An-nie Call-a-han, An-nie Call-a-han, An-nie Call-a-han. Whoo-hoo!*

# CHAPTER FOUR

Feeling happy, comfortable and most of all full of good home cooking, Mutt arranged a bed of straw for herself in an unused horse stall in the Callahan barn and took off her jacket, draping it over the side wall. She hung her hat on a nail, smiling at the sleek chestnut gelding in the next stall.

"This is fine, ain't it?" she said to the horse. "Finer than a frog's hair, yessir." She yawned and stretched her arms above her head, feeling the weariness of her muscles and the pain of the bruises she'd gotten from her earlier mishap. "We'll sleep good tonight!"

The horse shook his head and snorted, as if in agreement. Mrs. Callahan had been kind and generous with the plate she had sent out for Mutt this evening, piling on roast beef, potatoes and gravy and adding a thick slice of cherry pie. It was the best meal Mutt had had in a long time, eaten on the back porch while the family had their supper inside in the dining room.

Mutt had hoped to see Annie Callahan again, but she'd only glimpsed her once from afar as she and Mr. Callahan returned from fencing in the pasture. As they approached the house, she saw Annie in the backyard unpinning laundry from the clothesline with the pink glow of sunset framing her. She carried the clothes basket into the house, unaware that she was being watched. Her body moved with each step in the same way a dandelion seed floats through the air on its dainty umbrella, softly swaying from left to right, carried in relaxed arcs on wind currents.

Mutt didn't know why she was so preoccupied with Annie. All she knew was that she felt agitated just knowing she was nearby. She had never felt this way about anybody before, so on edge and a little breathless, and all of a sudden filled with longing for something she didn't understand. She just wanted to look at her, that's all. Each time she'd gotten the chance, she hadn't been able to stop looking at her.

One other time, she thought she might have seen Annie peeking out a window at her, but it was such a brief glimpse of a face, it could have been a cat or just her imagination.

After supper, Mutt had been given a bar of soap and a wash tub. She had placed the tub in a thicket of trees behind the barn, anxious to have a bit of privacy. It was dark by then, but the moon was up, three-quarters full and giving enough light to make her nervous about being seen. After carrying several buckets of water to the tub, she undressed and hung her clothes in the branches of the trees like screens. After her bath, she had put on her new white shirt to sleep in and rolled her old mud-stained one up in her bedroll.

The shirt felt cool and soft against her skin. She ran her hands over the front of it, luxuriating in the fine weave of the material, pressing down when her palms encountered the negligible lumps of her breasts. The shirt was roomy enough to hide them, and despite her long arms, the sleeves were about an inch too long. She rolled the sleeves up to her elbows, then lay down in the hay, her body feeling light and ready to float away into slumber. The audible breathing of the horse in the next stall was regular and gentle and would be just the thing to lull her to sleep.

She had only just closed her eyes when a sharp creaking startled her. She sat up to see a shaft of light widening as the barn door opened. The horse uttered a gentle whinny. When the door closed again, there was silence. Mutt got to her feet and looked over the gate of the stall to see a ghostly white figure in the dim interior of the barn. It moved like a sheet in a breeze.

"Hello," she called tentatively in the direction of the specter.

"Hello," came a whispered reply, a soft feminine voice.

Mutt's heart began to pound rapidly, her fingers clenched around the top of the stall gate. She realized this ethereal visitor must be Annie Callahan. A bolt of terror shot through her as she remembered Mr. Callahan's stern warning to stay away from his daughter.

Annie opened one of the shutters, allowing enough moonlight in to reveal herself to Mutt. She wore a dress like the one she'd had on earlier, and around her shoulders she held a flowing white shawl. It looked like a tablecloth but she wore it like a cape. She suddenly swept it off her shoulders with a flourish, then twirled around in front of Mutt's stall as if performing for her. When she came to a stop, she raised herself to her full height. In an artificially lowered voice, she said, "How do you do? I'm Bianca Montclair."

"Bianca…huh?"

Annie giggled and flung herself onto the stall gate, causing Mutt to hop back.

"What're you doing here?" she asked.

Annie leaned over the gate, her eyes dark and wild looking. "Your name's Mutt, isn't it? That's a funny name. Daddy said you're a hobo. I've never met a hobo before. He said, stay away from that hobo, Annie. I mean Bianca." She looked defiant, as if daring Mutt to call her on her blunder. "I snuck out after everybody went to bed." She giggled at her own indiscretion.

"Oh, you shouldn't oughta be here."

Paying no mind to Mutt's objection, Annie unlatched the gate and let it swing wide. Mutt backed away, stopping only when her back flattened up against the wall. Annie spread the tablecloth on the straw and sat on it, crossing her legs and arranging her skirt demurely to cover her knees.

"Sit here," she said, patting the cloth beside her. "Don't worry. Daddy's dead to the world asleep."

Bewildered but intrigued, Mutt coaxed herself to take the offered seat, her nose catching a whiff of lavender. She tucked her legs up to her side self-consciously.

"What're you doing here, Annie?"

"My name is Bianca," she corrected haughtily. "You must call me Bianca. Or you may call me Miss Montclair, if that pleases you." She smiled and held out her hand, as if she expected Mutt to kiss it. Not knowing what else to do, she touched her lips to Annie's hand lightly, and that seemed to satisfy her, as she then tucked it under her leg.

Mutt stared at her, marveling at the way the moonlight made her eyes look darker and her skin lighter. Her peaches and cream complexion glowed like the moon itself, the palest blue imaginable. The contrast of her lips, shimmering and plum-colored, drew Mutt's eyes to her mouth. Why's a girl wearing lipstick on a farm in the middle of the night? she wondered. She felt queasy and jumpy. Annie was small, but she seemed to fill up the whole space, making it hard to breathe.

"Tell me what it's like to be a hobo," Annie asked, startling Mutt's gaze away from her mouth and back to her eyes.

"It's not so bad."

"Have you been a lot of places?"

"I been all over. I only been a hobo for a while, but I saw the Pacific Ocean last year when I was picking apples in Washington. And I saw a seal." The way Annie's eyes lit up chased away some of Mutt's nervousness. "It was alive and everything. Sitting on a rock in the water and making an awful racket."

Annie gasped. "A seal! I wish I could see something like that! What did it sound like?"

"A sort of yelp like a dog that got hurt. You know how a dog hollers when you step on its tail? Accidental, I mean. I'd never step on a dog's tail on purpose." She thought briefly of her little dog Tippy back home and how much she still missed his soft brown eyes.

"Can you do it?" Annie asked with excitement. "Can you make the sound?"

Mutt thought back to the seal, slapping a flipper on a rock and calling out across the waves. Feeling foolish, but anxious to please, she decided to attempt it and uttered three barking yelps in a row. Annie clapped her hands together, delighted.

"It was a lot louder than that," Mutt said. "If there was a seal here now, he'd wake up the whole house carrying on like that one did."

"I've never been anywhere but Nebraska." Annie sounded frustrated.

"I might see the ocean again this summer. I'm on my way to California. They got an ocean too."

"California?" Annie's eyes grew big and she bounced up to a kneeling position.

"There's a lotta pickin' to do there. You can pick all through the spring, summer and fall. It never gets cold there. Never snows or rains or nuthin'."

"I know! I know all about California! That's where I'm going as soon as I graduate high school."

"You are?"

"Yes! I'm going to be a movie star like Irene Dunne." She pitched her chin up, put her hand on her heart and froze as if she were posing for a painting.

Suddenly Mutt understood the flourish of the tablecloth and the pretentious name. Annie had grand aspirations.

"Who's Irene Dunne?" she asked.

"You don't know Irene Dunne?" She looked incredulous. "Everybody knows Irene Dunne. *Magnificent Obsession*? *When Tomorrow Comes*? Oh, Mutt, tell me you know *When Tomorrow Comes* with Charles Boyer."

Mutt shook her head, sorry to let Annie down.

"Do you know Joan Crawford? Vivien Leigh? I love Vivien Leigh."

"I've only been to the pictures one time. When my brother Ray was going off to the army, me and my daddy and Ray all went to the picture show before we took him to the train station. The Three Stooges were in it. Do you know about the Three Stooges?"

"Sure, I do! That's the only movie you ever saw?"

"Uh-huh. It made us all laugh."

Annie regarded her indulgently. "Well, that's fine, but that's not the kind of movie I'm talking about. I'm talking about beautiful romantic stories that end tragically." She laid a hand over her heart and fluttered her eyelashes. "That's the kind of movie I'm going to star in. Me and Clark Gable. In the end, after he's broken my heart, he'll turn his back on me and say, 'I don't give a damn, Bianca!' and walk away." She giggled nervously, looking around as if somebody might have heard her say "damn."

Mutt wondered if she'd get her mouth washed out with soap if her father heard her.

"Why do you call yourself Bianca?"

"That's my movie star name. You know you can't use your real name if you're a movie star."

"Why not?"

"It's just how things are done in Hollywood. You have to change your name. Joan Crawford's real name is Lucille Fay LeSueur. Can you imagine?"

She's a funny kind of girl, Mutt thought. Funny, but fascinating. "Do you know a lot about motion pictures?"

"Yes, I do," Annie said matter-of-factly. "Why don't you go to them? Don't you like them?"

"I reckon I would if I could, but I don't have money to go to pictures. Maybe after I make some money in California this summer, I'll see one."

"If you do, try to see one with Irene Dunne. She's my idol." Annie leaned in closer and asked, "Do you think I'm pretty enough to be a movie star?"

Mutt sputtered nervously, then finally said, "Sure!" realizing her opinion was worthless, as she didn't know what movie stars looked like other than Moe, Larry and Curly. But Annie smiled with satisfaction at her answer.

"I like the way you sound," she said. "Where do you come from?"

"Mississippi. I was raised on a farm like you."

"Why'd you leave?"

Mutt's shoulders tensed as she considered her answer. "There was no money. I had to get out on my own and go to work."

"You got family back there? Mom and Dad?"

"Just my daddy. My brother's still in the army. Ma's been dead a long time."

Annie's pretty face grew momentarily sad, then she asked, "Do you like being a hobo?"

"Sure. I can go wherever I want and do whatever I want."

"I wonder if I'd like it."

Mutt shook her head. "Too hard for a girl like you. You couldn't wear a dress like that. Or lipstick."

"Hobos can't wear lipstick? Is that a rule?"

"I'm pretty sure it is."

"Can't a woman be a hobo?"

"Sure. There are some. Some women can take this kind of life."

"I bet I could take it."

"I bet you couldn't."

Annie bit her bottom lip and frowned, narrowing her eyes as if she were getting ready to throw a punch. A second later, her face relaxed and she asked, "How'd you get that cut on your face?" She reached over and touched Mutt's chin gently.

"I got throwed off a moving train." Annie's fingers on her skin made Mutt nervous. She worried that her smooth skin would give her gender away. She reached up and folded Annie's hand into hers, settling it on her knee.

Annie smiled. "It sounds exciting to be a hobo."

"The best part is riding on the trains. You can travel all over the country and see everything. Some of the fellas get on at one end of the country, ride across to the other, then get on and go the other way, and they just keep doing that. They like to keep moving. Some others do it just for the fun of it. They don't all do it 'cause they have to. Some of them have a nice home and family to go back to if they want to. But most are looking for work and have no other place to go."

Annie looked troubled. "It worries me to hear about people who have no place to go. People who have no home. It worries me because I feel like I should do something about it. I saw a movie once about a man who lived under a dock in the Boston Harbor. During the day he worked unloading ships and he barely made enough money to eat. At night he slept on the ground, and one night he froze to death. Another man took the coins he had in his pocket and rolled his body off into the bay. I'll never forget that. I thought, if somebody had just given him a warm blanket, he wouldn't have died. If I ever see a man like that, freezing on the ground, I'm going to give him a blanket. It's hard to think a man's life could have been saved by a blanket and nobody gave him one."

"You got a tender heart, Annie."

She smiled. "It was just a movie, wasn't it? I think if it was real life, it wouldn't have happened that way. People wouldn't let somebody freeze to death like that, would they?" She looked concerned. "Where do you go when it's freezing out?"

"Different places. Sallies. Uh, Salvation Army, I mean. Sometimes missions. But my favorite place to go is the library."

"Really?"

"Almost every town has a library. It's dry and warm and free."

"Do you like to read?"

"I love to read. I read all kinds of books. Besides, what else you gonna do in a library?"

Annie smiled serenely. Her face was so soft and beautiful in the moonlight, and the look in her eyes so intense. She looked right inside Mutt, churning her up like a batch of cream into butter. She'd never felt like this before, so flustered and confused. She noticed she was still holding Annie's hand and abruptly released it.

"You're awfully cute," Annie whispered, the tone of her voice almost secretive. "I really like you. Do you like me?"

"Uh, I...well, sure, I reckon I do."

"You're shy, aren't you?"

"Not as a rule."

"Do I make you nervous?"

"Uh-huh."

"Why?"

Mutt swallowed hard. "Don't know."

Annie smiled like she was pleased with herself. "Mutt, do you believe in love at first sight?"

She opened her mouth to answer, but only a tiny squeak came out. It was getting harder to think and harder to breathe and her heart raced.

"I believe in it," Annie whispered.

She leaned in close and offered her lips up like a ripe fruit, like one of those shiny red Washington apples. Mutt's stomach hit the floor. Staring at Annie's expectant, puckered lips, she realized she wanted to kiss them. But it wasn't fair to kiss her when she thought she was kissing a boy. She'd never have to know, Mutt reasoned. There was no harm in a little kiss. And it seemed an awful shame to disappoint her.

Mutt touched her lips to Annie's, pressing gently, afraid but wanting, lingering over the smooth silky sensation of her mouth and the lavender scent of her. Then she sat back and opened her eyes to see Annie smiling at her.

"I never kissed a boy before," Annie confessed.

"I never done neither," Mutt whispered. "I mean, I never kissed a girl before. I never kissed anybody before."

"Did you like it?"

Mutt nodded, not entirely sure that what she was feeling was positive.

"Me too. Let's do it again."

Mutt prepared herself, this time putting her arms around Annie's tiny waist and pulling her body closer. They kissed again, longer this time, and gradually the awkwardness of their mouths lessened and they fit together more naturally. She pulled Annie closer still, holding her against her chest so she could feel her supple breasts flatten against her rib cage. Annie's mouth was warm and tender, her body light and yielding. Her touch stirred up a yearning deep inside that made Mutt want more and more of her.

Feelings of fear and guilt crept in through her pleasure, forcing her to break away.

"Annie," she said gently, "we shouldn't ought to be doing this."

"You do like me, don't you? You said you did."

"Sure I do, but your daddy said he'd kill me if I touched you. And I don't want to die. I nearly got killed once already today."

Annie sighed a deep, contented sigh and rolled onto the tablecloth, lying on her back and looking up with a silly smile. She lay with one hand behind her head, her hair splayed out like a golden mane. She was the most beautiful thing Mutt had ever seen.

"Kiss me again," Annie said. She raised one arm up to invite Mutt to her side.

Against her better judgment, Mutt obliged her by lying next to her and touching their lips together. She floated in the soft embrace of Annie's arms while their mouths learned how to kiss.

Between rounds of kissing they talked, their heads close together, both of them fighting against sleep. Eventually, Annie lost the fight and lay in Mutt's arms breathing heavily. She waited unmoving for several minutes, listening to the sound of crickets outside the barn and the snuffling of the horse in the next stall.

She wondered why she felt so happy when she knew she'd never see Annie again after she left this place. That was nothing at all to be happy about. It seemed strange that yesterday she hadn't known Annie existed, but tonight all she wanted in the world was to stay here with her. Finally, reluctantly, she shook her gently awake and said, "Annie, you need to go in now."

Her eyes fluttered open and they both sat up.

"Do you have to go tomorrow?" she asked. "Couldn't you stay a little longer?"

"You and I might get in a heap of trouble if I did. Y'all know what your daddy would do if he found you with a hobo."

"He'd be just as mad if you were a preacher or a schoolteacher or the prince of Persia. He doesn't think girls should even talk to a man before they're married. He's very old-fashioned."

"Still and all, I reckon he wouldn't want you to *marry* a hobo neither."

"Would you marry me?" Annie asked teasingly.

"I would!" Mutt said decisively. "If there was any preacher in the world willing to marry us, I'd find him and stand up in front of him and say 'I do!'"

Annie smiled gratefully, then wiped lipstick off of Mutt's face with her handkerchief.

"But you and me don't belong together," Mutt said, as much to herself as Annie. "That's just the way it is."

Annie looked suddenly serious and grabbed Mutt by both wrists. "Take me with you! Take me to California."

"Oh, no!" Mutt leapt to her feet. "I can't do that."

"Why not? I'll be going there anyway on my own in a couple years. Why not now?"

"Because you're too young and I can't take care of you. That'd be like jumping into a big ol' barrel of knotted snakes. You gotta stay here and finish school and do what your daddy says. You got a good father. He knows what's best for you and he loves you. You got no reason to run away."

Annie put her arms around Mutt, holding tight. "I don't want you to go."

"I don't want to go neither." Mutt held Annie's face between her hands and kissed her tenderly. "But I have to. And you have to stay here."

If I were a man, Mutt thought, could I take her with me? Even then, it would be wrong. There was a better life ahead for Annie Callahan than living on the iron road. It was okay for some folks, but that wasn't what Annie wanted. She wanted the life of a movie star. Besides, Mutt wasn't a man, so there was no decision to make anyway.

What would she think if she knew she was hanging on a girl? Mutt wondered. She wouldn't be standing here looking up at me with love in her eyes. *Best to get out fast before she figures it out.*

They kissed one another for a long time before Annie moved reluctantly toward the barn door.

"Thank you, Annie Callahan," Mutt called after her.

"You can call me Bianca," she said, then slipped out of the barn.

For some time afterward, Mutt lay silently staring at the high rafters in the shadows above, still overwhelmed and full of wonder at what had happened to her, that *love* had happened to her. She had never believed in love before, despite how often and how easily it happened in books. It was something that happened to other people. She had never considered that it could happen to her. She didn't even recognize it when she had first seen Annie and it had hit her square between the eyes. But now she knew that this deep ache in her gut and the muddled thoughts in her head were the side effects of falling in love. As strange as it was, she knew she loved Annie Callahan.

She wished thinking about love didn't make her think of her daddy, but there was no way around that. He used to tell her he loved her over and over like he was trying to convince somebody. "Ah, Mutt, you know I love you." He said it a lot and she hated hearing it because that was one of the ways he excused himself.

Not when she was younger. He never said he loved her then. He had nothing but criticisms for her then.

*Why don't you ever wear a dress? Why don't you curl your hair? Why can't you be like your mother? She was such a fine woman. Why are you so tall?*

He called her Mutt, she supposed, partly for the way she looked and partly for the way she acted. Together, that made her somebody that displeased him most of the time. Maybe that was why he took his belt to her backside so often, because she liked to climb trees or because she was too tall for his liking. Her brother Ray was tall too and he climbed trees, but none of that was wrong for a boy. Still, Ray got whipped plenty of times too. They'd both dabbed Mercurochrome to one another's raw hind ends now and then.

If that's all there had been, belt whippings, she probably wouldn't have left. She could take a belt, even when he was stinking drunk and didn't know when to stop, beating her like he wanted to beat all the bitterness out of his heart. She could even take that. Maybe, she had sometimes thought, he had made her tough with all those whippings. She *was* tough. She could take care of herself.

Ray had complained once to their father that Mutt was too old to get her ass whipped like that. Girls her age should be punished other ways, he insisted. She was thirteen at the time and in trouble for ditching school. She and Tippy had gone fishing instead. She figured her father would never notice. By the time she got home with her stringer full of catfish, he'd be out to the world and she and Ray would have a fish fry. But somehow her father was still awake at four in the afternoon when she and Tippy came sauntering in, obviously having been nowhere near the schoolhouse.

"I'm gonna stomp a mud hole in your ass," he roared. "You get yourself in the kitchen and pull down your britches."

"Daddy," Ray said, standing as tall as their father. "Mutt's too old to get her ass whipped. You gotta punish her some other way."

"She's too old to get whipped?" he had answered, slurring his speech. "Is that what you think, you smart-ass boy? How'd this get to be any of your business? You don't got the brains God gave a goose, you know that? Well, you're older than she is and you're not too old for a lickin'. I'm gonna knock your head into the middle of next week."

Ray also got a whipping that day for being insolent. A year later, he left for the army. When he said goodbye to Mutt, he apologized. "I'm sorry to have to leave you here alone with him, but I got to get away or I'm gonna kill him."

It was okay, she assured him. She didn't think it would make any difference whether he was there or not. Kirby Hopper would still be mean and worthless and spend what little money they had on drink. But when she was fifteen, even Mutt's low expectations proved optimistic. Things did get worse.

One day she was being punished for smoking a cigarette with one of those belt whippings. As it turned out, it was the last time he took a belt to her. Sprawled over a chair, her pants around her ankles, her backside was bare and stinging from the bite of the strap. He was so drunk he stumbled as he pulled back for another blow, crashing into the kitchen table.

"Ladies don't smoke!" he spat at her when he had righted himself. "I'm gonna teach you to be a lady if I have to strip your hide to the bone." Whack went the belt again. She flinched, gritting her teeth and waiting for the next strike.

Seconds passed and it didn't come. She heard his heavy breathing, so she knew he was still on his feet behind her. Finally, instead of the belt, she felt his hand on her, tracing one of the new welts with an oddly gentle touch. Then she heard the belt fall to the floor. She tried to get up, but he held her down with a strong arm, firm against the wooden chair seat, wordless but inflexible.

"What are you doing?" she yelled through her teeth.

He didn't answer, just held her in place with his mindless, powerful body while she struggled.

# CHAPTER FIVE

The horse beside her whinnied with excitement, waking her up. The barn door swung open and Mr. Callahan stood in the doorway in overalls and straw hat, carrying a bucket. "Good morning, horses and hobos!"

He seemed to be in a good mood. Mutt bolted up and faced him.

"How was your night?" he asked.

"Fine as a frog's hair," she said, feeling guilty. "I'm much obliged for your hospitality, sir." She grabbed her jacket and hat. "I aim to be on my way now. Can you tell me how far to the nearest train station?"

"Five miles due west. Little town called Milton. A freight stops there once a day in the early afternoon. I'll get my missus to pack you a lunch."

"Y'all been so kind to me."

"Think nothing of it. You were a big help yesterday. I respect a man who earns his board doing honest work."

A half hour later Mutt stood in front of the house shaking Mr. Callahan's hand. Mrs. Callahan and Annie stood on the porch. Annie looked like the tragic movie star of her fantasies, mutely enduring the loss of her beloved. What was it she had wanted her hero to say when he left? "I don't give a damn!" That seemed awfully cold. Why would she want that?

Mutt communicated silently to her with her eyes, a message of appreciation and love. Then she turned and left the Callahan farm behind.

As she got farther and farther away from it, the sadness of leaving Annie was replaced with gratitude. Mutt wasn't generally prone to sadness. She was the sort who looked ahead and made the best of whatever came along. So she turned her mind to the future, and her future had nothing to do with Annie. That was just the way things were. It was enough to have learned that love did exist in the world, sweet and unselfish, whether or not she would ever encounter such a thing again herself. But she was happy to have felt it at least this one time.

The only real concern she had in the world was where to get her next meal, and with two sandwiches in her pack and a canteen full of water, she had no worries about that today.

She had been walking less than an hour when she stopped under a cluster of trees to eat one of the sandwiches, pressed ham and Velveeta neatly wrapped in wax paper. She figured she'd already gone halfway to Milton and had plenty of time to linger. As she sat on a log listening to the buzzing of insects, she thought about Annie's soft skin and lips. An ache like hunger crawled around in her belly. But it wasn't hunger. It was a new kind of ache she'd never felt before last night. It was an ache that had to do with Annie and only Annie. She didn't know much about the hollow space growing inside her but she knew she couldn't fill it with a ham and Velveeta sandwich.

As she shouldered her pack to resume her journey, she heard somebody hollering from the opposite direction. She climbed onto the railroad tracks and saw Annie running toward her. She knew it was Annie, even though she wore trousers and her golden hair was stuffed up under a cap. As she got close, waving frantically, Mutt could see that she wore no lipstick today. Her face looked as fresh and natural as a newborn kitten and just as sweet.

Mutt waved back, wondering why Annie was chasing after her like this. She had a bag slung over her shoulder. Maybe she'd brought some clothes or some other useful farewell gift. Whatever the reason, Mutt was overjoyed to see her again.

When she arrived, she doubled over, panting. "I knew I could catch you."

"What're y'all doing here, Annie?"

"I'm going to California with you!"

"Oh, no! I can't let you do that. You can't come with me. I thought we done settled that already."

Annie stood up straight, still breathless. "You can't stop me. We were meant to be together. I'll walk ten paces behind you if you won't let me walk beside you. After you hop on a train, I'll hop on it too. When you get off, I'll get off. Pretty soon you'll see there's no point arguing. So let's just skip all that and go to California together."

"Oh, Annie, why do you want to go and follow me?"

"Because I love you, Mutt."

Looking into Annie's big blue, swimming-with-tears eyes, Mutt felt her heart melt. She dropped her pack and held out her arms. Annie ran into them and held on tight. Then she was kissing Annie and Annie was kissing her back, and the hollow ache inside her filled up with warm happiness. She knew this was crazy, but she was too overcome with emotion to worry about the problems that lay on the road ahead.

"Promise you'll never leave me again," Annie begged, searching her face.

"I promise. I'll never leave you...if it's any choice of mine."

"I'll never leave you either. But if God or man ever tears us asunder, I swear I'll spend my last penny and my dying breath to find you again."

Mutt didn't know what "asunder" meant, but it sounded like Annie was serious about staying together.

They started walking hand in hand alongside the tracks.

"You can't just hop on a train," Mutt explained. "There's a right way to do it or you'll lose a leg. You have to know how and when. And you have to do it so you don't get caught. There's some railroad cops out there who'd just as soon kill you as pick a piece of corn out of their teeth. And there's rules. Hobo rules. You gotta know how to behave with the other hobos, learn how to talk and such."

"You can teach me all that."

Mutt's heart was full with Annie by her side. She had never had so much feeling for anybody as this girl with her bright, powerful spirit shining with joy and love and a thirst for life. She knew she'd never been so happy before.

But amid all that good feeling, an unwelcome thought crept into her mind. What would happen when Annie found out she'd given her heart to a girl? Maybe she'd run back home as fast as she could. That wouldn't be the worst thing that could happen. Mutt wondered if she could keep that secret for a week, maybe two. It wouldn't be easy, not with the way they wanted to be so close to one another.

It wouldn't be fair either, she reflected, glancing to her side to see Annie's contented smile.

"Look," Mutt said, stopping and facing her. "Before we go on, there's something you gotta know. If you still want to go with me after what I gotta tell you, I'll be happy to have you. More than happy. Because…well…I reckon I love you too."

"I don't care what it is. I want us to be together forever."

"Well, still and all, Annie, this is important." She held her loosely, reluctant to chase away the look of devotion on her face. "I hope this don't make you mad, but…"

A cloud of dust on the horizon caught her eye. She turned to see a man on horseback galloping toward them. She recognized the chestnut gelding she had shared the barn with. Two other horses emerged from the dust cloud following close on the first.

"It's my father!" Annie yelled.

Mutt let go of Annie and turned to face the approaching men. The lead horse arrived in moments, coming to an abrupt stop ten feet away and spraying dirt as his hooves dug in. Mr. Callahan sat in the saddle, a shotgun across his arm. He laid the reins aside and aimed the gun at Mutt's head as the other two horsemen arrived, flanking him.

"Down on your knees, boy!" he ordered.

"Daddy!" Annie pleaded, running up to him and grabbing hold of his leg. "Don't hurt him!"

"You shut your mouth, girl! Daniel, take her."

One of the men dismounted and grabbed her by both arms. She struggled against him insolently and ineffectually.

Mr. Callahan dismounted, his gun still aimed at Mutt, his eyes steely and his jaw set firm like she'd never seen it before. "I said, down on your knees."

Mutt sank to her knees in the dirt.

"Hands on your head!"

She locked her hands together on top of her hat as Mr. Callahan approached.

"You got some kind of nerve for a tramp," he said, "taking advantage of my hospitality like that, then stealing my daughter away."

"It wasn't Mutt's fault," Annie exclaimed. "He told me to stay home. I followed him."

"And why would you do that, Annie?" Though he addressed his daughter, he kept his eyes and his gun on Mutt. "Why would you be so bent on following a complete stranger to parts unknown? What did he do to you that you would want to follow him like that?"

Mr. Callahan walked slowly up behind Mutt and touched the gun barrel to the base of her skull. She felt the unmistakable sensation of cool steel against her skin.

"Daddy, you don't understand!" Annie whined, straining against Daniel's grasp.

"A drifter like this," Mr. Callahan said, "is basically worthless. No family. No home. No morals. Takes what he wants, what don't belong to him." As he spoke, he slowly moved in a circle around Mutt, ending up in front of her again, the double barrel of the gun looking her in the eyes. "Steals a man's chicken if he's hungry and steals his innocent daughter if he's got an itch in his britches. There's lots of folks having a rough time these days, but there's still plenty who'll do the right thing. No matter how much they don't have, they don't steal somebody else's. As far as I'm concerned, a man like this doesn't deserve to live." The gun barrel settled against her forehead. "I believe I made you a promise, boy, about what would happen if you touched my daughter. Well, against all good sense and decency, you touched her. Now I'm going to keep my promise and blow your head off. You'd better make your peace with the Lord real quick like, if you're a God-fearing man."

"Stop!" Annie screeched.

"I told you to be quiet! You can stand there and watch me put a load of shot in this worthless son-of-a-bitch and maybe next time some sweet-talking bum catches your eye, you'll think twice."

Mutt closed her eyes and tensed up, waiting for the explosion of the gun, hoping she would die fast. Of all the ways of dying, she never predicted she'd be killed for stealing a man's daughter. Life was kind of funny like that, she reflected, and concluded that God had a peculiar sense of humor. He liked to surprise folks.

"Daddy!" Annie's voice was desperate. "Mutt isn't a man! Mutt's a girl! She's a girl!"

Stunned, Mutt opened her eyes to see Annie break free of her captor. She dashed over and flung her arms around Mutt's neck.

"Get her out of here!" Mr. Callahan ordered.

"Daddy, she's a girl! You're all wrong about her! You got it all wrong!"

Mutt stared wide-eyed at Annie, who nodded encouragingly.

"What?" her father asked. "What are you talking about?"

"Mutt's a girl," she repeated, her eyes filling with tears. "No man's touched me, Daddy."

"What kind of trick are you trying to pull?"

Annie stood and pulled Mutt to her feet. "It's not a trick. See for yourself."

Mr. Callahan looked uncertain, then addressed Mutt. "Is she telling the truth?"

Mutt nodded, shocked at this turn of events. How did Annie know? she wondered. And when?

Mr. Callahan stepped toward Mutt and took hold of her chin, running his hand over it. "So you've got no beard. That doesn't prove anything. You're young."

"Drop your trousers for Daddy," Annie suggested.

Mutt felt her face blush hot and noticed Mr. Callahan's did the same. He removed his hat, looking like he didn't know what to do next. Mutt decided Annie was right. It was better to be embarrassed than dead, so she unbuckled her belt and let her pants slide down over her undershorts. She took hold of the elastic around her waist and prepared to pull the shorts down when Mr. Callahan's hand shot up. "Stop!" he said. "Those are women's knees if ever I saw any."

He seemed relieved when Mutt let go of her shorts and pulled her pants back up. She heard one of the other men laugh, but Mr. Callahan still had a seriously stern look on his face. However, the shotgun was now pointed at the ground.

"If you're a woman, what did you want with my daughter?"

Annie intervened. "I told you, Daddy. It was my idea. She didn't want me to come. She told me to stay home."

"But why'd you want to go with her?"

Annie turned to Mutt looking lost. She clearly didn't know how to answer her father's question without plunging them both into trouble again.

"She wanted to go to California," Mutt offered, using her natural voice. "She told me she's always dreamed of going to California and that's where I'm headed."

A smile of relief appeared on Annie's face. "Yes!"

Mr. Callahan frowned. "It's California again, is it? How many times have I told you to get that nonsense out of your head? The only place you're going is to your room and you're going to stay there for a week."

Mr. Callahan mounted his horse. He reached down for his daughter's arm and pulled her up behind him, then gave Mutt a look of perplexity before riding away. Annie turned around and waved, a mournful look on her face, before the dust from the galloping horses hid her from view.

Mutt lowered her gaze to the ground, feeling like the world had just closed in on her.

# CHAPTER SIX

Mutt walked into the hobo jungle as the sun set. Over a dozen fires burned alongside the South Platte River. She approached one where four men sat huddled around a cook pot. The aroma coming off their meal made her mouth water.

She removed her hat, saying, "Good evening, 'bos. I'm Mississippi Mutt."

One of the men looked up at her with one eye open and one nearly closed. He stuck his arm up toward her, a matchstick between his thumb and forefinger.

This was the hobo signal for *move on, we don't have enough*. She took the match and walked down river. She was about to approach another fire when she heard a gravelly voice say "Mutt? Is that Mississippi Mutt?"

She turned to see Frogman puffing on a cigarette and smiling wide under his big frog eyes.

"Frogman!" she called, happy to see him.

He reached up to shake hands, then turned to his companions. "Look here, you 'bos, it's my friend Mississippi Mutt."

He introduced her to the others around his fire. There was John the Baptist, a lean, delicate-looking young man with thin blond hair and small, close-set eyes. Then there was the much more grizzled Cannonball Carl who lay on his side on a piece of cardboard, cleaning under his fingernails with a penknife. He grunted in her direction as he was introduced, his mouth shut tight in a permanent grimace. The last person Mutt met was a stout middle-aged woman with hair the color of rust pinned on top of her head in swooping curls. She was thick around the waist and bosomy, wearing men's work trousers and a woman's paisley blouse.

"This is Boxcar Betts."

Mutt tipped her hat.

"You're a young one," Betts observed, lighting a cigar. "Sit down here next to me, little lamb."

"I'm seventeen," Mutt said, taking the offered seat. "Born in the year of our Lord nineteen twenty-four!"

Betts put a heavy arm around Mutt's shoulders and squeezed her tight. "Aren't you a sweet thing?"

"Sweet as Tupelo honey," Mutt said with an involuntary giggle.

She let herself be nuzzled deep into the older woman, feeling comforted amid the sweet smell of tobacco.

A five-pound coffee can hung suspended over the fire with something promising simmering inside. Frogman stirred it with a ladle.

"You got anything for the mulligan?" he asked.

Mutt pulled a wad of newspaper out of her pack and unwrapped it to reveal a half dozen dinner rolls. "Somethin' to sop it up."

He nodded his satisfaction. "I thought you'd be afar west by now, Mutt. Didn't you catch Big Charlotte like I told you?"

"I did catch her, but I got throwed off her."

"You got throwed off Big Charlotte?" Betts asked, her tiny eyes blinking through the cigar smoke. "Was she moving?"

"You bet she was moving!" Mutt declared, warming up to the chance to tell her story. "She was moving at forty miles an hour! But I had to jump or that cinder dick woulda for sure put a bullet in my head. He was a mean son-of-a-bitch." She glanced at Betts. "Beg pardon, ma'am."

Betts sputtered. "Cursing don't bother me none, son."

Cannonball Carl huffed. "Ain't it the truth?"

"Go on," Betts urged, "tell us what happened."

Everyone around the fire gave their full attention to Mutt as she related the details of her encounter on Big Charlotte, enjoying the nods and chortles of her companions as well as their sincere appreciation of her bravery in taking such a deadly leap and coming out of it with no broken bones. Each of them admired the cut on her chin, a mark that pegged her as a true member of the hobo fraternity.

When her story was done she learned a bit more about her companions. John the Baptist had been traveling only two years. He had been a Baptist preacher in Alabama until his flock had dwindled away to nothing when hard times came. His neighbors had packed up and moved out west looking for work. He eventually did the same, riding the freights. Along the way he took a liking to the hobo life. John had discovered that he could make a humble living as an itinerant preacher. Mutt liked listening to his voice, thick with a lazy Southern drawl that reminded her of home.

Cannonball Carl was an old-timer who rarely took a job, living exclusively in hobo jungles. "Jobs are hard to come by these days," he said. "Why should I take one and deprive another man of his livelihood?" He grinned, displaying a grand total of two teeth, both uppers and both of them the color of dried mustard.

Boxcar Betts was one of those rare creatures on the hobo circuit, a long-time road sister. Most of the women riding the rails were on their way to some new life, plunged by desperate circumstances into wandering until they could find somewhere to settle. But Betts had been hoboing off and on nearly twenty years. She provided something often lacking in the hobo jungles: a mother figure. Even the toughest, most hardened of men would soften to a woman like Betts. She seemed good-hearted and generous, but Mutt knew she had to be tough to survive this kind of life.

"You got a husband?" Mutt asked her.

She shook her head and wrinkled up her nose as if she smelled something foul. "I had one once, years ago. I'll try anything once, son, but once is enough for me when it comes to husbands. A woman don't need a husband to get on in this world. I'm doing just fine without one."

Betts pulled Mutt's head down to her thigh and stroked her hair. Mutt relaxed in the warmth from the fire and the pillowy support of Betts's body. The campfire flames danced in front of her, casting off heat and light.

After staring into the fire for a few minutes, she thought she could see a face, a face of flames like the Devil himself. It was a sallow face with dark circles under bloodshot eyes, hollow cheeks and a stubbled chin. It opened its thin-lipped mouth and looked like it was trying to speak. *Ah, Mutt, you know I love you.* With an involuntary jerk of her leg, she kicked toward the fire ring.

"Watch it," said Frogman. "You'll get dirt in the mulligan."

"Sorry. Is it ready yet?"

"Yeah." He ladled the stew into tin cans and passed them around the group.

John the Baptist softly intoned, "For what the Lord hath given us may we be truly grateful."

Mutt took a spoonful of the brew. It tasted like onion-flavored water with some hunks of carrots and potatoes. No meat. She dunked one of the bread rolls into the broth. They were stale, given to her at the back door of a bakery, but they softened right up as they soaked up the liquid.

Cannonball Carl turned up his can and drank his stew, chugging it down like it was a shot of whisky, his Adam's apple jumping up and down until the can was empty.

The cool night air was softened by the strains of a harmonica and the subdued voices of conversation broken by an occasional hearty laugh. Mutt was happy to be here. The pain of losing Annie that morning gradually slipped away as she listened to the familiar sounds of the camp at night. This felt like home to her now. She was especially happy to find Frogman here, but even when she didn't know anybody, the camps were comforting and the hobos welcoming. It was a community like any other, held together by their common needs and common foes.

"I'll wash up," she offered when they were done eating. She collected the dishes in the empty stew can.

"That's a fine boy," Betts muttered, leaning back against a log, her eyes half closed.

Mutt walked through camp past several fires and men in good spirits, talking, drinking, smoking and playing cards. She took the dishes to the river and washed them, then hung them from hooks in the branches of trees alongside the pots and pans of the rest of the camp. The tree branches, flush with spring growth, were laden with camp cookware, clean and drying, ready for the next meal and whoever came into camp tomorrow. Someone had mounted an American flag on one of the tree trunks. From the looks of its frayed edges, it had been there a while.

Returning to the fire, she added a few birch branches to it, then sat cross-legged in front of it, holding her hands out for warmth. John lay on his back wearing round wire-framed glasses, reading a well-worn Bible by the firelight. The harmonica was still playing, clear in the cool night air, and the smoke of a dozen fires curled into the sky above the camp, hanging over them like gauzy fog.

Frogman took a draw from his flask, then handed it to Betts who did the same. She pushed it toward Mutt.

"That boy doesn't partake of spirits," Frogman informed her, taking back the flask.

"Good for you," said John, looking over his reading glasses. "Keep your head clear and you'll always have money in your pocket."

"But I ain't got any money in my pocket," Mutt said.

Betts laughed. "You should find a trade to do to pick up extra change."

"That's right," Carl said. "You gotta have a trade. Now me, I'm a locksmith. If you ever lock yourself out of somewhere, I can get you in." He held his fingers near his mouth and blew on them while Frogman looked at him askance.

"Oh, I have something," said Mutt. "I do barbering."

"Barbering?"

"Haircuts and shaves."

John sat up. "I could use a shave. Sure could. Frogman, did you know Mississippi Mutt was a barber?"

"No, sir, I was not aware of that. I will keep that in mind should I ever decide to get shorn."

"Short hair'll keep away the walking dandruff," Mutt pointed out.

John laughed and Frogman huffed, then poked at the fire with a stick.

Mutt unrolled her shaving kit and took out a razor, strop, scissors and a small can of MacGregor Brushless Shaving Cream. She ran the blade of the razor across the strop a few times.

"That's a razor that's been around a while," John observed. "Looks older than you. I declare, it looks old enough to have shaved Jerusalem Slim himself."

Betts let out a tickled whoop. "Jerusalem Slim," she muttered, shaking her head.

"It used to be my daddy's," Mutt replied, not bothering to say she had stolen it from him when she left, one of the few things she took that she thought would come in handy. It had an inch-wide blade that locked into place when open and a handle made of buffalo horn, burnished by time to a rich walnut color.

"Is your daddy dead?" Betts asked.

"Yep."

"May his soul rest in peace," John said quietly.

Betts gave her a maternal look of sympathy. "What about your mother?"

"She died when I was a right young'un."

"Poor little orphan."

"I'll get me some water." She ran down to the river and grabbed a tin can from a tree, then dipped it in a clear pool of water. Then she ran back to the fire where John sat on a tall stump with his legs crossed, waiting for his fine, pale stubble to be shaved.

After lathering him up, Mutt drew the razor along the preacher's jaw, scraping off hair and shaving cream and leaving behind smooth pink skin. She dipped the razor into the water can to rinse it off and thought back to when she was twelve or thirteen years old shaving her father's tanned, deeply creased face with its stiff bristles. His beard was so different from this man's. It was one of the best memories she had of the two of them together. She would stand behind him where he sat contentedly with his head tilted back, a towel around his shoulders. He said she was the best barber in the whole county. For sure, she was the cheapest. But she didn't mind. It was one of her favorite chores. She enjoyed those few minutes, some of the most tender and peaceful there ever were between them. Looking back, she might even say that was the most loving act they had ever shared.

The last time she had shaved her father, she had stood behind him looking down at his sweaty bald spot, her hand shaking, her anger so huge it sparked up and down all her nerves and muscles straining to get out. The razor wanted to dig in deep and she had to use all that raw, angry power to hold it back. All it managed to do was scratch him, and a trickle of blood spilled onto his neck.

He had jerked back and put his hand up to the tiny wound, coming away with blood on his fingers. She had nicked the skin over his Adam's apple. It was the first time she had cut him since he first taught her how to use a razor. He was surprised, thinking it was an accident, and was annoyed at her. He was completely unaware of how close she had come to slicing into his throat. She had dropped the razor to the floor and fled the room. That was the day she realized she had to leave before she did something unforgivable.

"That's nice," said the preacher, running his hand across his chin. "You do a fine job."

Mutt wiped his face clean, then wiped off the razor. He handed her a nickel and said, "There, now you got money in your pocket."

"I do admire a clean-shaven man," Betts pronounced, eliciting a grunt of discontent out of Cannonball Carl, who absent-mindedly fondled his disorderly beard.

"You don't drink and you don't smoke," Frogman pointed out, "so what will you do with that nickel?"

"Maybe he'll get himself a woman," Carl suggested with a lascivious grin. "You ever had a woman, Mutt?"

"Leave him alone," Betts said, encircling Mutt in her massive arm. "Any woman you can get for a nickel ain't worth getting."

"There is some just the same," Carl said. "I saw two of 'em in the jungle in Cincie. They was sashaying through camp offering any 'bo with a nickel a right proper—"

"Oh, be quiet!" Betts pulled Mutt deep into her side. "This boy has no interest in your cheap whores. Besides, if he wants a woman, he don't have to pay. He's a handsome young fella. A real pretty little thing." She fondled Mutt's neck. "Why, if I wasn't so old, I—"

"You'd what?" asked Frogman, raising one eyebrow. "Haven't we heard you say plenty of times how you've got no use for the males of the species?"

"A girl's allowed to change her mind…when it suits her." Betts smiled down at Mutt, then winked. "This sweet child's going to sleep with me tonight."

Mutt figured Betts had seen through her disguise and would make sure nobody else got any ideas about messing with her during the night. In the company of men, she often slept uneasily, but tonight she would sleep soundly and hopefully dream about Annie Callahan.

"What will you do with your nickel, Mutt?" Betts asked.

"Save it. I'm saving up to go to a picture show."

"That's sweet."

"How much is a picture show?"

"Two bits."

She stretched out with her head on Betts's broad thigh, figuring she would have plenty of nickels to go to the picture shows once she got a job in California. She closed her eyes, feeling the heat of the fire on her face and Betts's comforting hand stroking her hair.

John the Baptist's melodic voice reached her from the other side of the fire. "The Lord is my shepherd; I shall not want. He maketh me to lie down in green pastures: he leadeth me beside the still waters. He restoreth my soul: he leadeth me in the paths of righteousness for his name's sake."

"Let's not have any preaching here, John," Frogman objected. "You can read your Bible to yourself. We've no need for it, not even on an empty stomach, and most certainly not on a full one."

"I second that!" Cannonball Carl grumbled.

"It's not for the sake of your soul I'm reading this verse," John said. "I know y'all's souls been sold to the Devil way back in the days of Methuselah. But our young friend Mutt here is innocent in the ways of the world and still in the arms of our Lord. There's no reason to deprive him of his salvation. We hobos need a preacher every bit as much as town folk."

Frogman muttered unintelligibly and folded his face into a powerful frown.

Mutt sat up. "I ain't as innocent as y'all think, Preacher John."

"You ain't old enough to have gone down the road of perdition completely, though you're in the company of lost souls. The Lord will protect you and listen to your prayers."

"You watch out there, Mutt," Frogman said. "This preacher might expect you to put that nickel right back in his collection tin."

Betts laughed.

"Ah, go on," John said. "There's no harm and no cost in listening to the wind, as they say." He bent his head to his open Bible. "Yea, thou I walk through the valley of the shadow of death, I will fear no evil; for thou art with me; Thy rod and thy staff, they comfort me."

John's voice was pleasant and his text poetic, but Mutt didn't understand it. She certainly didn't understand why she might be comforted by a rod and a staff. She'd had enough of that in her life. In her experience, rods and staffs and belts and switches were no comfort at all. So she was content when John went back to reading to himself. They listened instead to a banjo at one of the other fires playing "She'll Be Coming 'Round the Mountain."

She nestled back into Betts's lap. What comforts me, she thought, is the weight of Betts's arm around my shoulder, the aroma of her cigar, the heat of the fire, and the musical jangling of pots, pans and tin cans in the trees on the riverbank.

Betts softly hummed along with the banjo and a few minutes later Mutt fell asleep.

# CHAPTER SEVEN

Standing on a high rung of a ladder in the boughs of a peach tree, Mutt wiped her forehead with her sleeve and lifted her face to the clear sky to feel the full force of the Northern California summer sun. She then returned to plucking white peaches, trying to ignore the itch of the peach fuzz creeping up her arms and across her back.

"Five years ago," said Topeka Slim from the ladder in the next tree, "I made three hundred dollars one summer loading cargo ships on the docks of Richmond, Virginia."

"So you're a rich man," Mutt quipped.

"I *was* a rich man." Slim's tanned face grinned through the branches, revealing the gap in his bottom row of teeth.

Mutt had known him for a week. Of the fellas who worked here, he was her favorite, an easygoing man with a ready laugh and a lot of stories to tell.

She had already heard the story of how he got his teeth knocked out by a sheriff's deputy in a Louisiana jail years ago. Thrown in a cell for vagrancy, he'd been given nothing to eat but corn mush for three days and sent out to work in the cotton fields all day. On the fourth day, the mush had weevils in it so he complained to the deputy, who replied with, "If you don't like the food here, Mister, you can eat my boot!" Then he kicked Slim in the mouth, knocking two teeth clean out and rattling a few others plenty loose. Sometimes when he spoke, his words came out with short whistles, and when he ate an ear of corn, he had to make a second pass over each row, picking up the kernels he'd missed.

Behind every scar and missing tooth is a story, she had learned. Like the scar on her chin. The wound had healed, but a narrow white line remained to mark the spot.

"What happened to the money?" she asked.

"I buried it in a coffee can in one of the jungles. Too dangerous to carry that kind of dough around. You know what I mean. Jackrollers would be all over ya."

"Which jungle was it?"

"Well, see, that's the problem. I plumb forgot. I've been looking for that coffee can ever since. Mighta been St. Louis or Chicago. Or maybe Boise." He chuckled, wiping his hand on the front of his shirt.

Topeka Slim was in his early sixties and he'd been riding the freights for decades. His colorful stories helped pass the time on a long, hot day in the orchard. Mutt had met him once in a camp in Iowa, so when he turned up here on the Gemgiani farm, she was glad to see a familiar face. He remembered her too and immediately asked for a shave and a haircut. He was a good-hearted old fellow who'd spent his life wandering, and the years of traveling showed in the deep lines of his face. As lifers on the iron road went, he had been one of the lucky ones. He was still alive and healthy minus a couple toes he'd lost to frostbite and those two missing teeth.

Mutt had no aspirations of being a professional hobo for a lifetime like Slim, but it was working out okay for now. She hadn't thought much about the future. It loomed like a featureless gray cloud in her imagination.

Her plans encompassed nothing more than this season. California had turned out to be less than the paradise she had imagined it to be. There were a dozen men for every job, the work was hard and the pay was meager. The rooms that came with the jobs, when there were some, were as bad as most jails. But she had stuck with it, moving from orchard to orchard, following the crops as they ripened through the spring and into summer.

The other thing she'd discovered about California was that it was an improbably big territory. The area they were harvesting in was near a town called Marysville, over four hundred miles north of Hollywood. She was sure Annie had been as ignorant as she was regarding where places were in California. All she'd cared about was getting here when she decided to go with Mutt. Wouldn't she have been surprised to find herself still so far away from her destination?

Mutt had been lucky to land this job. It was better than most. There was a bunkhouse for the pickers and two meals a day. She'd stay here until the peaches were done. Altogether that would be about two weeks.

"Where you going after this?" asked Slim.

"Tomatoes. They say there's more tomato fields in California than Carter's got liver pills."

"True enough."

"I hear there's nuts to pick in the fall. You know anything about that?"

"Sure. Down around Modesto, Turlock. Lots of walnuts. Almonds too. That'll take you through to October. Then you got your oranges down in Southern California. Take you through December. After that, you sit back and smoke 'em if you've got 'em until spring rolls around again."

"Yep. That's how I figured it. After that, I was thinking I'd head back to Mississippi, maybe get back by Christmas."

"You gonna visit your folks?"

"I got some relatives, cousins. I thought I'd pay them a visit."

She wondered if Cousin Opal knew she'd run away. Or was she still sending those birthday cards like she'd always done? Last month, Mutt had turned eighteen. Maybe a birthday card had shown up at the farm for her. She wondered how that would have made her daddy feel, getting that birthday card with nobody there to give it to.

Now that she was an adult, she figured she could go visit Cousin Opal without any danger of being sent back to her father. Even if they tried to make her go, she wouldn't have to because now she knew how to take care of herself. With Ray still in the army, Mutt knew that the only people in the whole world she had to visit were Cousins Opal and Fred. Her mind drifted toward a farm in Nebraska but she yanked it back. There was nothing there for her. It had been three months since she'd watched Annie ride away on the back of that horse, but waking and sleeping her face still came regularly to mind. She held on fast to the memory of Annie's lips on hers and the bright sparkle of her eyes. Every night she tried to dream about Annie but she usually failed. She dreamed her up less and less and that made her sorry. She wondered if Annie ever dreamed of her.

When she went to see Fred and Opal, she'd tell them it would be okay if they wanted to let her father know she was still alive. She didn't mind about giving him some peace of mind but she would never go home again.

She had no home.

She climbed down the ladder with a full bucket and emptied it into a lug box. The sound of laughter distracted her and she looked down the row of trees to see two young men in overalls and short-sleeved shirts walking through the orchard. They were the Gemgiani twins, Luke and Joe, the twenty-year-old sons of the man who owned this orchard.

"Hey, old man!" called Luke, pausing just long enough to give a hard kick to Topeka Slim's ladder, knocking it sideways and causing Slim to latch his arm onto a tree branch to keep it upright. "Better watch it or you're gonna fall."

Both boys laughed, their handsome, olive-complected faces full of mirth.

His tone dismissive, Joe Gemgiani said, "Stupid Okie." Then, noticing Mutt, he said, "What are you looking at, Sissy-Boy? You got something to say?"

"No, sir," she muttered, taking her empty bucket back up the ladder.

The boys walked on and Slim frowned, muttering, "Spoiled brats. I'm no Okie. Those boys don't know their ass from a red rooster."

The Gemgiani twins were college boys on their summer break, supposedly working on the farm, but all they really did was make trouble. Their father was a fair and decent man, but as Slim said, his sons were spoiled brats.

Back up in the tree, Mutt caught the aroma sloughing off the fruit in the heat of the afternoon. She pulled a peach off a branch and held it in the palm of her hand, admiring its perfection. It reminded her of Annie, its bashful blushing skin covered with pale, velvety hairs. She touched the peach to her cheek and closed her eyes, imagining the sensation of Annie's face pressed against hers.

"Payday today," Slim remarked. "It's gonna be a little short this week because of the Wobblies."

Mutt frowned, thinking about the red union card in her pocket. "Wobblies," she muttered. "I don't understand why I gotta give them money I earned fair and square."

"It's the union dues. This is a union operation. You want to work here, you gotta join."

"I know. But what good does it do?"

"It's why you get your two squares a day and a roof over your head. That's what good the Wobblies do for you. I been around a long time, Mutt. Believe me, the unions are a good thing for poor working stiffs like us. It's protection."

Mutt shrugged, realizing she didn't know much about the Wobblies one way or another. All she knew was that she had been told that if she wasn't a card-carrying member of the Industrial Workers of the World, she wouldn't be working on this farm. So she'd signed up.

"I'm going into town for a hot, juicy steak tonight," Slim said. "How 'bout you?"

"I'm fixin' to get myself a new razor. The one I have is old and the handle's cracked. Barbering brings in a few dollars, so it'll pay for itself."

"That's a sensible thing then. But what about fun? A nice steak dinner? Maybe some good whiskey?"

"I don't drink."

"Well, that's sensible too. You're real sensible for such a young fella. But you ought to have a little fun. What do you like to do for fun?"

"There's one thing I'd like to do."

"What's that?" Slim peered around the tree to see Mutt's face.

"See a picture show."

Slim's eyebrows went up. "Yep, yep, that would be a fun time. I wouldn't mind that myself. I know they got a movie theater in Marysville. I've been there. We could hitch a ride into town on Sunday, have a nice meal and see a picture. If you wouldn't mind the company."

"I wouldn't mind a bit."

"It'll be like a regular date!" Slim declared, then buckled up laughing so hard he nearly pitched himself off his ladder. Steadying himself, he said, "Just so you know, I'd rather take a girl to the show, and if any presents herself, wanting to go out with an old, shiftless wanderer like me, I'll be off with her in two shakes of a lamb's tail."

"In the meantime, I guess you're stuck with me."

"What kind of picture do you want to see?"

"One with Irene Dunne in it."

"Sounds like you got something particular in mind."

Mutt shrugged. "I just want to see something romantic is all."

"No surprise there, you being such a young man and all. All right then. We'll find us a love story to watch!"

*  *  *

In the dark of the movie theater Mutt sat next to Topeka Slim with her handkerchief in hand, sobbing quietly as Vivien Leigh, reduced to prostitution by the severity of war, was reunited with her true love played by Robert Taylor. Believing she was besmirched beyond redemption and unfit to marry him, Vivien Leigh killed herself on the spot they first met, *Waterloo Bridge*.

The lights came on in the theater as the credits rolled by. Mutt blew her nose and wiped at her face, embarrassed by her emotions but too caught up in the tragic events on screen to control herself. She wondered if Annie had seen this film. She'd seemed so tenderhearted she'd most likely need two or three handkerchiefs to make it through.

Slim slammed his palm playfully into her shoulder. "Aw, buck up. It's just a story."

Mutt sniffed. "When they said it was a love story, I thought for sure it'd have a happy ending."

"Since when did a love story have a happy ending? As soon as a fella falls in love he may as well throw happiness out the window."

"But they could have been happy. He wouldn't have cared what she done. He loved her."

"Nah, she was right. He would have cared. Once the honeymoon was over, he would have cared."

Slim led the way out of the theater and into the warmth of a summer evening.

"Why does a love story have to be sad?" Mutt asked.

"Ah, it doesn't have to be. It just usually is. Lots of things don't work out." A soft whistle came through the gap in his teeth as he spoke. "Life never follows the road you laid out for it. It goes its own way, like a stubborn mule. So what's the point trying to plan it all out?"

"But if you don't make plans, how will you ever get anywhere?"

"That's the thing about fellas like me, Mutt. We don't get anywhere. That's why they call it drifting. But you, you're young and you should think about your future. If you're figuring on marriage and a family and all that, why, that's real nice. It's worth thinking about." Slim put a hand on her shoulder. "You're a good worker and you got a good head on your shoulders. There's no reason at all you shouldn't make a plan like that. Now let's get on out to the main road and catch a ride back."

They walked side by side through downtown Marysville, passing a saloon full of boisterous men spending their paychecks on a good time. A lot of men Mutt had met in her travels had no plans beyond that. Topeka Slim was one of them. She knew she didn't want to live her life like that, but she didn't know what she wanted instead. She would like a place to call home. What he was talking about, though, marriage and a family, that wasn't for her. She didn't want to get married, not so long as she had to marry a man. She thought about Annie and how she'd asked Mutt if she would marry her.

"I would!" Mutt had answered without hesitation.

That would be the sweetest thing ever, but that was just a fool's dream.

# CHAPTER EIGHT

Alone in the bunkhouse, Mutt opened the handkerchief that held her new straight razor. The handle was gleaming maple with a mother-of-pearl inlay. The blade flashed silver, sharp and clean, never used. She intended to break it in on Topeka Slim. His bristly white whiskers and leathery skin would be a fine test for it. She'd never bought herself anything nice before. Talking herself into spending the money had not been easy. But it wasn't rash, she assured herself. It was a tool of her trade and would earn its worth many times over.

Since it was Monday, the mattresses in the bunkhouse were bare, all of them thin, stained and lumpy. They lay on nets of wire and were filled with chicken feathers and covered with gray and white striped cloth. The sheets and towels were washed every Monday. To some of the pickers, that was a luxury they could hardly believe. Clean sheets once a week! She wondered if that was one of the things she could thank the Wobblies for.

She sat on her bunk and took off her hat and the handkerchief around her neck. It was soaked through with sweat. She unbuttoned her shirt and noticed the perspiration stain on her undershirt, between and under her small, pointy breasts. It had been another hot day and some of the pickers had taken off after supper for a swim in the river. That sounded good, but for obvious reasons she couldn't join them. After a short rest, she'd go out to the shower and clean up.

The hardest thing about passing as a man in a communal setting was handling the off-duty hours. Bathing was always a challenge. But the after-supper time in the stiflingly hot bunkhouse was also hard. Most of the men lounged around in various stages of undress and slept in the nude. After over a year in disguise, Mutt had developed numerous tricks for obtaining the privacy she needed. But in rare moments like this, amid the luxury of solitude, she still kept up her guard. There was too much at stake to risk discovery. Her livelihood depended on maintaining the deception.

She often thought about how hard it was to live independently in the world if you were a woman, calling to mind those she had met and how they had managed. There were a few, like some of her teachers back in Jenner Springs, who were educated women making a decent living, but they were in the minority, at least in Mutt's experience.

There was Boxcar Betts, she reminded herself, who had carved out a niche in the society of wanderers. They accepted and respected her and she survived. But there were far more women who had nothing to live on but their bodies, and the longer they plied that trade, the cheaper and sorrier they became. In *Waterloo Bridge*, even the beautiful Vivien Leigh had had no choices left. What happened, Mutt wondered, when nobody wanted these women anymore? Did they all kill themselves like Vivien Leigh?

On her way to California, Mutt had shared a train car with several other hobos, including two young women traveling together, their eyes wary and watchful as if they were fugitives from the law. She had watched them with such curiosity that one of them, the younger one, thin-faced with a sharp chin and defiant brown eyes, had asked, "What are you staring at, boy?"

What she was staring at was the first female couple she'd ever seen, for that's the conclusion she came to after watching them for several hours.

They didn't talk to anyone. They didn't even tell their names. They sat huddled together under a thin wool blanket as the train climbed over the Sierra Nevada Mountains with its snowy peaks of granite and its vast pine forests. Mutt could only imagine their story, as they gave little away. One thing she did figure out was that they were in love, and that realization made her happy because she hadn't known that women could love each other like that. Except for the extraordinary case of herself and Annie, which she had previously considered unique. But these two women also made her sad because there was something about them that smacked of hopelessness. They were running away together, trying to escape a hostile world where the two of them were an impossibility. She wanted to ask them so many questions. Where were they going? Where would they not be an impossibility? Did they even know? What would they do when they got there? It was obvious they had no money. In their eyes was the fear of the unknown.

She had wanted to know their story so badly that despite their aloofness she had asked, "Where you two headed?"

"None of your business!" replied the one with the wild brown hair.

Mutt had often thought of them since and wished she knew what had become of them. She had seen desperation many times over since she'd left Jenner Springs, but the wretched look of women, homeless, friendless and penniless, was the thing that haunted her most.

Over the months of being on her own, she had concluded that pretending to be a man had been the right thing to do. She enjoyed a kind of freedom these women could never know.

The bunkhouse contained four bunk beds, accommodations for eight men, a couple of wooden chairs, a table for card games, and lockers where they kept their belongings. The floor was bare wooden planks and the token windows contained dirty glass with no screens. There was a never-ending fight between those who wanted to open the windows at night for air and those who wanted to shut them to keep out the mosquitoes. It was usually too hot to sleep either way, and Mutt spent hours each night tossing on her bunk, hiding under a sheet from the aggravating buzz of mosquitoes and trudging through the night to the revolting outhouse to relieve herself.

The food was about the same as you could get at a mission—weak coffee and oatmeal for breakfast, and at the end of the day a plate of beans with a slice of bread. But at least here you didn't have to listen to a sermon along with your beans. All in all, it was tolerable.

She turned the new razor over in her hand, noting the reflection of her eyes in its blade. They were elongated by the curve of the steel. She tipped the blade slightly to pass over her freckled nose and focus on her pale, straight lips. She smiled at herself.

Hearing a sound at the door, she closed the razor and slipped it into her pocket, pulling her shirt together over her chest just as the door opened. The Gemgiani twins burst in with the freshly laundered towels and sheets. They dropped them on the nearest bunk.

"Hey, look," Luke said, stepping toward Mutt. "It's Sissy-Boy. What're you doing in here all alone, Sissy-Boy? Won't the other boys let you play with them?" He laughed like he'd made the world's all-time best joke.

Mutt gave him an indulgent smile and started past him, intending to get out of the bunkhouse and away from these troublemakers as fast as she could. Luke caught her by the arm as she passed, bringing her up short and yanking her around to face him.

"Where do you think you're going?" He kept a firm grip on her arm, his gray eyes full of contempt.

"Shower."

"Good idea. The stench in here is enough to knock a man over. Don't forget your towel." He let go of her arm.

She grabbed a towel from the stack as she passed the bunk, wary of the other twin near the door.

"Aren't you going to say thank you?" Joe asked.

"Thank you," Mutt said grudgingly, reaching for the doorknob.

Joe slammed his boot against the door, preventing it from opening. "Is that any way to talk to your employer? Where's the respect?"

All Mutt wanted was to get outside. The bunkhouse felt like a trap. These boys were like cats with a mouse. As long as she struggled, they would keep playing with her, so she knew she had to make it no fun for them.

"Thank you, sir," she said, looking Joe in the eye. He had the same eyes as his brother, cold and gray.

The boot didn't budge. Apparently they had nothing better to do tonight than harass her.

"Did that sound respectful to you, Luke?" Joe asked.

Luke tipped his hat back on his head. "Not hardly. I don't think Sissy-Boy is appreciative of our hospitality."

"Fellas," Mutt said, "I don't want no trouble. I just want to go about my business."

Joe's boot moved away from the door and Mutt reached again for the doorknob. Joe caught her and swung her around, pinning her by both arms with her back against him. The towel dropped to the floor at her feet and pain ripped through her shoulders as he jerked her arms back even tighter.

Luke lunged toward her, his right hand balled up in a fist. He pulled back, about to throw a punch at her face when suddenly he stopped, his eyes fixed on her chest. With her arms pinned, her shirt was fully open and the thin, damp undershirt clearly revealed the shape of her breasts. For a woman they were smallish, but for a rail-skinny young man they made no sense at all.

Luke stared in confusion. His fist dissolved.

"What's the matter?" asked Joe, his breath hot in Mutt's ear.

Luke glanced from Mutt's chest to her face while she struggled fruitlessly against his brother. "I don't think Sissy-Boy here is a boy at all," he finally said.

"What are you talking about?"

Luke grabbed the undershirt and pulled it up to her neck. Seeing her naked breasts, he caught his breath. She stamped hard on Joe's foot, causing him to holler and release her. She pulled her undershirt down but it was too late to prevent her secret from being revealed. She stood facing them, breathing hard and gauging her chances for escape. Joe stood directly in front of the door, the only way out.

"You can see plain as day," Luke marveled. "Look at her face. Hell, this is a girl!"

"Imagine that." Joe whistled.

"You belong to one of these other bums?" Luke asked.

She shook her head. "Y'all don't have to tell your daddy. I do a good day's work. I earn my money just like any of these men do and I don't cause no trouble."

Luke turned his head to grin at his brother. "I don't see any reason *we all* got to tell anybody, do you?"

Joe shook his head. "I think a girl is better than a Sissy-Boy any day."

"Bolt the door," Luke said in a low tone. He came toward her, a determined, mean look in his eye.

She knew what this was about even before Luke unbuckled his belt. She backed away from him, hearing the deadbolt slide into place.

"Please," she said, "just leave me be. I'll be outta here. You don't have to pay me what's owed. Just let me go peaceful like."

Luke said nothing, but continued his advance. When she was backed up against the far wall and couldn't go any farther, he grabbed her by the waist and threw her roughly down on the nearest bunk. Then he crawled on top of her, struggling to get her under control while she beat at him with her fists. His head banged into the top bunk several times as they fought.

"Hold her down," he hollered to his brother.

Between them, they were able to subdue her, pinning her down flat on her stomach. Joe sat on her back, weighing her down heavily and effectively immobilizing her. Luke yanked her pants down to her knees. Then he ripped her undershorts apart.

"Jesus!" he said. "Look at this."

"What?" Joe asked, irritated. He was facing the wall, unable to see what his brother was so fascinated with.

"Her backside's all scarred up. Welts all over it."

She felt his fingers on her skin and fury welled up in her. She bellowed into the pillow, a low, guttural animal growl like nothing she had ever heard come out of herself before.

"Quit wasting time," Joe ordered. "Just do it. She's like a wildcat."

When Luke stood up beside the bed to undo his pants, Mutt summoned all the rage stored up in her to throw Joe off with one mighty heave. He tumbled off the bunk and onto the floor, banging his head into the bed frame. She rolled over and sprang up, yanking up her pants and stumbling away from Luke. He moved rapidly toward her. Her hand searched her pocket desperately as she ran for the door. She pulled the razor out and opened it in one clean motion as her other hand reached for the deadbolt, fumbling with it in frenzied panic. Luke latched onto her shoulder and spun her around, tearing her hand from the doorframe. They stood face to face, both of them breathing hard. His lips curled into a self-satisfied sneer.

He lunged at her and she lashed out with that fine sharp blade and slit his throat.

# PART TWO

*Spring, 1950*

# CHAPTER NINE

Mutt felt conspicuous climbing the steps into the Greyhound bus. A suitcase weighed down her left arm and brushed against the stiff navy blue wool of her new skirt. With a matching jacket, a simple white blouse, pale stockings and brown flats, she imagined she couldn't have looked more unremarkable. Still, as she handed the driver her ticket, her throat closed up with anxiety. She scanned the passengers—men in working clothes, women in cool dresses, a few children trying to use the bus as a playground. She avoided meeting anyone's eyes as she moved down the aisle, wondering if there was anything about her, like the cut of her prison-issued suit or finger-wave hairstyle, that would tell them she had just walked through the gate of the California Institution for Women. The locals in this dusty desert town must see it all the time, women with a look of uneasiness getting on a bus at the Tehachapi Greyhound station, headed for Los Angeles where they could get lost in the anonymity of a big city. To the locals, if not to everyone, she was sure she stuck out like a hog with two heads. She inadvertently caught the eye of a whiskered man who nodded curtly, his expression unrevealing.

She instinctively followed Zetta's prim white hat riding high on the thicket of her charcoal-colored hair. They didn't know one another well, but were now comrades through the coincidence of being released from prison on the same day. She and Zetta had not belonged to the same social group. The women segregated themselves when they were able to, like at meals, and Zetta, whose family had originally come from Portugal, had aligned herself with a handful of other women from Portuguese families. Though the inmates divided themselves along ethnic lines, the population of Tehachapi wasn't that large. For somebody like Mutt who had been there for many years, nobody was a complete stranger.

She felt like a trespasser on this bus, like she didn't belong here in the company of ordinary people. If they could recognize her for what she was, they would shun her…or worse. But one way or another, her life had always been like that, lived without a sense of belonging, furtive and protective of her real self. She was accustomed to being different.

Zetta took a seat halfway back and Mutt sat down beside her after slipping her case overhead. Wearing a navy blue suit identical to Mutt's, Zetta crossed her legs and fanned herself with the envelope containing her release papers. She seemed perfectly at ease, defiantly so with her upturned chin and resentful brown eyes. But Zetta had been inside only six months on petty larceny charges. Her homecoming would be significantly less traumatic than Mutt's, especially since Zetta was actually going home. Her home was Southern California, so she had friends and family there. Mutt had nobody. She'd never even been to Los Angeles. But she'd been told it was a big city where she could find work.

In her bag were all the credentials she needed to get a job, proof that she could type and take dictation, and that she had completed all the coursework equivalent to a high school diploma. For the last eight years, she had been groomed with the skills necessary to become integrated and successful in society. Though there were no certificates for it, she had also been trained in other essential skills for women, learning how to walk, talk, dress, put on makeup, cook a pot roast, darn a sock and bathe a baby. Possessed with all of these talents necessary for running an office and a home, she had been assured that she was equipped to return to the world. She could get a job and a husband. They had even trained her to dampen her Mississippi accent and give up Southern phrases like "y'all" and "finer than a frog's hair," as that sort of thing was considered undesirable to employers and presumably to any potential husband worth having. During the course of her internment, she had been transformed in countless ways.

*If my father could see me now*, she thought for one absurd moment, *he would fall on his knees and praise God*. What he had never been able to do with her, the State of California had achieved. At least superficially. There were many ways in which Shirley Hopper had not changed at all. Under her sedate new demeanor was the same lost and lonely Mutt, the same awkward, wary girl who had no idea where to go or what to do with herself. But she had also retained her essential hopefulness. Amid all of the uncertainty of the road ahead, there was an excitement stirring in her, the promise of a new kind of life. She couldn't say what it would be like, not in any detail, but that didn't keep her from the honest belief that it would be better than anything that had come before.

"This outfit is shit!" Zetta complained, wriggling in her seat.

"I think it's kind of nice," Mutt remarked. "But hot."

They both took off their jackets as the bus left the town of Tehachapi behind. Mutt watched out the window as the prison complex came into view in the distance, nestled in the low hills of the desert, surrounded by beige dirt and scrubby brush. That had been her home for eight years. It was hard to believe she was leaving it behind. The buildings and high fence of the prison dipped out of view below a hill and she turned her head forward.

"So, Hobo," Zetta said, using the nickname she'd been pinned with in prison, "what've you got lined up?"

"Nothing yet. I'll get someplace to live first thing, then try to find a job."

"In the City of Angels?"

"City of Angels?"

"That's Los Angeles. That's what it means in Spanish."

That was a hopeful beginning, Mutt thought. She could use an angel about now. "Yes, in the City of Angels. I don't have anywhere else to go."

"Do you have any money?"

"I have a little. I've saved up. With that and what they just gave us, I'll be all right for a while."

As she had always done, Mutt had spent almost nothing on herself in prison. She had been paid a token wage while working in the business office as a secretary, on-the-job training for what was to come after she was paroled. Since she didn't smoke and didn't need much of anything, she had saved almost all of the money she made over the length of her incarceration. She had also put away the five-dollar bills that had been arriving on her birthday for the last several years. It had taken Cousin Opal nearly two years to find out where to send those cards after Mutt's sentence began. But on her twentieth birthday, a card arrived for her addressed to "Miss Shirley Hopper" and signed, "Love Fred and Opal." Then, just as before, a card came each year with its five-dollar prize, all of which she had kept in anticipation of this day, the day often described by the inmates as being "free." Although she was allowed to walk out the front gate and head any direction she chose, she didn't yet feel free. That was going to take some time.

She had spent the last eight years surrounded by iron and brick and hard women and not much beauty or tenderness. She had spent all her time looking forward to the day of her release, which her lawyer had assured her would arrive long before she had served out her full twenty-year sentence. She spent her time thinking about the things that made her happy: tomatoes fresh off the vine, chickens scratching in the dirt, the mournful sound of a train whistle. Most of all, she thought about Annie Callahan and all the things she represented: love and innocence and the joy of living. Her memory of Annie reminded her of how good life could be. She didn't expect to meet Annie ever again or even anybody like her, but just knowing that the world held such a possibility was enough to give her hope for the future. That was what had kept her from despair. Especially after what happened to Ray.

After that first birthday card from Cousin Opal, Mutt had also received a postcard from Ray. He had re-enlisted in the army, and in the summer of 1944 he was stationed in the Philippines. The postcard featured a beach scene with palm trees. As she read the words he'd written, she could practically hear his cheerful voice. "Hi, Mutt. Having a swell time in the army. Will come visit you when the war's over. Love, Ray."

She had taped that card on the wall beside her bunk and used its exotic scene to transport herself to imaginary places. More importantly, the promise of a visit from her brother gave her something to look forward to.

In the autumn of that year she received a telegram from Opal saying her brother had been killed in a munitions warehouse explosion at his base. It was a terrible shock. She had been devastated, especially because she wasn't allowed to attend the funeral. She'd felt that Ray was her family connection to the planet, and now he was gone. Technically, her father was still alive, but that was merely a fact, not anything she could hang on to. Still, as she had lain in her bunk mourning her brother, her heart had been moved to feel sorry for Kirby Hopper. He had lost everyone—his wife, his son and his daughter. She didn't understand how she could feel sorry for him and hate him so much at the same time.

As if to remind Mutt that she was not alone in the world after all, Opal and Fred sent her a Christmas package that year that contained a wealth of cheerfulness. There were cookies and chocolate bars, a hand-knitted shawl, a set of dominoes, and a 45 rpm record of Bing Crosby's "White Christmas." For all its beauty, that song was just too sad for a young woman spending her third Christmas in a desert prison. She gave the record away. But she'd kept the shawl Opal had made her. It was tucked into the bag riding above her head.

Getting out of prison brought a whole new wave of grief to Mutt. She knew that if Ray had lived through the war, he would have welcomed her to his home. By now he would have a wife and a couple of children and she would have an entire new family to be a part of. She knew she would never be a mother, but she had looked happily forward to her role as aunt to her brother's family. But that wasn't the way it was going to be.

"Do you know anybody in LA?" Zetta asked.

"No. Well, actually I know a fella. He's an old hobo friend of mine. Topeka Slim. But nobody else."

"If you want to, you can always go back to hoboing, can't you?"

"I could if I had to, but I'm hoping for something more settled. What about you? What are your plans?"

Zetta shrugged. "I'll go back to my old job."

"What's that?"

"Bartender at a nightclub downtown. Great bunch of gals there."

"What's it called?"

"Bumpers. It's on South Central. Not the best neighborhood, but it's nice inside. Clean and friendly." She lowered her voice and furtively added, "For women like us. Come by if you get lonely."

"Thanks."

Mutt leaned her head against the back of the seat and tried to get comfortable for the hot two-hour ride to the city. *I'll be all right*, she assured herself. *Just fine. I'll be finer than a frog's hair.*

# CHAPTER TEN

As soon as she walked into the diner, Mutt spotted Topeka Slim sitting alone in a booth with his hands folded in front of him like a choirboy in prayer. His hair had gone completely white and the bags under his eyes were noticeably baggier than the last time she'd seen him—in the witness box at her trial. Otherwise, he was easy to recognize in his white shirt and brown coat, possibly the same brown coat he had worn the night they went to the picture show all those years ago.

She walked directly to his table and drew his eye, but there was no sign of recognition there. It didn't surprise her. She didn't look much like Mississippi Mutt anymore, wearing a tailored suit, legs in stockings, her hair touching her shoulders and her figure filled out. Even though he'd seen her in a dress during her trial, this just wasn't the Mutt he had known.

"Slim," she said with a smile. "It's so good to see you again."

He stood up, staring into her face in disbelief. "Mutt?"

"It's me, sure enough." She drew him into a hug, then sat down opposite.

He fell back onto his bench, his mouth hanging open, showing off his two missing teeth. "Yeah, I can sort of see it now. By golly, you've changed! You even got a few curves on you now."

It cheered her to hear the soft whistle of his speech. "I'm not the girl you knew eight years ago."

"Well, now, to be accurate, Mutt, you weren't a girl I knew then." He chuckled. "You're not a bad-looking woman, you know that? I was real glad to hear you got out. Real glad. Good behavior, is that it? They let you out for good behavior?"

"I guess. Somebody on the parole board must have believed my story, that it was self-defense. You didn't have to come all the way over here. I just wanted to say thank you for what you did for me. On the phone was good enough."

"I know. But I wanted to see you, Mutt, to see if you were okay. I need to get out of the house once in a while anyway. I'm retired now, you know. Too old to ride the rails with the rheumatis' and all."

The waitress came by and they both ordered coffee. Slim ordered a piece of apple pie.

"Nobody called me Mutt in there," she said. "It feels kind of funny hearing it again after all these years."

"What'd they call you in the joint? They use your real name? What was it? Something Hopper. Some girly name. I remember that from the trial."

"It's Shirley. But don't you go calling me that!"

He nodded and rolled his eyes. "You bet."

"The other women called me Hobo. After they heard my story, that's the nickname they gave me."

"You've got more names than anybody I ever knew," declared Slim.

"In there I had a number too, so I guess I can add that to the list."

"What'd you do in there all this time?"

"This and that. They give you jobs to do and classes to go to. I read a lot. There was a library. I always liked libraries. They seem safe to me."

"You know, you don't even sound the same, Mutt. More high falutin' or something."

Two steaming coffee mugs were set between them.

"They tried to take Dixie out of me," she explained.

"That's a right shame."

"Don't you worry none. It's still in there." She winked at him. "As sure as a hog's rump is made of pork."

Slim nodded with a smile and stirred sugar into his coffee. Then he shook his head. "It still boils my blood thinking about what they did to you. That son-of-a-bitch Joe Gemgiani sitting up there with his hand on the Bible lying through his teeth. Saying that when he and his good-for-nothing brother found out you was a woman and said they was going to tell their father, you attacked them. And that son-of-a-bitch lawyer saying you was some kind of hobo camp prostitute."

Mutt patted his forearm. "Don't go getting all riled up again, Slim. It's all over and done with." She lifted the mug to her lips and tasted the coffee. "I never got a chance to thank you for testifying, especially seeing as how it was against your boss."

"I wouldn't have worked another day for that son-of-a-bitch. I'd rather have starved. Not that they listened to me. I told them you were not a prostitute. Far from it. You were a legitimate road sister, honest and respectable, and those boys were mean and worthless. But nobody listened to me. I was just a hobo. That son-of-a-bitch lawyer kept calling me a bum. Did you hear that?"

"Yes, I heard it. But it's okay. That's all in the past. I paid my debt to society for killing a man. I never wanted to kill anybody, but I did, so I paid for it."

"If anybody ever deserved to be killed..."

"Slim, let's talk about something else that doesn't make your face so red. Tell me how you've been."

He visibly relaxed and waited while his pie was delivered. "I don't get out much anymore." He sunk his fork into the flaky crust. "I've got a little place down by the river. My legs bother me a lot, so catching the freights is too hard. Ah, I miss it sometimes. I can hear the whistle at night calling my name."

"Do you keep in touch with any of the others?" Mutt asked.

"Oh, sure. We write, talk on the phone. And I wander down to the jungle there to visit sometimes and take the boys some beer and hot dogs so we can have a little wienie roast. You remember

Slo-Poke? He's still out there on the iron road. Whenever he comes my way, we get together for a laugh. And Frogman…you knew him, right?"

"Yes." Mutt recalled Frogman's wide-eyed signature stare. "I did know him. How is he?"

"He caught the Westbound last winter." Slim shook his head, knowing Mutt would understand the hobo slang for death.

"Oh! I'm really sorry to hear that. He was so nice to me. He's the one who gave me the name Mississippi Mutt."

"He knew you were a girl," Slim said before shoveling in a mouthful of pie.

"He did?"

"Oh, yeah. After they sent you down to Tehachapi, I met up with him riding the Pennsy line and told him all about it. He said he knew you was a girl the minute he met you."

Mutt recalled that day, nine years ago, when she had happened into Frogman's boxcar. He'd showed no sign he recognized her as a female. But he had been kind and helpful, and maybe that was the reason.

"He was real sorry about what happened to you." Slim spoke with his mouth full, unwilling to stop eating long enough to talk.

"What about Boxcar Betts? Any word of her?"

"Oh, sure!" he mumbled, waving his fork. "She's doing good. She doesn't ride much anymore. She's getting on you know, like me. She built herself a little shack there at the Omaha jungle and lives there permanent. She's like the hobo queen of Nebraska. Every time I've been through there, she's added onto that shack. Damned if she didn't build herself an indoor john with a shower and toilet and everything. A few more years and she'll have a regular mansion down there on the riverbank."

"I'd like to see that!"

The last hunk of pie went into his mouth. "So now what'll you do? You gonna stay here in LA?"

"For a while. I've got myself a room. It's not much, but I don't need much."

He nodded and scraped the crumbs off his plate. "Good for you. I was about to steer you down to the hobo jungle. You'll always be welcome there, you know. Folks has heard about you.

And if they don't treat you right, they'll have me to answer to."

"It may sound strange to you, Slim, but I'm going to play it straight from now on."

"No more freights?"

"I won't say never, but for now, that's right. No more freights."

"Maybe that's best. If you show up at the jungle looking like that, wearing your Sunday go-to-meetin' clothes, they'll kick you out anyway. Figure you's some kind of schoolteacher or something, lost your way."

Mutt chuckled. "This is my job interviewing outfit."

"You got an interview?"

"Not today, but I thought you'd get a kick out of seeing me in my suit."

"It's real nice, Mutt. What kind of job do you interview for dressed like that?"

"Secretarial. Clerks and typists. Things like that."

"You know how to type, do ya?"

"I do now. Seventy words a minute and not a single mistake."

He whistled, on purpose this time. "Well, I'll be. Seems like you'll be moving up in the world real soon."

"Speaking of moving up in the world, did you ever find out where you buried that three hundred dollars?"

He shook his head. "It's still out there somewhere. Unless somebody else dug it up." He shrugged. "Easy come, easy go."

No regrets, Mutt thought. That was the hobo philosophy. She liked it and would do her best to live by it. What's done is done. She was looking to the future now.

When their visit was over, Mutt hugged Slim goodbye on the sidewalk in front of the diner.

"Maybe we can go to a picture show together one of these days," he suggested. "Now that I know you're a gal, you'd make a heck of a better date than the last time we went."

She laughed. "I'd like that."

# CHAPTER ELEVEN

Mr. Dix, the gaunt young man conducting the interview, seemed ill at ease, as if his stiff white collar had too much starch. He wore a gray suit, blue and yellow tie and black wing-tip shoes. His sandy hair already started well back on his forehead though he looked to be in his early thirties. He tapped the end of a pencil absentmindedly on the edge of his desk as he nodded in her direction, his thin lips pressed tightly together.

Mutt believed the interview was going well. In the two weeks she had been job hunting, she had filled out a dozen applications for clerical jobs but had had only two interviews. They had seemed okay too but she had heard nothing yet from either. This morning, June 21, 1950, believing that good things are supposed to happen on your birthday, she had decided to skip the written application and apply in person. It had been a good strategy. She had been invited in to answer questions about her qualifications.

It seemed she had the knowledge and skill required for the job. She was beginning to hope that she might actually be hired and become an independent working woman with a steady income and a respectable life. That had seemed utterly impossible a few weeks ago as she looked ahead with uncertainty toward her freedom.

Suddenly she could imagine taking the bus downtown every morning to the Stanton Community Bank and Trust, walking in and saying "Good Morning" to everybody, then sitting at her designated spot with her own personal coffee cup beside her typewriter. The bank manager and loan agents would walk up and address her as "Miss Hopper" with polished professionalism. Men in crisp suits would say, "Miss Hopper, would you type this, please?" And "Miss Hopper, can you come into my office and take a letter?" With equal professionalism, she would say, "Of course, Mr. Dix." At lunchtime she would go to the break room where the other women gathered to eat and smoke and gossip. These women, the straight-backed typists she had seen on the way in, would become her friends. Maybe they would even invite her to their homes and their children would call her "Aunt Shirley." On her birthday next year, everyone in the bank would take a brief respite from work to present her with a cake and sing to her. This imposing, high-ceilinged building with its sparkling chandeliers and gleaming wood rails would become a place she belonged. It would be the focal point of her respectable life.

From the moment they had shaken hands, Mr. Dix had been enthusiastic about her. She wasn't one of those silly young girls just out of school. They were so unreliable, he said, and he was looking for someone more stable, a girl who was not simply looking for a husband. Mutt had assured him that she was not looking for a husband at all, that she wanted a career, and he had said, "Excellent!"

"You didn't finish high school, is that right?" he asked.

"That's right. I dropped out at the beginning of my junior year. But I've completed the coursework and passed all the tests. The paperwork is there." She indicated the folder she had given him that lay closed under his folded hands.

"You went to night school? Is that it?"

She had been waiting for the right moment to tell him about her prison time. She realized there may never be a right moment, but his question did present the opportunity. There was no possibility of avoiding it. She knew the bank wouldn't hire her without checking her out.

"No," she said. "I didn't go to night school. You see, Mr. Dix, I've just gotten out of prison. I was in Tehachapi for eight years. That's where I finished my schooling and learned secretarial skills."

He looked confused. "What? Prison?"

"I worked in the business office there for two years, so I do have job experience. One of my references is from the supervisor of that office. She can tell you about the quality of my work."

He stuttered. "I…I…yes, of course." He narrowed his eyes, staring hard at her. "So when exactly did you get out?"

"Two weeks ago."

He recoiled, looking surprised. "I see." He twisted and stretched his neck in that stiff collar again, then regarded her with a nervous wince. "Um, what were you…what was your offense?"

"Second-degree murder," she said in an undertone, hoping the softness of her voice would temper the effect of her words.

He didn't attempt to disguise his surprise.

"I didn't mean to kill anybody," she said. "It was self-defense."

"But you were convicted."

"That's right. The jury didn't believe me."

He took a deep breath. "Look, I'm going to be perfectly frank with you, Miss Hopper. You're an attractive young woman and present yourself well. I'm sure you are competent in the required skills." He paused and smiled unconvincingly. "But this is a bank and we simply don't hire people with a criminal record. It's the nature of the business. Trust is paramount for our staff. It's even a part of our name. Stanton Community Bank and *Trust*. We're handling people's money here."

"I understand that," she said hesitantly. "But you wouldn't make an exception? I'd work hard and I'd gain your trust. You'll see."

He sighed. "If it were just me, I wouldn't have a problem giving you a chance. But it's the image we have to portray to our customers. Surely you can imagine how they might feel if they heard that one of our employees had served time in prison. One of our most important jobs is to reassure people that their money is one hundred percent safe with us. This is a bank policy and I must adhere to it."

Mutt could see there was no point arguing. It didn't matter how many words a minute she could type or how exceptional her punctuation was. Nothing mattered except that she had been in prison. So what was the point of all those years spent learning job skills she couldn't use?

She was embarrassed. "I'm sorry I wasted your time, Mr. Dix."

"It's okay." He stood and extended his hand. "Good luck to you, Miss Hopper. I hope you find something that suits you."

She walked through the opulent bank building with its neat rows of workstations. At each desk sat a clerk or secretary, women in business attire with their hair made up, typing or rapidly fingering the buttons of adding machines. They worked amid a clatter of keys striking platens and ringing typewriter bells, a symphony of tinny dings that reminded her of the business office at Tehachapi, though that had been a much smaller operation.

She passed the highly polished mahogany railing that separated the secretarial pool from the teller windows and its line of customers. Stepping onto the sidewalk outside, she sucked in a lungful of sooty city air and wondered why she had wanted to work in a place like this anyway. Just because that's what she'd been groomed for at Tehachapi, that didn't mean she was, in Mr. Dix's words, suited for it. It would suit some women well enough, but she'd never liked the job at the prison, sitting at a desk and typing for hours on end—*Dear Mr. So-and-so, Ding. We are writing regarding visitation rights with your wife. Ding.*

Why would she like this job any better now? The prison staff had done its best to prepare the non-professional women for one of two things: marriage or office work, in both cases stressing the need for femininity and mildness, two things that Mutt knew she didn't come by naturally. Picturing the typists at their desks in the bank, she tried to imagine herself as one of them. Suspending her natural Mutt-ness for a half hour during an interview was one thing, but to do it every day for years on end…

Maybe a smaller office, she thought. A one-woman office where things were more casual and friendlier and they didn't have any inflexible policy against hiring people who'd made

long-ago mistakes. Some family business where she could do all
the paperwork, the books and everything. She was good at math
and she could handle a job like that.

Encouraged by her new plan, she walked to a small
neighborhood park and found an unoccupied bench where she
could look through the newspaper wants ads. She pored over the
notices under "Help Wanted - Women."

Secretaries, girl Fridays, waitresses and babysitters.

Waitress was always a possibility, if nothing else panned out.
Maybe a restaurant wouldn't be as choosy as a bank.

Her eye wandered to the column titled "Help Wanted -
Men." Out of curiosity, she scanned the jobs listed there and
saw there were far more options. There were ads for laborers of
all sorts and heavy equipment operators. There was even an ad
for a barber. The thought of it made her cringe. That was one
occupation she would stay away from. The last time she'd seen
her razor was in the courtroom with a tag tied to it—Exhibit A.

A dog barked and she looked up to see a woman leading a
cocker spaniel past on the sidewalk. She was dressed smartly in a
skirt and jacket, beige stockings, a wide-brimmed hat and high-
heeled shoes. The dog pranced and the woman did likewise in
step with it, her heels clicking rhythmically on the sidewalk.

Mutt set her paper down and glanced around. The street was
wide with a strip of grass separating the north- and southbound
lanes. Every so often, a palm tree topped with an umbrella of
graceful fronds rose high up out of that patch of green. The
straight row of palms extended into the distance as far as she
could see. A lot of people were out, walking, driving, going about
their business. It was a mild June day with a cloudless sky, much
like every day she'd seen here so far.

She wondered if she would ever get used to this place. It was
so big, so noisy, so full of activity. Not especially friendly. Other
than Topeka Slim, nobody had yet shown the least bit of interest
in her. Once she had a job, she knew she'd meet people and make
friends. Maybe she'd even get an automobile someday. Wouldn't
that be grand! She smiled to herself, watching the cars go by,
a steady stream of Fords and Chevrolets with their polished
chrome bumpers, many driven by women with scarves over their

hair and big sunglasses shading their eyes. Everybody seemed to have somewhere to go. They walked and rode with such an air of intent.

She picked up her newspaper, noticing that it was open to the gossip columns. She was about to turn back to the want ads when a photograph caught her eye. It accompanied the main story on the page and showed a gorgeous-looking man and an equally attractive woman, both dressed sumptuously and formally, clasping one another's hands. The headline read, "Sterling-Montclair Wedding Talk of the Town!"

The name *Montclair* hit a chord deep inside her, so she started reading the article, stunned to see the woman's full name: *Bianca Montclair*.

There was nothing about Annie Callahan that Mutt had ever forgotten, not a single word that she had said, or the expressions of her mouth, or the lavender perfume of her. Or her fantasy stage name. *"How do you do? I'm Bianca Montclair."*

A chill ran down her spine. Was it possible there actually was an actress with that name? Had Annie been imitating her? Mutt had been so ignorant about movies back then, she'd never even heard of Irene Dunne. But she'd heard of her since. She'd seen her in movies in prison. She even knew the name Clive Sterling. He was a popular romantic leading man. But since that night in the Callahan barn she had never again heard the name Bianca Montclair.

She stared intently at the woman in the photo, through the mascara and eyeliner that made her eyes look large and unnatural. The longer she stared, the better she was able to swim through the layers of time and artifice to get to the sixteen-year-old farm girl underneath.

*It was her! It was Annie!*

Her heart pounded with excitement and amazement. She leapt off the bench as if she suddenly had somewhere to go. She stepped one direction, then the other in agitation. Finally she sat down again and read the article, devouring every word. She gradually understood that Annie was a newlywed. She had married Clive Sterling and they had moved into a suite at the elegant Rutherford Hotel. The reporter anticipated that the happy couple would split their time between the city and Clive Sterling's beach house in Malibu. Mutt zipped through the background information on Sterling to read the one paragraph about Bianca Montclair.

"Raised on a farm in Nebraska, Miss Montclair came to Hollywood some years ago with aspirations of becoming an actress. She and her future husband met on the set of *Coming of the Dawn* in which he starred and she had a supporting role. Since then, the happy couple has often been seen out on the town together, so it was no surprise when they announced their engagement six weeks ago."

Dumbfounded, Mutt sat on the bench for ten minutes, so isolated from the world around her that even traffic noise didn't reach her. Finally she roused herself and walked to the bus stop in a mental fog. She was overwhelmed to think that Annie was right here in Southern California, maybe even in this city at this very minute.

Leaning against a light pole waiting for the bus, she shook her head. What difference did it make? Regardless of where she was, Bianca Montclair was living in another world. Ten feet or ten thousand miles away, it was all the same.

If Annie ever thought of Mutt at all, it was probably with regret and shame, or at least disbelief that she had allowed herself to get carried away over someone so unworthy. It was an episode of her life she had probably tried to forget. Maybe she had forgotten it.

Just be happy for her, Mutt told herself, climbing the steps of the bus. She made it to Hollywood. She became a movie star and she married a movie star. She accomplished what she had set out to do, and that must not have been easy. Mutt recalled with fondness how spirited Annie had been. She'd had such a powerful urge to go to Hollywood she'd been ready to run away with a stranger, risking everything to chase her dream. Mutt had been her ticket to California. Maybe that's all she'd ever been for Annie, she reflected. Now more than ever that seemed the most likely way of looking at it.

She slid into a bus seat and looked again at the newspaper

photograph, at Annie's ecstatic smile. She was a princess in a fairy tale, living the life every little girl dreams of.

*I'll be happy for her later*, Mutt decided. *Right now, I'm going to be sad.*

# CHAPTER TWELVE

Without planning it, Mutt found herself standing on the sidewalk opposite the Rutherford Hotel. Somehow, instead of going home, she had ended up here. It wasn't that much of a surprise, considering how preoccupied she had been ever since reading that Annie lived here with her new husband.

After getting off the bus, she had stood in this one spot watching people passing under a maroon-colored canopy on their way in and out of the ten-foot tall gold-framed glass doors. The building was made of a pinkish brown stone, eighteen stories high with ornate carvings on ledges at the base of every story. It was a monstrosity of a building. Everything about it was heavy. Though not beautiful, it was remarkable.

For all this, it wasn't the architecture of the building that held Mutt transfixed. It was the idea that behind one of those windows Annie could be sitting at this very moment powdering her nose or listening to music or drinking a cup of tea, and the mere width of the street and the thickness of that hulking building's wall was the only thing between them.

The thought filled her with wonder and drove her imagination in wild circles.

Smartly dressed men and women continued to pass through those doors, and each time they opened, Mutt examined the women to see if she could find Annie in faces obscured by hats and veils of black netting. Although Annie's face remained vividly familiar to her, nearly a decade had passed and she wasn't sure she would recognize her even if she walked right past her on the street. Not with the clothes and makeup typical of the women going in and out of the Rutherford Hotel. The girl she remembered didn't look like these women at all.

After a half hour standing on the sidewalk in front of an Italian deli, she crossed the street and stood ten feet from the hotel entrance. Tentatively she moved closer to the doors, looking through the glass into the lobby. When she saw two women coming toward her in elaborate feathered hats, their shoulders wrapped in furs, she pulled the door open and held it for them. They walked through, giving her a brief nod. She stood with the door handle in her hand, the door wide open, gazing into the lobby. The interior was luxurious, carpeted in plush red and gold with dark wood. A high ceiling rose up at least three stories and murals of cherubic figures surrounded the central rotunda. She'd snatched only a brief glimpse when a man in a dark uniform appeared in front of her and asked, "Are you going in, Miss?"

She looked him over quickly, realizing he was the hotel doorman. Somehow she hadn't noticed him before, or perhaps he had been away from his post. His uniform was trimmed in gold braids and tassels. A nameplate on the lapel read "Chatham."

Embarrassed, she gave control of the door over to him and stepped back. "No. Sorry."

She hurried away, returning to the bus stop.

On the ride to her building in a worlds-away different part of town, she sat with her chin in her hand and stared out the bus window, seeing nothing as city streets flowed by. She might have stayed like that through the entire trip if a little boy hadn't plunked himself down beside her. She glanced up to see his mother, her hand holding that of a kindergarten-aged girl, arrange herself and her daughter in the seat opposite Mutt. The woman smiled briefly in Mutt's direction. The boy was about ten, fresh-faced and carefully groomed. His hair lay well controlled on his uncovered head and his shoes were black, shiny and unscuffed. He held a toy airplane in his lap.

"Look what I got from my grandpa!" he said, holding the toy up to her face. "The propeller turns and everything!" He wound it carefully with his index finger, checking to make sure she was watching before letting it go. The propeller spun rapidly with a whirring sound as the rubber band unwound.

"That's swell," Mutt remarked, smiling down at him. "Is it your birthday?"

He nodded vigorously.

"Happy birthday! It's my birthday too."

"I'm eleven," he announced proudly. "How old are you?"

"Georgie!" his mother snapped across the aisle, her brows knitted together in disapproval.

"It's okay," Mutt assured her. "I'm twenty-six," she told Georgie, who seemed to be still confused about why he wasn't supposed to ask.

When she reached her nondescript brick building, she stopped inside the front door to check the message board above the telephone. As usual, there was nothing there for her. She walked up a flight of creaking stairs without seeing anyone, then turned right to reach her room at the end of the landing. Despite the small size of the room, it was uncluttered. She had accumulated almost nothing in the couple of weeks she'd lived here. The room had come furnished with the most rudimentary items. Next to the door was a plain wooden table and one chair. A twin bed with no headboard occupied the wall on the other side. A lamp with a discolored shade stood next to the bed and above that she had taped Ray's postcard from the Philippines. There was one tiny window with clouded glass and no curtain that looked across an alley at the exterior wall of another such building.

The only other tenant she had met so far was Oliver Krantz next door. She had run into him in the hallway a week ago as he returned from the bathroom, barefoot, wearing trousers and a yellowed undershirt. All she knew about him was that he drove a delivery truck for a beer company. She heard him cursing now and then when both of them had their windows open in the evening. If he sometimes also laughed, she might think he was listening to a radio, but he never laughed. He only yelled, "Damn you!" and "Go to hell!" Thinking he might be insane, Mutt did her best to avoid him and always locked her door.

She chose this place because it was cheap and because the landlord, Mr. Wakely, had asked few questions and required no references other than cash in hand. With the money she had saved from her prison job and the gate money they had given her, she estimated that she could live here for as long as six months before things got desperate. But by then, she would surely have a job.

She had bought herself a few clothes and some bed linens. Even if there had been more money, there wasn't anything she wanted to buy. After eight years in a tiny space with only a bunk, a shelf and a toilet, she'd grown used to an austere environment and hadn't yet adapted to the idea of having things of her own. Before living in a cell, she had lived on the road for a long time, carrying only a few essential items. She had learned how little a person really needs to live in the world. No canopy beds or Chesterfields, she remembered Topeka Slim saying. Understanding what one really needed was a good lesson to learn.

The sparsely furnished room with its bare, ochre-colored walls actually seemed spacious, even luxurious, to Mutt, and she was still trying to get used to the idea of having it. In some ways, it was almost frightening not to be confined in a tiny, impenetrable cubicle. But she was happy to be here, to be out and in charge of her life again. In time, as she became more accustomed to freedom and wide open spaces, she would think about putting some pictures on the walls and a vase of flowers on the table and making this place look like it belonged to someone. Maybe she'd get a radio too. It would be nice to listen to music and radio programs. Meanwhile, she had library books to keep her company.

She felt glum and restless. It was her birthday and nobody acknowledged it except a little boy and his mother on the bus. There wasn't even a card from Cousin Opal. But that wasn't

Opal's fault. Mutt hadn't given Opal her new address. Opal didn't even know Mutt was free. There was probably a birthday card sitting there at Tehachapi with her name on it: *Miss Shirley Hopper*. It would be returned and that's how Opal and perhaps Mutt's father would learn of her release from prison.

She thought of the nightclub that Zetta had told her about and wondered if she would enjoy a night out for a change, a little private celebration. Since she didn't drink, she found it awkward to go to bars, but it would be nice to see someone she knew for a change. The thought of staying home alone on her birthday seemed sad. Besides, she was curious. Zetta had said the club was for "women like us." Mutt wasn't sure what she'd meant by that. Did she mean ex-cons? Or was it possible she meant women who love other women? Could there be such a place? Could there be such a group of women?

Mutt had never thought much about these questions, about the larger context of her private reality. She knew she had fallen in love with a girl on a farm in Nebraska. She knew she thought of women differently than other women did. She had discovered in prison that in the absence of men, women found ways to satisfy their physical desires with one another. They often mimicked the relationships of men and women, one of them taking the role of the male partner and the other the female partner. She had assumed this sexual activity between women was peculiar to prison or perhaps any environment where women had no access to men.

Mutt had no interest in men, in prison or out. During one of the few times she'd spoken to Zetta, during a child-care class, she had learned that Zetta felt the same way. As she had fumbled with pinning a diaper on a doll, she grumbled, "Why the hell do I have to learn this shit? I'm never getting married. I'm never having a kid." Then she'd laughed derisively and said, "Unless they invent some way for my girlfriend Lottie to knock me up."

As the class proceeded with bathing the doll in a tub of warm water, Mutt had ventured a question. "You have a girlfriend on the outside?"

"Sure. Lottie. She's waiting for me. How about you? You don't go with men. I can tell."

Mutt hadn't answered because at that moment the instructor had hollered, "Hopper! You just drowned your baby!"

Most of the women at Tehachapi weren't like Zetta. They missed men desperately and were driven to relationships with women only because they ached for human interaction and needed an outlet for their physical desires. Mutt knew she was different. Maybe she had always known. Maybe that's why she was never the kind of daughter her father had wished for.

When she had first been incarcerated, Mutt believed she had no need or desire for sex, that it simply wouldn't ever be a part of her life. Her brutal introduction to it at the hands of her father had left her with feelings of shame and loathing. During his drunken, nauseating attacks on her, she had learned to disassociate herself from what was happening, to separate her mind from her body and become a stone, feeling nothing.

But gradually she had become drawn to certain women in prison and had allowed them to make love to her. In the beginning, she went through the motions without emotional involvement, just to please her partners. But with time and experience, she had learned to enjoy her body in the arms of another woman, and her sexuality had awakened. She had learned about the gentle, loving side of physical desire.

Though she had been fond of her lovers, she had not fallen in love. That had happened to her only once, suddenly and surprisingly, and had taken her over completely. But she knew beyond doubt that if it were ever to happen again, it would happen with a woman.

Yes, she was curious, very curious about this club where Zetta worked and what exactly she had meant by "women like us."

# CHAPTER THIRTEEN

One minute she was standing on the sidewalk in a seedy section of Los Angeles with the winos and bums, sad men who were touchingly familiar to her, and the next she was in a dark, low-ceilinged room crammed with people, the city outside completely blotted out. As her eyes adjusted to the low light, her head snapped this way and that to take it all in. On the crowded main floor, couples danced under a stagnant layer of smoke. Farther in, a scattering of tables were occupied by people drinking, smoking and talking. On the right side of the room was a bar lined with backless stools, some of which were occupied. Loud music blared from a jukebox against one wall. She recognized the voice as Ella Fitzgerald, a jazz singer who had been popular with some of the women at Tehachapi. But the song, sultry and a touch angry, wasn't one she recognized.

At first she hadn't realized that the "men" she had seen inside were actually women wearing men's clothing, their short hair slicked back with pomade. But as she looked more carefully at their faces, she began to understand. The occupants gradually unfolded like blooming roses into femaleness: soft cheeks, slender wrists and full mouths, their bodies smooth and graceful, moving swan-like across the floor. Many of their partners were earnestly feminine, wearing dresses, stockings, lipstick and eye shadow, their hair voluminous and unapologetic, their creamy bosoms spilling over the tops of their dresses, the same. Unapologetic.

There was a wide spectrum of women here, dressed in a variety of styles and encompassing several ethnicities, but all of them, it finally became clear, were women.

Standing just inside the doorway, Mutt felt self-conscious, taking mental stock of her own appearance and wondering if she would look out of place. Was there anything about her, she wondered, that would give away the fact that she had never been here before, had never been anyplace like this before? She didn't know if there were rules, cues or taboos, as there were in both hobo and prison culture.

She glanced down at her navy blue suit, white blouse and pale stockings. She had worn this outfit because it was the nicest thing she had. But now that she saw what the other women were wearing, she began to think this was an unfortunate choice. Observing the haircuts and waxed hair of some of these women, she was even second-guessing her hair style. Her hair fell loose to her collar with a natural wave, not like she used to wear it when she was Mississippi Mutt, but more feminine and full. She had let her hair lie naturally ever since the day her lawyer had said, "We'll want to emphasize your femininity, such as it is, so the jury will be more sympathetic." That strategy had fallen flat. Or perhaps it wasn't her appearance that had turned the jury sour on her. Perhaps it was her speech. Her lawyer would have preferred that she not take the stand, but she was the only witness for the defense who had actually seen what had happened.

"Why won't they like me if they hear my Mississippi accent?" she had asked.

"There's a lot of prejudice against Southerners in California these days. So many of them have come here competing for jobs. But it's mainly like people anywhere. You're different. People don't like different."

That had been the first time she'd been told to drop the "Southernisms." She'd had only a few weeks to prepare for her trial. It wasn't long enough to change that much, especially when the prosecutor started badgering her and it was all she could do to keep her rage in check, let alone her y'alls. In prison she'd had considerably more time. She still had an accent but she knew nobody would laugh at her speech now the way they had in the courtroom.

That lawyer had been right. People don't like different.

She looked around the room, struck by the fact that she was in a crowd of people who were different. But here, all together, they weren't.

Through the noise and haze of the nightclub, she recognized the woman behind the bar pouring drinks. She wore an official-looking white coat with a starched collar and a plain black tie hanging from her neck. Her dark hair was pinned on top of her head austerely except for one loose curl that adorned her left temple. Her full lips were deep crimson with lipstick and her eyes were amplified with evening makeup. She looked sexually provocative in a deliberate way.

At the sight of Zetta's familiar figure, Mutt felt tremendously relieved. She edged through the crowd to the bar and waited to be noticed.

"Hobo!" Zetta exclaimed, her face lighting up with recognition. "You came. Welcome to Bumpers!"

"Thanks." Mutt slid onto a stool.

"How are you? How are you enjoying freedom?"

"It's not bad. I'm getting used to it." From the safety of the bar, Mutt glanced around briefly, scanning the faces and bodies of the women nearby. "This is something! I never knew there were places like this."

"Oh, sure. Maybe not where you come from." She laughed lightheartedly. "How about a drink?"

"I'll have a root beer."

Zetta did a double take, then pursed her colorful lips and opened the refrigerator to fetch a bottle of root beer. She poured it into a frosty mug. Mutt wrapped both hands around it, glad to have somewhere to put them.

Zetta leaned over the counter to be heard above the noise, her penciled-in eyebrows pitched at a radical arch, making her look mildly surprised. "Found a job yet?"

Mutt shook her head.

"Too bad. But you will. Persistence, that's what it takes. I thought maybe you'd come from work, seeing as how you're dressed."

Reminded of her suit, Mutt stuttered with embarrassment. "I…I didn't know what to…"

Zetta waved and made a sputtering sound. "Oh, don't worry about it. Nobody cares. You see everything here. This is a great bunch of women. Something for everybody's taste, if you know what I mean." She winked.

Mutt wasn't sure she did know what Zetta meant.

"You don't have a girl, do you, Hobo?"

Mutt felt herself color. So it was really true, all the women here were like her, at least in that one way, and she marveled all over again at the thought.

"No," she said. "I don't have a girl." She glanced nervously around to see if anybody was listening, but nobody seemed to be. "Zetta, the only place anybody ever called me Hobo was in the joint, so I'd like to leave that name behind now, okay?"

"Okay, sure. What should I call you?"

For the last eight years, she had been known by the prison staff as "Hopper" and by her cellies as "Hobo." They had never known a genuine female hobo before and the idea fired their imagination and gave Mutt an easy route into a social circle. She had stories to tell, even if they weren't her own stories, of life on the road and the danger and romance of riding the rails. But there was one story she had never told, though she had often been asked.

*Who did you kill?*

She was afraid that if she told that story the other women would celebrate her. They would turn her desperate act into something heroic, and she didn't want it to be seen that way. There had been nothing heroic about it. She'd taken a life in a moment of panic. She was sorry for it, as anybody would be who had been there and seen that boy fall to the floor with his blood gushing out around him. But many women in prison had a lot of bitterness and resentment toward men who had done them wrong one way or another. Rape was not an uncommon experience among them and many of them had fantasies about killing a villain in their past, much as Mutt herself had once had about her father. They would have felt it was their own personal revenge in a way if they had known her story. But if they had actually killed a man, they would know it was nothing to celebrate.

So she had never talked about that. Instead, she had told happier stories. The women were particularly fond of hearing about Boxcar Betts, and Mutt had found herself making up many remarkable adventures for Betts to keep the women of Tehachapi entertained, as if Betts had been some sort of heroic figure like Superman. She recalled that Zetta hadn't heard these stories, so maybe she'd be able to use them all over again here at Bumpers. With that thought, she realized she was already planning to come here again.

"I'm Mutt," she finally answered. "That's what I've been called since I was a little kid and I guess it's what feels most natural to me."

"Mutt?" The startled arch of her eyebrows angled up even further. "Okay, then. Mutt it is."

She drank her root beer with deliberation, taking in her surroundings and watching women dance. The jukebox never went silent, offering up songs by Nat King Cole, Peggy Lee, Doris Day and Eddy Arnold. Everything she knew about popular music she had learned in prison. Hobos didn't play this kind of music. They sang old ballads about whiskey and loners and lost love, similar to the songs she learned in school as a child, with roaming buffalo and mules named Sal, except that the school songs were decidedly less vulgar. A hobo fraternity could be quite a crude congregation, especially when they believed there were no women present.

When Mutt was halfway through her drink, a woman slipped between the barstools to order and looked her over with deliberate interest. She extended a smile that was an odd mixture of perplexity, curiosity and flirtatiousness. The woman was young, just out of her teens. She was only five feet tall with short brown hair and a trim, boyish build, dressed in denim pants and a blue shirt, tucked in and topped off with a wide leather belt sporting a silver, Western-style buckle. Mutt glanced down to see cowboy boots on her feet.

"Another round, Baby?" Zetta asked, running a cloth over the counter between them.

Noting the term of endearment, Mutt glanced from Zetta to the other woman with curiosity, wondering if this youngster was Zetta's girlfriend Lottie.

"Yep," the newcomer replied. There was nothing in her demeanor that hinted of intimacy. While Zetta made the drinks, the other woman turned her attention to Mutt and introduced herself. "Hi. I'm Baby."

Grasping the situation, Mutt gave her own name.

"Why don't you introduce Mutt around?" Zetta suggested. "She's never been here before."

Baby nodded enthusiastically and Mutt helped her carry the drinks back to a table in a dim corner of the room where three other women were seated. Mutt was introduced to Anya, Maggie and Tully, a jolly group that had obviously already had a few drinks. They urged her to join their table.

As Mutt took her seat, she said, "Nice to meet you all. Nevermind this outfit. I had a job interview today and haven't been home to change."

"Ah," Tully said, looking enlightened.

Anya, a dark-haired beauty with lustrous brown skin and a lipstick-drenched mouth, clung possessively to Maggie's arm, leaning into her. Maggie smoked a cigarette, a pack of Pall Malls at her elbow on the table, the smoke curling up toward the ceiling into the diaphanous cloud hanging above them. She shook her head, tossing long bangs off her forehead. Her dark hair lay straight, falling just below her ears. She smiled at Mutt before clinching her pale lips around the cigarette for another drag.

Tully had an unusually straight nose in a rounded face. Her small blue eyes appeared passive but not unfriendly. She looked solid and heavy like an antique chest of drawers. She wore tan slacks and a loose dockworker-style blue shirt, under which a tremendous pair of breasts were only marginally concealed.

She peered with intelligence and discernment at the stranger among them, hinting that she had not yet formed an opinion. She reminded Mutt of a type of woman she had known in prison. They were the ones in charge, perhaps only because of the low tenor of their voices or their sheer bulk. They looked like they could flatten you with their pinkie, but they weren't all bullies. Some of them were totally sweet, even motherly. But when you first laid eyes on them, especially if you were of a twig-like shape as Mutt was, you felt like running. Because she had known women like Tully intimately, she wasn't intimidated by her. Besides, she was, like the rest of them here at Bumpers, welcoming.

As the conversation continued, centering on gossip about other women and their relationships, Mutt learned that the clientele at Bumpers was a mixed bag, women from all different backgrounds and social classes, women who as a collective had only one thing in common: they were all lesbians.

Mutt was surprised to learn that Maggie worked as a taxi driver. "Disguised as a man of course," she explained. "Women don't drive taxis."

"You should see her in her makeup," Anya said, glancing admiringly at Maggie. "She's a master at it. Nobody ever guesses. She's got the clothes, voice, everything down pat."

To illustrate, Maggie sunk her head slightly toward her chest and said, "Where ya goin', Mac?" in an indifferent, working man's voice.

"That's good!" Mutt remarked.

"They never look twice at you anyway," Maggie said. "Cabbies, doormen, waiters. The slave class, you know. We're all interchangeable to them, so I could probably drive my cab looking like this and never raise an eyebrow."

"Doormen?" Mutt uttered almost to herself, reminded of the doorman at the Rutherford Hotel.

"Oh, sure, anything like that. You're tall and slim like me. No hips. Easy to turn you into a handsome young man."

"I've done it before," Mutt said, "but I don't think I was very good at it. People guessed."

"If you ever want to try it again, give me a call and I'll show you a few tricks."

After fifteen or twenty minutes had gone by, Mutt realized she was enjoying herself. The social culture at Bumpers wasn't so different from that of Tehachapi. The same male-female role playing was clearly in evidence and she had already heard a few familiar slang words that she had previously thought were unique to prison culture.

She began to realize that this subculture had existed on the outside all along. She just hadn't known about it.

She told her story about getting thrown off a fast-moving freight, and for the first time ever she didn't leave out the part about the farmer's daughter.

"She was the most beautiful girl I ever saw," Mutt said with a breathy sense of freedom. "She had long golden hair and dreamy blue eyes. Her skin was like peaches and cream and her mouth…" Mutt paused, seeing that her new friends were waiting expectantly for a description of Annie's mouth. It was clear that they all understood and approved of her feelings toward Annie.

"What happened?" Baby asked, her eyes wide with anticipation.

"I kissed her," Mutt said. "A lot."

"And?" Baby urged. "Did you undress her in the moonlight and kiss her all over her naked body?"

Mutt felt her ears get hot. "Uh, well, I—"

"You don't have to say," Tully assured her. "Baby's never done it so she always wants to hear all the details about everyone else's love life."

Baby frowned, clearly unhappy that Tully had revealed her virgin status. She folded her arms across her chest and petulantly slammed herself against the back of her chair.

"So what happened with you and the most beautiful girl in the world?" Tully asked.

"The next day after I left, she came after me. She wanted to run away to California with me and become an actress."

"Everybody out here wants to be an actress." Anya rolled her eyes and Mutt wondered if she too had acting aspirations.

Mutt could have said that Annie did become an actress after all, but of course she couldn't reveal Annie's identity.

"Did she make it to California with you?" Baby asked, leaning back into the table.

"No. Her father caught up with us and would have shot me right there on the spot, but Annie saved my life. She said, 'No man has ever touched me. Mutt is a woman.'"

A boisterous round of laughter erupted around the table.

When the laughter died down, Tully narrowed her eyes. "But you were disguised, right? She didn't know you were a woman."

"It turns out she did know."

Maggie gasped. "She did?"

Mutt nodded. "And her father nearly made me get naked to prove it."

Everyone at the table laughed again and Mutt sat back to bask in the good feeling. She hadn't expected ever to be able to tell that story. Though there were plenty of female couples in prison, there was an assumption that most of them were making an exception because of the circumstances. They were playacting and still didn't generally approve of homosexuality or even admit to it. Even there, Mutt hadn't felt free to express her true feelings out loud.

She was indeed in a new kind of place among these women, and it was a wonderful kind of place.

"Mutt," Tully asked, "would you like to dance?"

As Mutt stepped onto the dance floor to the romantic, smoky voice of Dinah Shore, she thought that her birthday had turned into an excellent celebration after all, much better than she could have imagined.

She was not a good dancer. She'd had so little experience. But Tully, a couple of inches shorter than she was, took charge. As soon as she relinquished herself to Tully's control, she no longer thought about her feet or her body's perpetual awkwardness. She floated around the room in Tully's secure embrace, pressed lightly into her inescapable bosom. She began to relax and enjoy the closeness of another woman's body, something she thought she had left behind for good when she walked past the guard tower on her way out of Tehachapi. She had never guessed at this shadowy world of women who love women. She felt buoyant and giddy, as if she had been drinking gin instead of root beer.

*I'm not alone!* she thought exultantly.

After Tully, she danced with nearly everyone as word got around that it was her birthday. The women of Bumpers wanted to make her night special. And they did. She was happy beyond her expectations. There was only one thing that could have made her happier than finding a place to belong, and that was if she had been dancing with Annie Callahan. But, she thought, that would surely be too much happiness to bear.

# CHAPTER FOURTEEN

From the day she had learned that Annie was in Los Angeles, Mutt had been compelled to get a look at her. In between her efforts to find a job, she lurked outside expensive dress shops and scanned the entrances of prominent restaurants and nightclubs that she imagined movie stars might frequent. But most of all she haunted the sidewalk across the street from the Rutherford Hotel, often leaning against a particular lamppost in front of Fiore's Italian delicatessen. Through the hot days of summer, the spicy aroma of cured meats wafted out of the building, and when the deli door was open, the bark of a man with a pronounced Italian accent rolled into the street like periodic thunder.

This particular spot on the sidewalk afforded the best view of the entrance to the Rutherford. After being scared off by the doorman during her first visit to the hotel, Mutt felt more comfortable observing from the other side of the street.

So far, despite many vigilant hours, she had not seen Annie. She had studied the newspaper photo of the Sterlings at length, hoping to be able to recognize one or the other of them if they appeared. She thought she saw Clive Sterling exit the building one morning with another young man, and the two of them walked up the street together. She wasn't sure it was him. The man wore a hat and she didn't see his face clearly but it gave her encouragement that if she stood here long enough, she would eventually catch sight of Annie going in or out.

Through the hours, Mutt kept herself distracted by watching the Rutherford's doorman, Chatham. His uniform, with its yellow epaulets and braided cords, gave him a somewhat military look, but he was much less disciplined than a soldier at his post. He had a habit of flipping a quarter off his thumb to keep himself occupied when no one was in need of him. He did this incessantly and absentmindedly He occasionally missed catching it and chased his quarter about on the sidewalk or in the gutter. In addition to his quarter-flipping habit, he had another, more sinister one. Inside his jacket he kept a flask that he drank from surreptitiously throughout the afternoon. By the end of his shift, he was visibly intoxicated and spent more and more time rooting around on the ground for errant quarters.

Chatham was only marginally respectable at his best and not even close to respectable later in the day. She had seen him fall asleep more than once, leaning against the stone wall with his mouth agape. After watching him for a couple of days, Mutt had decided that she could do a much better job as the Rutherford's doorman. With that realization, she began to imagine how she would do things differently and how perfect it would be if she actually were the Rutherford's doorman. For one thing, she would get paid for standing around waiting for a glimpse of Annie, which she doubtless would get. More than a glimpse. She would get to speak to her. The more she thought about that, the more she wished Chatham would fall down drunk in the gutter and be swept away for good.

Today she was here earlier than some days and he appeared alert. He stood flipping his quarter, catching it on his closed fist every time. The smell of salami coming from the deli behind her merged with gasoline fumes as she shifted from one foot to the other. She glanced down the street at the Birmingham Bank and the huge, gold-handed clock with Roman numerals that she used as her personal timepiece.

After the first couple of days on the Annie watch, she had decided she had to limit her time here, as it was both discouraging and unproductive, taking her away from her important search for work. She'd imposed an hour and a half limit on herself, after which she had to leave. Today she'd arrived at ten o'clock. It was twenty-five minutes past eleven, so she had five minutes left.

The unfortunate thing about the time limit was that it had turned into a time sentence. She'd found that she was now compelled to serve out the entire hour and a half regardless of how she felt about standing here in the salami fog listening to the barking of an overwrought Italian chef.

She was glad the time was nearly up. There was a job she was anxious to apply for. It was a low-paying position for a girl Friday in a small business that provided janitorial services to other businesses. It was just the sort of thing she was looking for, but she no longer had much hope that any of these leads would pan out. Everybody was suspicious of a woman who had done hard time. She had to shake her head now at her earlier aspirations like the Stanton Community Bank and Trust. That had been incredibly naïve.

Just as she was preparing to go, Chatham sprang toward the doors of the hotel and opened one of them to a woman in a powder blue skirt and jacket over a white, ruffled blouse. On her head was a wide-brimmed felt hat of the same cheerful blue color, trimmed with a white sash that hung off the back and trailed behind her like a banner.

Mutt's heart stopped. She clung to the light pole with both hands, watching through the moving cars in the street. Chatham spoke with the young woman briefly, then stood at the curb and raised his arm to signal a taxi. The woman peered out at the street, vaguely looking in Mutt's direction. It was Annie! It was surely Annie! Her pale cheeks and bright, full lips were as familiar to Mutt as sunshine in August. Feeling light-headed, she pulled herself up to her tiptoes with the light post. She strained to see over the yellow cab that stopped in front of the hotel and obscured her view of Annie.

"What you doing here?" demanded a gruff and heavily-accented voice behind her.

She spun around to see an overweight, red-faced man in a soiled white apron scowling at her.

"What?" she asked, confused and irritated. She turned to watch Annie's hat as it ducked below the roof of the cab.

"Why you stand here all the time?" the chef asked. "This no bus stop. This my place and I no want you here. I call the cops. You go and don't come back. Capisce?" He stamped his foot to punctuate his commandment.

Without responding, Mutt hurried farther up the street, walking rapidly as the taxi entered the stream of traffic and approached her. She held her breath and bit her lower lip, then stopped walking to get a better view into the backseat of the cab. Annie sat looking out the window, her mouth curved into a detached smile. Their eyes didn't meet. Annie didn't see her. If she had, Mutt knew, she wouldn't have recognized her. All she would have seen was a stranger in a navy blue suit, pale stockings and brown, sensible, working woman's shoes, her hand raised to her cheek and a look of dumbstruck wonder on her face.

# CHAPTER FIFTEEN

In the stifling heat of late summer, Mutt stood at attention on the sidewalk, positioning herself in the shade of the maroon canopy outside the double doors of the majestic Rutherford Hotel. Her slacks were crisp, her black shoes shone like mirrors. She wore a smart navy blue jacket with yellow epaulets on the shoulders, stripes on one sleeve and a nametag over the breast pocket. Her hat was like that of a policeman—stiff with a black bill and a decorative golden cord circling it. Her hair lay close to her head, greased back from her face and out of view under the hat. On her hands she wore white gloves. She stood at attention at her post, guarding the doors.

It was no surprise to Mutt that Chatham had been fired. Although she had often fantasized about marching into the hotel to complain about him herself, she had nothing to do with his dismissal. The hotel management had finally caught on to his drinking problem. Or so she assumed. All she really knew was that one day he was gone and a Help Wanted sign had appeared in the front window of the hotel. As soon as she'd seen that sign, she knew that Providence was smiling down on her.

She had immediately flown into action. Within a few hours, after enlisting Maggie's help, she was back at the hotel as Mick Donovan being interviewed by the hotel manager. Desperate to get the job, she didn't tell him about her time in prison. She felt it was irrelevant. Mick Donovan had never been in prison. Mick Donovan had a spotless record. As the youngest son of a poor mill worker in Alabama, humble Mick Donovan was tailor-made for this low-paid, no experience necessary job.

"No, sir," she had assured the manager when asked if she liked a beer or two on a Friday night. "I don't drink. Never have and never will."

"You're hired," the man had said, and pointed her to a closet where she could change into the uniform.

This disguise was much more convincing than she had managed on her own in those early years of train hopping. She wore a dark brown mustache under her nose and the suggestion of a five o'clock shadow on her chin. Her eyebrows were emboldened to look darker and heavier than her own. Her shoulders were padded, her chest flattened with a binding cloth. She wore a man's ring, a bulky setting holding a round red carnelian gemstone that looked natural on her large hand. A yellow silk handkerchief peeked shyly from her breast pocket. Everything about her appearance had been diligently addressed by Maggie's astonishing makeup skills. No one seemed to have any suspicions about her gender. She could have fooled her own father, she thought.

During the few weeks of her employment as the Rutherford's doorman, she had learned how to conduct herself in such a way as to be helpful and attentive but inconspicuous. She thought she was a fine doorman and she loved the job. It amused her to think that this was not at all what they had in mind at Tehachapi during those several years of skills training with the typing, dictation and how to make the perfect cup of coffee. But even with no training, she felt that this job was a better fit than the ones they'd groomed her for.

Nobody had checked out her story. The job wasn't important enough. Maggie had been right about the invisibility of the servant classes. It was the perfect occupation for somebody with something to hide.

Elderly Mrs. Pennington approached the door from within, toddling as much side to side as forward, carrying her toy poodle in a white woven basket. Mutt reached for the door and swung it open for her.

"Good afternoon, Mrs. Pennington," she said, using her old Mississippi Mutt voice. "Is your car coming?"

Mrs. Pennington peered up with her powdery white face and squinting eyes and said, "Yes, Donovan." She looked up and down the street expectantly.

"There it is," Mutt announced, pointing toward the long black sedan heading their way.

She escorted Mrs. Pennington to the curb and helped her into the rear seat. The elderly woman placed a silver dollar in the palm of Mutt's glove. "Thank you, Donovan," she said.

After several weeks, Mutt was used to her new name. It seemed that every time the road of her life took a turn, her name changed along with it. With a new name came a new persona, as if she were an actor playing a role. It was fitting for Hollywood, she had decided.

Mrs. Pennington's car glided off down the street. Mutt retired to her station, standing with her arms at her sides, watching an endless stream of automobiles pass by. Across the street at Fiore's Deli, the familiar voice of perpetually exasperated Signor Fiore reached her ears through the open door. He and his wife, first-generation immigrants from Genoa, worked long hours at their store, arriving before Mutt each morning and leaving after her at night. She sometimes visited their shop for a sandwich or a box of ravioli to take home for dinner. She was familiar now with many of the shopkeepers on this street and they knew her too. Or thought they did. They knew Donovan. It was the same with the staff at the Rutherford Hotel: Charlie the bellboy and Bleeker the desk clerk. And Annie.

It was solely because of Annie that she had renamed herself Mick Donovan. Though she didn't look anything like the Mutt Hopper Annie had known for only one day, she couldn't take a chance on arousing her suspicions by using her real last name. After all, she had disguised herself as a man before. Annie might even expect something like this from her. If she thought about her at all. That was doubtful, Mutt realized, considering how thoroughly Annie's life had changed since then. Still, Mutt had taken every precaution to make sure she wasn't recognized. This was the best way she could think of to be near Annie without intruding on her life.

Like everyone who stayed at the Rutherford, Annie, or Bianca Montclair, as she must now be called, entered and exited from this entrance, so Mutt had seen her many times already. The first few times she had almost been unable to contain herself. But it had gotten easier. She was no longer afraid she would collapse at Annie's feet like an idiot and smear her shoes with kisses. Today, she was actually looking forward to three o'clock when Annie would emerge for her visit to the home of Mrs. Riley Hampton where she went each Wednesday to something called The Women's Welfare and Literacy Society. Mutt knew that a British-style high tea would be served at Mrs. Hampton's house, but whatever else these women met for, she couldn't guess. The Women's Welfare and Literacy Society sounded like it served some purpose other than merely social. Perhaps, she thought, it was some sort of book club. She was explicitly forbidden from asking questions about such things. Even if it wasn't forbidden, she wouldn't have risked showing that much cheek and drawing attention to herself.

Whenever Annie went out, Mutt tried to imagine what she did. Sometimes it was easy to guess, like when she and her husband appeared in their formal attire on their way to the opera. Or when they left for the Mocambo nightclub for an evening of dancing. Often, they were off to a party for people who worked in the motion picture business. These were occasions for Annie to enrobe herself in fine furs and silky gowns. She emerged from the interior of the building luminous, lighting up the street like a comet.

Her husband was a beacon of brilliance as well. Clive Sterling was extremely handsome, refined and well-mannered with a thin mustache in the style of Clark Gable. It was no wonder Annie found him attractive, Mutt decided, as she had wanted to star opposite Clark Gable from the beginning. Clive Sterling also had many social engagements, with and without his wife, and was always dressed to the nines. Mutt had never seen him in ordinary street clothes. Despite his fame and fortune, he was always polite and friendly to Mutt, as he was to the entire staff. He always gave a tip and sometimes a hearty pat on the back, asking, "How is your day going, Donovan?" with an attentive expression suggesting he really wanted to know. It was hard not to like Clive Sterling. The only thing Mutt had against him was that he was married to Annie. But even that wasn't much of a gripe. If Annie was going to be married to somebody, who better than a rich, dashing, thoughtful fellow like that?

It was the best possible life for Annie no matter how much Mutt ached for her. She had nothing to offer her in the face of all this. She never hoped to be more to her than her congenial doorman.

Aside from the impossibility of Annie, Mutt had no aspirations on the romance front. The mere idea that women could be coupled was still new to her. She had met several such couples now. Though they lived their lives in secret pretending to be sisters or merely friends, they seemed happy. One couple she had met did not live in secret, but that was because one of them was an heiress and her parents were deceased. She had everything she needed and didn't have to make excuses to anyone. If you were self-sufficient, Mutt concluded, you could live however you wished to, and that seemed like a reasonable goal in life.

On the side of the Birmingham Bank building a half a block away, the big hand was just a few ticks away from three o'clock. She prepared herself mentally for Annie's arrival, aware that as much as she liked seeing her, there was also always pain in these brief encounters. It was the pain of having to hold so much feeling inside, pushing it back and damming it up. There was also the pain caused by Annie's perfunctory behavior. She treated Mutt like she did any other member of the staff. Not that she was unkind. She was just detached. That was the only appropriate way to be with the doorman, Mutt understood. The look of joy she remembered so vividly from the day they had set out together for California never came her way now. But still she remembered it and still she yearned for it.

She steeled herself, then put her gloved hand on the thick bar of the door and pulled it open as Bianca Montclair approached and passed through. She wore a yellow dress, precious white shoes and a white cape. Her small hands were encased in white silk gloves. A choker of diamonds lay like stars on the pale skin at the base of her neck. Her hair was swept up and hidden inside a grand hat decorated with melon and rose-colored silk flowers. She was a tableau of beauty and elegance, shimmering and pulsating with vitality.

"Hello, Donovan," she said. "Mr. Sterling has the car today. Can you get me a cab, please?"

"Certainly, Mrs. Sterling," Mutt replied, bowing slightly. She walked to the curb and flashed a hand signal to a taxi parked half a block away. Then she returned to Annie who smiled at her cheerfully. "Going to Mrs. Hampton's as usual?"

"Yes. My WWLS meeting. My goodness, it's hot out here today."

"Yes, ma'am."

"How can you endure it, Donovan, standing outside all day long?"

"It doesn't bother me so much. I'm used to it. I've worked in the outdoors all my life."

"You're a very tough fellow."

The taxi slid up to the curb.

Annie made no move for the cab, but stared at Mutt, her face wrinkled up with a look of consternation. "You know, Donovan, I've said it before, but I can't get over this feeling that I know you from somewhere. There's something about you that strikes me as familiar. It's disturbing in a way to have a feeling like that and not to be able to figure out why. Maybe I should get myself hypnotized so I can remember who it is you remind me of. Have you heard of that? Hypnosis? When you get hypnotized, they say you can remember everything that's ever happened to you all the way back to your birth. Do you believe that's possible?"

"I wouldn't know, ma'am." Mutt swallowed hard, pushing back the urge to wrap herself around Annie and squeeze her close. Her nerves tingled with the thought of how wonderful that would feel.

The taxi waited at the curb while Annie gave Mutt one more searching look, then shook her head regretfully. Mutt helped her into the cab, supporting her arm, then gave the address of the Hampton house to the driver.

Watching them drive away, she wondered for the first time if this job had been a mistake. Maybe she should be a doorman at another hotel. She saw Annie several times a week, always looking gorgeous, hanging happily on the arm of her flawless husband, enjoying the best life had to offer. None of it had anything to do with Mutt. She didn't begrudge Annie any of these things, but she wondered if she would be happier if she didn't witness them.

The plain truth was that nothing Annie did was any of Mutt's business. Maybe she would be better off making a clean break and trying to find someone new to fix her heart to. She wasn't against finding someone new. She had met several women at Bumpers and some of them were really something. But she knew that you couldn't make a decision to fall in love. It has to happen on its own. As long as Annie owned her heart, she didn't expect it to happen again.

Leaving Annie, she concluded, was unthinkable. Seeing her this way was better than not seeing her at all, whatever the emotional cost.

# CHAPTER SIXTEEN

There was something different about Tully tonight. She didn't seem to be enjoying herself as much as usual. She was never boisterous. She was a reserved woman who observed more than talked, so her silence was only a subtle change from her typical self, but it was enough for Mutt to notice. She had learned that Tully grew most talkative when it was just the two of them, so she waited until Anya and Maggie left for the dance floor before asking, "How was your day?"

Tully shrugged and took a long drag on her cigarette. Mutt had found it easy to talk to Tully. She'd told her about Luke Gemgiani and her eight years at Tehachapi. She had told her about her brother's death and what she could remember of her mother. She'd told her a little about her father, but as always, she stopped short of telling the worst of it. She supposed Tully was so easy to talk to simply because she listened.

"Is something wrong?" Mutt persisted.

Tully regarded her through the smoke she exhaled, her pale eyes unrevealing, then she abruptly stubbed out her cigarette and said, "Dance with me."

Mutt happily agreed. Dancing was what she came here for, dancing with women, and Tully was an excellent dancer. She'd been here many times since the night of her birthday and had discovered a new passion in dancing. She didn't care if the music was fast or slow, if she led or followed. She danced with anyone who wanted to and she had rapidly improved her technique so that she was now a sought-after partner on the dance floor. This was her hangout now. Her friends were here and this is where she sloughed off her cares.

She had adopted a signature style of dress for the club, androgynous but not as masculine as that of the women in suits and ties. She wore a flowing cream-colored shirt with long puffy sleeves and a string tie crisscrossing the V-neck like shoelaces. She left the tie untied and the shirt tucked in loosely at the waist over trim camel-colored pants tapered down to a pair of black, short-heeled boots. On the job, she wore her hair slicked back close against her head, but in the evening she wore it more natural, with bangs and no hat. Her costume made her look like a bit of a swashbuckler, she thought, her sleeves billowing as she led her partners around the dance floor.

Like herself and Maggie, whom she occasionally saw on the job in her taxi, she guessed that most of the women at Bumpers would look completely different elsewhere. For instance, Tully was a nurse at a hospital. Mutt tried to imagine her in a white uniform and cap, handing out pills and taking temperatures. Maybe it wasn't such a stretch, she decided, as Tully did have a reassuring confidence about her. She reminded Mutt of a teacher she had had in grammar school, Miss Ackerman. She had been stern and serious, a middle-aged woman who had never married, who had gone to college and had intelligence and abilities far exceeding her role as reading and math teacher to a room full of twelve-year-olds. In many ways Miss Ackerman was hard and impenetrable, but there were moments when a child was in need, emotionally or physically, that she softened in a remarkable way.

Mutt had experienced that firsthand one day when she had gone to the lavatory and discovered blood on her panties. Terrified, she sat in the bathroom stall sobbing in silence, believing that she was internally injured and going to die, and that her father, who had beaten her the night before with his belt, would go to prison for killing her. She stayed in the stall for an hour at least, waiting with alternating hope and despair for the bleeding to stop.

She never knew how Miss Ackerman found her, except that girls had been going in and out of the lavatory the entire time and maybe someone connected the dots when Mutt did not return to class.

When she heard the door open again, she assumed it was one of her classmates until she heard Miss Ackerman's voice, loud and formidable, exclaim, "Miss Shirley Hopper!"

Mutt was extremely intimidated by Miss Ackerman and did not want to cross her. So she answered in a pathetic little voice that must have barely cleared the door of the stall. "Yes'um."

"What is wrong with you?" Miss Ackerman demanded, her tone only mildly softer. "Are you ill?"

"Yes'um."

"In what way are you ill?"

"I'm bleeding."

"Bleeding? Did you get cut? How badly are you bleeding? Come out here so I can see."

Reluctantly, Mutt unlocked the door and emerged holding her underpants before her as evidence. Miss Ackerman looked momentarily startled, then she looked annoyed. "You've got your menses. Is this the first time?"

Mutt had no idea what she meant, so she just stared, still holding the panties out for inspection.

Miss Ackerman's expression softened. "Shirley," she said, "you don't have a mother, do you?"

Mutt shook her head.

"And no older sisters? No women around to explain the facts of life?"

"No, ma'am."

Miss Ackerman smiled in an unfamiliarly tender way. "I'd like you to stay after school today so we can have a talk. Can you do that?"

"If y'all don't think I'm gonna die."

Miss Ackerman raised one eyebrow. "No, I don't think you'll die any time soon. Meanwhile, you wait here and I'll be back with something for you. You can wash those out in the sink. Use cold water."

That afternoon, Miss Ackerman assumed the role of mother to Mutt, explaining things she would never have guessed at in a kind and soothing tone. She answered Mutt's questions, the ones she dared to ask, without hesitation or embarrassment. The ones she didn't dare to ask, Miss Ackerman anticipated and answered anyway. It seemed she understood everything that was in Mutt's mind and heart. She had never felt so well understood before, nor had she ever had a conversation remotely like this one.

Mutt was more than grateful. Her teacher had performed a necessary and practical duty, but Mutt had been the recipient of much more than information that day. She had felt the uplifting benevolence of a woman, a warm, protective cloak of compassion with which she was unfamiliar. After that day, she coveted every moment she had in the presence of Miss Ackerman. She cherished every word that passed between them and felt they had a special bond, though Miss Ackerman never again singled her out for that kind of personal attention. Looking back, she recognized it as a romantic crush, the first time she had opened her heart to a woman.

It was Tully's intelligent reserve and authoritative personality that brought Miss Ackerman to mind, though there was no physical resemblance between them. For just a moment, Mutt tried to imagine slow dancing to this Benny Goodman number with lean Miss Ackerman in her thin cotton print dress, her hair in a sober knot and a silver whistle around her neck.

"What are you smiling about?" Tully asked.

"Oh, nothing. I was just thinking about something that happened a long time ago."

"Was it that girl, the farmer's daughter?"

"No. It was someone else."

"Ah, the many loves of Mutt Hopper."

Mutt smiled. "Not so many."

"No? I would have thought after all those years in prison that you'd have quite a list of conquests behind you."

"You said loves, not conquests. Totally different."

Tully nodded, understanding.

She was a smooth dancer, if not a graceful woman otherwise. Pressed up against her overflowing bosom, Mutt felt comforted and cared for, and let herself be driven leisurely around the floor.

Tully gripped her close and laid her head on her shoulder, slowing the pace of their dance even more, no longer keeping time with the music. She seemed mournful tonight. Mutt wasn't used to this. Tully was normally so composed, a gentle but solid presence who seemed to anchor the world, or at least the world of Bumpers. As long as you were spinning around her, you felt safe. Tonight she seemed to be wanting, not giving, comfort.

Embracing Tully's broad back, Mutt could sense the need in her, and held her more tightly, offering herself, her closeness, as a silent balm. But Tully was needier than that. She brought their bodies together even closer, her hips tight against Mutt's, so purposefully that the accessory under Tully's clothes made itself fully understood against her. Mutt had felt it before when they were dancing, a hint of something stiff as their bodies grazed one another. Some of the butch women wore these appliances as part of their Bumpers' attire like other women wore earrings.

Mutt felt a hunger rising in Tully, the way her hand grew moist against her back and the way her mouth grazed her neck, her breath changed from its usual cadence.

Mutt knew the signs of arousal in another woman. She didn't recoil or resist the effect Tully's mute proposal had on her own body. They stood locked together on the dance floor, their blood growing hot, moving against one another in a carefully orchestrated grind that may have looked like dancing to anyone watching. The suggestive lump inside Tully's pants pressed deeper into her, and the idea of it excited her.

"Do you want to go somewhere?" she whispered near Tully's ear. "Your apartment?"

Tully broke away, her eyes full of purpose, and took Mutt by the hand, leading her off the dance floor. They passed behind a dark curtain at the back of the room and into a dimly-lighted hallway flanked by a door on either side. There was another door at the end of the hall. Mutt knew that door led to an alley behind the building. Like everyone who came to Bumpers, she'd been told that this was the escape route in case of a police raid. She had never been back here before, but Tully obviously had. She opened one of the side doors and pulled Mutt into a musty room, switching on a weak light to reveal a cluttered storeroom. The space was filled with furniture covered in shrouds of cloth, trunks and stacked boxes. The far corners of the room remained in the shadows. The discolored wallpaper, once an ivory field of cheery pink roses, was now yellowed by time.

Tully threw the bolt on the door, then pressed Mutt against it with her body, taking her mouth hungrily. Mutt returned her kisses, growing more and more aroused. Tully smelled of tobacco, gin and the subtle aroma of a spicy cologne. Mutt took her tongue deep into her mouth, embraced and restrained by the pressure of her body.

Tully unbuttoned Mutt's pants and pulled her shirt free of them, reaching under it to take her breasts in both hands. She continued kissing her mouth, ravenous, and squeezed and kneaded her breasts and nipples until they were as hard as marbles. Tully dipped her head down to take one of them into her mouth and sucked and flicked it with her tongue. Mutt leaned against the wall enjoying the sensations of Tully's hands and mouth on her skin as the ache in her grew more and more pronounced.

Finally she reached between them to undo Tully's trousers. She slid them down over her thighs. She ran her fingers over the cloth of her undershorts, feeling the shape and girth of the object concealed there. Tully bit her lower lip, her eyes on Mutt's hands between them. She was clearly excited.

Mutt slid purposefully toward the floor, kneeling eye level with Tully's undershorts. She curled her thumbs over the elastic and slid them off, revealing the ruddy-colored phallus she wore in a harness around her upper thighs. Mutt had never seen one like this. Prison dildos were often imaginative but crudely made. This one was made of rubber, exquisitely fashioned, pliable yet firm and obviously not homemade.

She gripped it in her hand, appreciating its smooth surface and eliciting a murmur from Tully as if her prosthetic had sensation. Tully stood unmoving as Mutt ran her hands over the tool, then around and behind the base of it, sensing the quivering of Tully's body with her fingertips.

She slid the dildo in her mouth, knowing Tully was watching her and becoming aroused. Her body had gone completely inert as she stood with Mutt kneeling before her licking suggestively down the length of the appliance. While she sucked and licked it, she stroked Tully's thighs with her hands.

When she rose and faced Tully, she looked mesmerized. Mutt removed her own pants and undershorts, her billowy shirt flowing loose around her like a nightshirt. She brought them close together again. They kissed and groped one another, working each other into a quick frenzy of desire. Tully took control again. She spun Mutt around, pinning her against the wall with the weight of her body, both hands cupping her breasts under the shirt as she bit the back of Mutt's neck lightly. The dildo teased and inflamed her with its bold insinuations between her thighs.

Tully moved one hand down across Mutt's stomach, then lower, her fingers raking through the curls of her pubic hair, then dipping into her wetness with an audible catch in her throat.

"You're ready for me," she whispered next to Mutt's ear.

"Yes!"

When she felt the tip of the dildo enter, a sudden panic gripped her. "Not from behind!" she pleaded.

"Okay," Tully said gently, easing back and turning her so they were face-to-face. "However you want it, honey."

Looking into Tully's concerned face, Mutt relaxed, then nodded to reassure her.

Mutt took her in, gasping at the sensation of being filled up. Tully thrust into her with a slow and deliberate rhythm. Mutt leaned heavily against the wall, relishing the deep, thick pleasure of their bodies connecting. The mustiness of the room combined with the musky scent of enraptured women surrounded her and heightened her senses. She closed her eyes and let her body fall into a natural rhythm. At the end of each thrust, Tully's female center touched her own in a burning kiss that left Mutt frantic until there was nowhere else to go but over. Tully merged with her, against and inside her, until Mutt released herself in a surge of mute celebration.

They stood together for a moment, locked tightly in one another's arms.

"That was beautiful," Tully breathed. She pulled free and led Mutt to a sofa covered with a dark green cloth. She sat on top of the covering and folded Mutt into her lap, holding her loosely in both arms.

Mutt played absentmindedly with Tully's hair, brushing it this way, then that way across her forehead. "Do you feel better?" she asked at length.

Tully sighed. "I feel good, thanks. I really needed that." She put her head against Mutt's shoulder. "And this."

They leaned into one another for a few moments, silent until Tully asked, "Do you want to talk about it?"

"Talk about what?"

"Whatever it was that spooked you a few minutes ago. You seemed really frightened there for a second."

"Sorry. It wasn't you."

"I know. That's why I asked if you wanted to talk about it."

If there was ever a time and place that lent itself to that kind of confession, this was it. Regarding Tully's compassionate, steady gaze, Mutt considered it, but she'd never felt the need to talk, so she shook her head and pulled Tully back into a close embrace.

After a few minutes, Mutt felt something fall on the bare skin of her thigh. She brushed at it and realized it was liquid. She lifted Tully's head to look at her face and saw that she was crying, silently and without any obvious emotion.

"Will you tell me what's wrong?" she asked gently.

Tully offered her a small, grateful smile. "My sister got married today."

"And that makes you sad?"

"She didn't want me at her wedding. I'd been looking forward to it for months now, ever since it was first announced. I wrote and told her how happy I was for her. My phone calls to my mother have been full of talk about this wedding. A couple of weeks ago I asked why Susie hadn't sent out her invitations yet. My mother said she'd sent them out weeks ago. That's how it came out that I wasn't invited."

"That's terrible! Why? Don't you get along with your sister?"

"I thought I did. She's my kid sister and we were really close as children. This was a complete surprise to me. My mother didn't want to talk about it. But I finally got the message that Susie didn't want me there because she thought I would somehow taint her pure and holy wedding ceremony with my depravity."

Mutt was horrified. She put her arms around Tully's neck and held on, not knowing what to say.

"It's clear now," Tully said, her voice breaking, "that she won't want me in her life at all from this point onward. She won't want me around her kids. I had no idea she felt so strongly about this. We never talked about it. I thought maybe she was a little uncomfortable with it, my relationships with women, so we avoided the subject, but I never guessed she was so disgusted by me that she'd want to erase me from her life."

Tully cried in earnest now. Mutt, feeling helpless and angry, held her protectively.

She didn't understand the horrible cruelty that families were capable of against one of their own, but she did know how painful it was. She knew how a strong woman could be demolished by grief when someone she loved with the unfettered trust of a child did something so inexplicably heartless. She had seen this sort of grief before and she had felt it herself.

She knew Tully would be okay and would bury this affront somewhere inside, unseen. But tonight she would grieve.

# CHAPTER SEVENTEEN

On Saturday, wearing no disguise, Mutt took a bus downtown to the corner of Wilshire and Grand Avenue where a rally was scheduled to start at noon. She didn't know much more than that. Annie had mentioned in passing that the WWLS, her women's organization, was marching in this rally. This was the first time Mutt had ever followed Annie to a place away from the hotel. Though she felt guilty, she couldn't resist the opportunity to know more about Annie's life, a life that sometimes seemed unreal to her.

As soon as she got off the bus, she heard a drum beating and followed it to a crowd on the edge of Pershing Square. Most of those assembled were women and many of them carried signs. One woman had a drum suspended on her body. She was on the move, apparently leading the procession, banging the drum with a regular beat. The other women and a few men fell in behind her. Mutt scanned the writing on the signs, reading "A Woman's Place is in the World." "I Am Not a Second-Class Citizen." "Give Rosie a Raise." "Equal Work Deserves Equal Pay."

As the crowd marched off, shaking their signs above their heads and shouting, Mutt moved rapidly alongside them on the sidewalk, searching for Annie. She finally spotted her walking in the center of the group. She wore a summery turquoise striped dress. Her head was uncovered and her hair was pulled back into a ponytail, giving her a youthful look. Sunglasses covered her eyes and she wore no jewelry, so she looked less like Bianca Montclair and more like the farm girl Mutt had first met. Above her head she carried a sign that read, "United We Will Win."

Mutt didn't want to be seen by Annie. She just wanted to observe her, so once she had identified her, she dropped back toward the rear of the procession. Making as much noise as they could, the crowd of women drew onlookers to the sidewalks as they passed by. Some of them handed out leaflets.

"Do you want a sign?"

Mutt turned to see a fiftyish woman waiting for her answer. Her hair was subdued by a red headband and she had sharp, intense brown eyes and fine dark hairs on her upper lip.

"Uh…" Mutt replied.

The woman turned her sign so Mutt could read it. It said, "ERA NOW!"

"What does it mean?" she asked.

"It calls for an amendment to the constitution," the woman explained. "The Equal Rights Amendment. It mandates that women will be treated equally and fairly. Among other things, it demands that a woman be paid the same as a man for the same job and prohibits discrimination based on sex. We've been trying to get this legislation passed for some time now. To have the same rights as men, that's what it's about."

Mutt studied the woman's face momentarily, noting her sober expression, then took the sign from her.

"I'm all for that!" she declared.

The woman smiled. "Of course you are. You're a woman. The WWLS is for equal rights for everyone regardless of race, sex or any other difference. I'm Dorothea Hampton, by the way."

Mutt shifted the sign so she could shake Mrs. Hampton's hand. "I'm…Shirley."

"Nice to meet you, Shirley. If you'd like to join our group, give me a call."

So this was Mrs. Hampton, the leader of the WWLS. And this, Mutt glanced up at her sign, was what they did.

She caught up to the parade of women, staying toward the rear and holding the sign high above her, occasionally getting a glimpse of the back of Annie's head. The thought that they were marching together at the same political rally filled her with happiness. The thought that she could, if she chose, join Annie's women's group made her feel like bursting. Of course she couldn't actually do it. Mrs. Hampton had extended the offer without knowing where Mutt stood on the social ladder. Bottom rung, or near, it anyway. But even more to the point, she couldn't let Annie know her, so she and Annie must remain in separate worlds.

But for today she was happy, sharing in her own way in Annie's real life.

She saw a man in coveralls frown at their group as they walked by. She made a point of waving her sign emphatically back and forth at him. She'd never done anything like this before. It was exciting, and she had a wonderful time. Annie seemed excited too, her cheeks flushed with passion, her fist pumping the air, her body full of vigorous intent. It was a joy for Mutt to see her like this and it brought to mind the young girl who had chased after her with stars in her eyes, love in her heart and defiance in her mind, ready to take on the world. Mutt hadn't seen that girl again before today. She had even wondered if she had been displaced completely by Bianca Montclair. But now she knew otherwise.

The flame in her heart blazed to the rhythm of the drumbeat and the cadence of angry women's voices, a chorus of righteous indignation that somehow felt like a voice emerging from her own gut. She began to chant with them, tentatively at first, but eventually unreservedly, letting her own buried anger inflect her voice. She had never let it speak before, but today it came out of her with force. The words they chanted were unimportant to Mutt. "Equal Pay for Women!" "Freedom for all!" She spoke the phrases of this cause along with the others, but her heart screamed out its own messages of protest, messages of rage against her personal injuries.

One of the women marching beside her put a hand on her shoulder and gave her an encouraging smile.

Mutt had started her day merely wanting to be close to Annie, but by the end of the march she was so caught up in the spirit of the protest she had nearly forgotten Annie.

When it was all over, she took a bus to Bumpers, hoping to tell her friends about her day, but it was too early for most of them. She sat at the bar and poured out the details to Zetta.

"It felt so good to be a part of something like that," Mutt said. "All those women standing up for the rights of other women and nobody stopping them."

"I'm glad you enjoyed yourself," Zetta said, dumping the contents of an overflowing ashtray. "I wonder if any of those women marching for the rights of working women were actually working women." She smiled ironically.

"I was," Mutt pointed out.

"Technically, you're a working man. You don't know what it's like to be a working woman in a man's world. I do. I've done it."

"Then you should be out there protesting."

"Maybe. I'm glad somebody is, but this group of yours… these women aren't like us, are they?"

"What do you mean?"

"If they knew you, knew all about you, that you're an ex-con and a homosexual, they'd run the other way. They'd give you about as much respect as they'd give a pile of steaming dog shit. These society bitches do these things because they're bored and they want to feel good about their snazzy-ass lives. But they don't want to be down in the shit with the women who really need help, do they? They wouldn't come anywhere near a real problem. They're self-righteous hypocrites." She leaned against the bar with a half-snarl on her lips. "So it's swell you got to march for women's rights, but you need to remember who these rich society bitches are. Today they're all about the rights of working women. But tomorrow they might be marching to shut down our place here and have all of us thrown in prison."

"They can't all be like that," Mutt protested.

"Probably not all of them," Zetta admitted. "But whatever they're like, they aren't like us."

Mutt thought about Annie and wondered how accurate Zetta's cynical view was of her. Would she be willing to get down in the dirt to help someone who was really in need? She was once willing to run away with a desperate character and live in the muck herself. But things had changed so much for her in the intervening years. Was it possible she had changed so much that she would even disapprove of Mutt and her friends here at Bumpers? From her position of legitimacy, would she be repulsed by them? The thought troubled Mutt, and all of the good feeling of the day slipped away from her.

# CHAPTER EIGHTEEN

Mutt was just about to knock off for lunch when a delivery van from Bullock's Department Store pulled up in front of the hotel. The driver jumped out and headed toward her with a clipboard in hand.

"Hey, Mac," he said, his clean-shaven face sporting an all-business expression. "I've got a living room set for Mr. and Mrs. Sterling. This is the place, right?"

"Yes," Mutt replied. "You'll want to pull around to the back to the service entrance."

"Sure thing. Can you let them know we're here while we unload this stuff?"

Mutt went inside and asked Bleeker to ring the Sterlings with the news.

"I'll show them to the service elevator," Mutt said.

"You stay with them," Bleeker ordered.

For the protection of the residents, it was a rule of the hotel that service people were not allowed to wander freely in the hallways of the upper floors.

Mutt accompanied the two men in their overalls as they loaded a chair and matching love seat into the service elevator. The furniture was elegant and graceful with carved legs ending in animal claws. The pieces had a feminine look about them and seemed vulnerable in the hands of these two burly, well-muscled deliverymen.

When they arrived on the fourteenth floor, Mutt took the lead, walking swiftly to the door and rapping with the back of her gloved hand. She had never been in the Sterling suite. Maintaining an outward calm, inside she was fluttery, feeling like she had entered a forbidden zone. At the same time she was intensely curious as to how Annie lived.

The door opened and Clive Sterling stood in the doorway, tall and willowy, wearing a flashy purple smoking jacket, his tiny mustache trimmed to perfection, his hair thick and tidy on his small, perfectly shaped head. He was a beautiful man, the sort who caused women to swoon just by walking past them.

"Ah, Donovan," he said with a friendly smile. "Are you with the delivery?"

"Yes, sir. They're bringing it down the hallway now."

He swung the door wide. "Come on in. I hope this works. We spent weeks looking for something."

Mutt crossed the threshold, glancing quickly around for Annie. Instead there was a young man smoking a cigarette in front of the glass balcony doors at the rear of the apartment. He wore casual white pants and a lightweight sweater, looking as if he were on his way to play tennis. He was fair and lithe with a pale, clean-shaven face and widely-spaced eyes that gave him a captivating appearance. He glanced indifferently at Mutt.

The main room of the apartment was spacious, suggestive of two rooms though there was no wall between them. At the back where the young man stood, there was a bar with glass shelves containing a multitude of bottles and glasses. It looked equipped to supply any drink request. To the right of that was a formal dining area with a long table and eight straight-backed chairs. Closer to the door was a sitting area where the new pieces were being deposited by the delivery men. A television built into a bulky walnut console stood against the wall and above it was a painting that drew Mutt's eyes. It was a bold depiction of Annie's head and shoulders, her mouth, bright cherry red, slightly puckered, her shoulders bare, dangly sapphire earrings framing her face and her eyes darkly dressed in blacks and blues, the undeniable focal point of the painting. Her hair, yellow and painted in curving, indistinct arcs, dissolved into a bluish, purplish background. The image was garish yet erotic. Though obviously modeled after Annie, it didn't seem to capture her at all. It's Bianca Montclair, Mutt decided, not my Annie.

The apartment gave the impression overall of being clean and spacious, full of new, expensive objects. It dazzled and sparkled like a brand-new penny.

The delivery was quick and efficient, over in just minutes. Annie did not appear. When the new furniture was in position in the center of the room, Mr. Sterling sat on the love seat and spread his arms along the curving back, nodding absentmindedly.

"What do you think, Gerald?" he asked the young man by the window.

Gerald shrugged. "I don't really know much about furniture."

Mr. Sterling rose from the love seat. "Neither do I, to be honest. Bianca chose this set. We'll see what she thinks when she gets home." He spun on his heel to face Mutt. "Donovan, when Mrs. Sterling arrives, don't tell her the furniture came. I want her to be surprised."

"Yes, sir."

Mr. Sterling gave a tip to the deliverymen, then one to Mutt. It made her uncomfortable, especially here in their suite. Whenever he gave her money she felt guilty or angry, depending on her mood. She felt guilty for taking money from a man whose wife she coveted and equally guilty for her unkind thoughts about such a friendly, generous and unsuspecting fellow. She felt angry because she was his inferior in every way and he must think of her that way even if he deftly avoided showing it. He had everything she would never have. He had everything anyone could want. He had given Annie a dream world to live in. He had made her happy.

Mutt knew it wasn't his fault that she was so inadequate. Even if Clive Sterling did not exist, it wouldn't improve Mutt's chances of giving Annie the life she craved where exquisite furniture cradled her body and the finest furs kept her warm and the world's rich and famous kept her company.

Even if she were a man, it was ridiculous to think Annie would want her. She wasn't beautiful. She wasn't rich. She wasn't refined. She was the doorman, a servant, as far distant from Annie as the moon—bleak, lonely and cold—was from the sun.

# CHAPTER NINETEEN

Baby's hand was moist in hers as they jitterbugged under the low ceiling, crammed into a throng of shuffling women's bodies amid the heat and noise of Bumpers on this typical Wednesday night. Mutt was here at least four nights a week, drinking soda pop and dancing with anybody who would consent. She loved the freedom of movement she could express on the dance floor. It was such a contrast from the well-mannered seriousness of her day job.

Though the place was packed, she felt more than usually lonely. Seeing Annie's hotel suite with its lovely furniture and air of elegance had left her feeling sad and hopeless. There was a big hole in her life and not even the noise of the nightclub could distract her from it tonight.

Baby was a full head shorter than she was but nimble and quick. Mutt cast a glance toward their usual table where Maggie, Anya and Tully leaned over their drinks, smoking cigarettes and watching the dancers. It had been a few weeks since Tully's sister's wedding and she was herself again. She seemed to have forgotten all about it, but Mutt knew she hadn't. That was something never forgotten, something that never stopped hurting. But it wasn't mentioned again by either of them. It was simply understood. The same was true of their tryst in the back room. Tully had a new, fond smile for Mutt that acknowledged that they had shared an intimate experience. Other than that, nothing had changed between them. They were friends, two people who cared about one another and supported one another, but they were not a couple. She had seen women reach out like that in prison, looking for a way to connect with another person if only for one needy moment.

In the months she had known Tully, Mutt had never seen or heard of a girlfriend. She didn't know if she had ever had a regular woman. She danced and was friendly with everyone, but she never flirted with any of the women and never asked anyone for a date. She was a loner.

Mutt wasn't a loner. Despite all of the hardships of communal living, first in the hobo camps and next in prison, she had always valued the camaraderie of the group. She had thought of the others as her family in a way she'd never had a sense of family before leaving home. Amid the impersonal monstrosity of the city, she had now found another such family in the microcosm of Bumpers. Baby, Maggie, Anya and Tully were her people, along with a handful of other regulars, as well as Zetta behind the bar and Ruby, the larger-than-life owner of the nightclub. They all knew Mutt and were happy to see her. At work, people were friendly enough but more distant—they didn't know her, the real her. It was the same for most of these women. This was one place they could be themselves.

For a few hours, they came here to escape the fear, suspicion and disapproval that lay on the other side of that door. Maybe it wasn't ideal, but it was something. It was more than a lot of people had in this city. It was the one thing keeping Mutt from despair. She didn't feel at home in Los Angeles. City life didn't suit her. Her heart longed for the wide-open countryside. Bumpers was her one small sanctuary.

It was impossible to leave LA and find a place that suited her better as long as Annie was here. That's what she had been telling herself all along, but lately she had been imagining leaving, imagining a life somewhere else without Annie in it. In the recesses of her mind she had begun to think that her goal in life would eventually become prying herself away from Annie. She thought of the future as a time when she would escape the bonds of her unrequited love. In many ways she had traded one prison for another and was still unable to do the one thing she'd always wanted to do—live free.

"Nice to see you, Mutt."

She looked toward the voice to see Ruby squeezing her way through the dance floor, greeting her guests. A big woman with black hair and pale skin, she advanced through the crowd by tossing her body into a crevice between people and widening it, using her bulk as a wedge. Ruby wore light blue eye shadow all the way up to her eyebrows and widened her lips with lipstick so that all of her features took on an exaggerated quality, designed perhaps to match her overall size. Everybody liked her. She was their queen and their mother. She was worshipped and adored for giving them this special place to congregate.

"Hi, Ruby!" Mutt called after her.

Ruby squeezed her way over to their table as the dance ended and Mutt and Baby returned to their chairs. Ruby leaned over the table, talking to Tully, displaying a good foot of cleavage and most of her pendulous breasts over the scooped neck of her dress, directing all eyes, surreptitiously, if not outright and unabashedly, to her bosom.

"You should all get in Maggie's taxi," Ruby suggested, "and go down there and see it right now."

"What are you talking about?" Baby asked.

"The movie I saw last night. It was *All About Eve* with Bette Davis."

"Oh, I love her!" Anya said, wriggling in her chair. "She's my favorite actress."

"Lauren Bacall!" Maggie interjected, announcing her own favorite.

"What about Bianca Montclair?" Mutt ventured, hearing the syllables aloud and startling herself. She had never pronounced that name before except in the privacy of her head.

"Who?" Ruby asked.

"I know who she is," Baby said. "She's Clive Sterling's wife."

There were looks of recognition around the table at the mention of Annie's husband.

"She's an actress too," Mutt explained.

"What did she play in?" Tully asked.

"She was in *Coming of the Dawn*. I haven't seen it. I was just wondering what she was like, if anybody had seen her in the movies."

Tully's steady gaze suggested mild confusion at Mutt's interest in an actress she had never seen.

"I saw that one," Ruby said thoughtfully. "I don't remember it much. I'll tell you what, my favorite movies are westerns. A brooding man on a horse, gazing out over a dusty, wide-open landscape, now that just gets me...right here." She touched her fist to her left breast and shook her head with feeling. "Then throw in a feisty gal with a pair of six-shooters...what more could you want?"

Maggie opened her mouth to speak but was distracted by raised voices near the front of the club. The music was cut in the middle of a song. Amid an excited chaos of voices, one reached them distinctly. "Cops!"

The door from the street flung open, hitting the wall with a bang.

"Out the back!" ordered Ruby, charging toward the front to intercept the cops.

As a group, they all jumped to their feet. Tully swept the hallway curtain aside and shoved Mutt through it just as a raucous commotion ensued up front. In the midst of it all, she could hear Ruby's raised voice saying, "You boys got no right coming in here and harassing my girls!"

In single file, Mutt's group rushed down the short hallway, the first ones to make it to the back door. At the front of the line, Anya threw open the door and burst into the alley, the rest of them following close. Behind them, others were now pouring through the narrow chute.

As soon as Mutt was out in the open night air, she saw three cops rounding the corner of the building, jogging into the alley to cut off the rear escape route.

"Hold it!" one of them hollered. "You're all under arrest."

Baby made a break for it, but a policeman caught her as she tried to run past him. She struggled in his grasp while the other two came toward the rest of them wielding billy clubs. By now two dozen women had streamed into the alley and were running, overwhelming the three cops, who must have realized they didn't have the manpower to contain this mob. Mutt was relieved to see that Baby had torn loose and was running full speed down the alley on her way to freedom.

The cops started swinging their clubs at anybody within reach. Mutt sprinted toward their line of defense along with most of the others, knowing her chances of getting by were good in the middle of the crowd. But just in front of her one of the cops swung his club and whacked Maggie on the shoulder. She went down at his feet. He raised his club over her head to give her another blow. Mutt lunged for him, knocking him off balance. Stumbling a few steps back, he recovered quickly. Then he snarled at her, reminding her of the railroad cops who hadn't bothered to hide their disgust for hobos.

"You filthy dyke!" he said, taking a step toward her.

She raised her arms too late to protect herself from the well-aimed swing at her head. A sharp crack rang out as the club connected. She went down, the world spinning around her.

Then suddenly she was lifted under the arms and half-dragged, half-carried to the next street where she was able to stand and face the woman who had rescued her. It was someone she didn't know, a short, muscular woman wearing a green tie and vest and a snappy porkpie hat.

"Can you walk?" she asked.

"Yes, I think so. Thank you. I'll be okay."

"Get going," the woman urged, and then ran off.

Mutt shook herself, reaching up to feel the tender bump on top of her head. She bolted rapidly from the scene, hoping that her friends were already long gone. She kept moving at a swift pace for four blocks until she arrived at a familiar bus stop. She slumped onto a bench to wait for the bus.

It was nearly midnight and cold. Her breath formed a fog in front of her face. Nobody else was around except the men who slept in doorways, and they were long oblivious to the conscious world. Some of these men, she thought, had probably been hobos before the war. Maybe she had even known them, had shared songs and stories with them in the jungles alongside the rivers of America. A lot of those men were heavy drinkers then. She could easily imagine that they had come to this, had become bums and winos, no longer able to work and still with no place that wanted them.

Her mind turned to Frogman. She had forgotten to ask Topeka Slim how he died. There were plenty of ways to die out there. Despite what she had said to Slim, it wasn't a life she could go back to. But she was still so much like the hobos. There was no place that wanted her either.

She was disheartened. Where could she go? What could she be? Where did she belong? It seemed like the world just didn't want her to live in it. There had to be something else, something where she could survive without disguising herself as a man or running from the police or constantly fearing for her life, somewhere she would feel wanted and loved. There must be some way to live free and proud and legal and still be herself.

Her head throbbed as she spotted the bus a block away, its welcoming lighted interior yellowish against the dim gray backdrop of the city. She stood, feeling dizzy, as the bus pulled up to the curb. It was nearly deserted at this late hour. She tucked herself gently into a seat, curled up and faced the window. She watched the buildings and streetlamps click by. She could see her reflection in the glass, opaque and ghostly, a pale round face with small ears and large eyes, messy hair and a downcast look to her mouth. In the glass, she looked almost identical to herself as a girl, a funny looking mutt of a girl.

She turned away from her reflection, troubled by the lost expression in her eyes.

# CHAPTER TWENTY

Before leaving for work on Thursday, Mutt used a pay phone to call Maggie and found out that eleven women from Bumpers had been arrested. As the owner, Ruby was also taken in. The rest, including everyone in her close circle of friends, had escaped. She was relieved to hear it. None of them would stay in jail long, but jail time wasn't the real threat in a raid like this. For someone like Tully, exposure was the danger. If she had been arrested, she would have certainly lost her job at the hospital.

For a woman with a career, it seemed like the risk of going to Bumpers to have a few drinks was too great. But it was more than drinking and dancing, Mutt knew. It was a place to escape a hostile world and be with others like herself, and that was worth a lot. It was worth the risk to Tully and many others.

Standing at her post outside the door of the Rutherford Hotel, Mutt felt light-headed. The knot on her head had grown overnight. She thought she might have to go home and lie down. She'd never taken a sick day. She didn't even know the terms of her employment contract, if sick days were allowed or how many. Feeling chilled, she pulled her collar higher around her neck. It would warm up as soon as the sun cleared the tops of the buildings, but this December morning had a distinctly winter feel about it. She smiled to think how soft she'd become. She remembered nearly freezing to death in the Midwest during winter, huddled on the ground under a thin blanket and waking up half-buried in snow. She hadn't seen a snowflake in nearly a decade, and the nights here never fell below fifty degrees.

Feeling dizzy, she leaned against the building and tucked her chin against her chest. She removed her cap to feel the bump on her head. It was bigger than ever and the pain was unrelenting. Finally, feeling that she could no longer stand without fainting, she decided to go inside and ask Bleeker if she could take a few hours off.

Before she reached the door, she saw someone approaching from within. She grabbed the handle and pulled the door open for…Annie. She looked gorgeous as usual, dressed in casual clothes today, a pair of black pants and a red cloth coat with a collar of black velvet. Her orange-red earrings matched her lipstick.

"Good morning, Donovan," she said, clutching a black pocketbook under her arm.

"Good morning, Mrs. Sterling. Is the valet bringing your car? Or will you need a taxi?"

"Neither. I'm going for a walk. It's chilly this morning, isn't it?" She laughed lightheartedly. "I mean for Southern California! Back home in Nebraska we'd call this a winter heat wave." She peered into Mutt's face, her expression one of concern. "Are you feeling okay, Donovan? You look frighteningly pale."

Mutt opened her mouth to reply. Nothing but a clipped croak came out. Then she felt her knees buckle.

She seemed to be falling through air, her body tumbling in slow motion. She went down, down, down until she sank into something soft and cold, like mud or…snow.

She lay cradled in a deep bed of powdery snow while tiny snowflakes drifted down from a solid black sky and landed on her upper lip, her eyelids, her forehead, immediately melting. One fell onto her eyelash and didn't melt. She tried to reach up to brush it away, but she couldn't move her arms. She couldn't feel her limbs at all. Maybe she was frozen, she thought.

Or dead.

A woman came into view beside her, standing over her, her expression unrevealing, her face pale and lovely and vaguely familiar. She had eyes like Mutt's own, big, round and bottomless. She wore a heavy winter coat and a knit cap over soft brown hair. It was her mother, Grace Hopper. Soon there was another figure, his expression neither friendly nor hostile, standing beside her mother, looking down where Mutt lay trapped in her snow cocoon. It was Kirby Hopper, unshaven but remarkably sober looking. One by one, her brother Ray arrived, then her second cousins, Fred and Opal Hopper, the latter with her hands clasped in front of her and her thin lips pressed into a tight horizontal line. The five of them stood on either side of her, all of them staring down at her wordlessly. They seemed not to see her as she struggled to ask them for help. But she couldn't make any noise. Her words stuck in her throat and the snow kept falling, landing on her family and herself, covering their heads, their shoulders, the tops of their shoes. Eventually she wasn't able to blink it off any longer and the snowflakes overwhelmed her eyes. She could see nothing but a bright white field. No sight. No sound. The only sensation she felt was cold.

*So this is what it feels like to be dead*, she thought. *It wasn't painful. It was just…nothingness.*

After a time, she began to notice a sound emerging from the emptiness.

It was a voice, a muffled, echoing female voice like that of an angel. She wondered if she had already gone to Heaven. When you're dead, time is probably not like time for the living. She might have been dead for a few seconds or a millennium.

"Donovan," the voice said gently. "Donovan."

Her body seemed to be floating, insensate. She couldn't see anything and she couldn't tell where the voice was coming from.

"Donovan, please," the angel pleaded, her voice becoming more distinct. "Donovan, can you hear me?"

There's something strange about this, Mutt thought. *Wouldn't an angel in Heaven know my real name?*

She felt a hand on her arm and forced her eyes open with difficulty. Hovering above her was a lovely face with skin like peaches and cream, reddish orange lipstick and a mantle of black velvet encasing her neck. This was the angel who was speaking to her. The beatific face, inches from her own, looked worried.

"Annie," she whispered. "I declare, Annie…you're an angel." Then she closed her eyes again, unable to keep them open.

As if from a tremendous distance, she heard the angel say, "Take him to my suite! And call my doctor!"

* * *

Mutt woke gradually out of a deep sleep to find herself in a white-walled room. As time passed, she realized she was lying on a wide bed covered to her shoulders by a soft and luxurious sheet. The room was dim and windowless. She heard a faint ticking and turned her head to locate a clock on the far wall. The movement caused her pain, reminding her of her injury. She turned to look at the other side of the room and saw Annie sitting in a chair beside the bed. Her eyes were closed and she was slumped down in an uncomfortable-looking position, a silky lavender robe covering her from neck to ankles. She appeared to be asleep.

Mutt was confused. *Where was she? Why was Annie here?*

She reached under the sheet to scratch an itch and felt an unfamiliar garment over her skin. She lifted the sheet to take a look, finding herself wearing nothing but a cotton nightgown. Alarmed, she touched her face to find no mustache. She pulled the sheet up to her chin, scanning the room to locate her clothes. If they were here, they were not visible.

Annie stirred. Her face took on a pouty frown as she opened her eyes, but the frown quickly transformed into a delighted smile as their eyes met. She leapt out of her chair and hopped onto the bed, taking Mutt's face gently between her hands.

"You're awake!" she said, then hugged her gingerly. "How do you feel?"

"Uh, I…"

"Dr. Freeman said you had a concussion. Does it hurt?"

"Where am I?"

"You're in my bedroom. You do know who I am, don't you?"

Mutt hesitated, then decided to say, "Mrs. Sterling?"

"Not to you, silly! When you called me Annie this morning, I immediately knew who you were. Nobody here uses my real name. Hardly anybody even knows it. And the way you said it, with that cute southern accent, I finally figured out why you seemed familiar to me." With a look of elated triumph, she announced, "You're Mutt!"

Mutt shrank back against the pillow. "You remember me?"

"How could I forget you? Why didn't you tell me it was you? Why have you been so mysterious? You do remember me, I know you do. I'm so happy to see you again, my darling, beautiful Mutt!"

Mutt was overwhelmed with gratitude that Annie remembered her with such fondness. The light in her eyes was reminiscent of the way they'd shone that day so long ago as they had prepared to run away together.

They smiled at one another for a silent minute before Annie asked, "Are you hungry?"

"I...no. What time is it?"

"It's almost five in the afternoon. You've been asleep for hours."

Panicked, Mutt moved to sit up and experienced a sudden jolt of pain like her head would crack open. "I have to get back to work."

"You can't work," Annie laughed, pushing gently against her shoulders to urge her back to the pillow. "Dr. Freeman said you have to rest and heal for a few days."

"But I have to tell my boss. I'll be fired."

"Don't worry, Mutt. I've taken care of that. I told the hotel manager you're ill."

"You didn't tell him who I am, did you? They wouldn't let a woman..."

Annie shook her head. "I didn't say anything about that. Just that you're ill and under doctor's care. Nobody knows about that except me and Dr. Freeman. And I'll have to tell Clive, of course."

"Your husband? You're going to tell him about me?"

"You're here in his apartment, aren't you? What do you expect me to do? Hide you under the bed?" She laughed giddily.

"I shouldn't be here. I should go. I can go to my own place."

"No. You're not supposed to travel. You need to rest. I won't let you wander all over the city with a concussion."

"But if they find out I'm a woman, I'll lose my job."

"Don't worry, Mutt. Clive won't tell anyone. Believe me. He can be trusted." Her expression was so tender and reassuring that Mutt relaxed and leaned back on the pillow.

"That's a nasty bump," Annie said. "Does it hurt?"

"Yes."

"How did it happen?"

Mutt gazed into her troubled eyes, too muddled to know how to answer that question. The answer was too long and complicated. There were too many other questions still unanswered. Mutt had no idea what Annie would think of Bumpers or the society of women there. Would she be on the side of the police? Did she even know about these things? How far back would Mutt have to go to explain? She wasn't capable of it just yet.

"I was in the wrong place," Mutt said, "at the wrong time." She attempted a smile. "Unlucky."

"My poor darling." Annie squeezed her hand. "I have so many questions for you. You know about me, obviously, but I know nothing about your life since I last saw you standing beside the railroad tracks all those years ago. Oh, Mutt, I can't believe you're here. I never thought I'd see you again!" She hugged her around the neck, then pulled back and smiled fondly. "But I can see you're barely awake. Dr. Freeman gave you something to help you sleep. He said rest is the best thing for you. So I'll let you rest." Annie moved to go.

"Wait," Mutt said, reaching for her hand. "There's one question I've been dying to ask you all these years."

Annie settled back on the bed beside her. "What is it?"

"When you told your daddy I was a girl and saved me from getting my head blown off…how did you know?"

Annie smiled and pushed Mutt's hair back from her forehead. "I spied on you the night before when you were taking your bath. I climbed up into the hayloft and watched you undress in the moonlight. I know I shouldn't have done that, but I was so fascinated with you and so curious. From the moment I first saw you, I knew there was something very special about you."

"Then you…you knew all along." Mutt was stunned.

"Once I knew you were a woman, I was more fascinated than ever with you. I went to my room and sat there for a long time thinking about you, a girl on her own and wandering the country disguised as a boy. What freedom you had! How brave and strong and independent you were! You captured my imagination, my heart and my dreams altogether."

"But…but…"

"Why didn't I tell you I knew?"

Mutt nodded.

"I didn't reason it all out at the time. It seemed like the best way to make you comfortable. Would you have kissed me, I wonder, if we hadn't been pretending you were a man?" Annie stood, then reached over to caress Mutt's cheek tenderly. Her smile was so full of affection that it felt like a warm blanket settling over Mutt's body. "Now get some rest. We'll have plenty of time to talk tomorrow."

Annie was right. If she had revealed what she knew that night, Mutt wouldn't have been able to kiss her or even speak to her the way she had. Such a thing would have been unthinkable to her back then. It was nearly unthinkable now to realize that from the moment Annie had entered the barn in her tablecloth cape, she knew the truth.

The next time Mutt woke, she heard voices from the other room. She recognized Annie's voice, but she wasn't sure who she was talking to until her husband blurted out, "Donovan is a what!"

Mutt slipped out of bed and stepped quickly to the closed door where she pressed herself against it to listen.

"Please keep your voice down," said Annie. "She's asleep."

"I think I need a drink," Clive said.

Mutt heard footsteps, then the tinkling of glass before Annie said, "Do you remember the story I told you once about a hobo girl named Mutt?"

"Of course! How could I forget that? It was one of the most interesting things about you. It was one of the reasons I felt I could trust you."

Mutt pressed her ear firmly against the door, surprised that Annie had confided this incident from her past to her husband.

"It seemed completely natural that I fell in love with that little hobo. I was so captivated with her, I would have followed her to China if my daddy hadn't locked me in my room for a week. I spent that entire week in tears. Honestly, I don't know what my parents made of that. I never told them how I felt about Mutt, but they seemed very anxious that I have a date for the Fourth of July dance. They must have put an ad in the newspaper because four boys asked me to that dance."

Clive chuckled.

"But they needn't have worried. Mutt was a singular experience. I've never felt that way toward another woman."

"You were young and your heart was open. Society hadn't yet managed to inflict its taboos on you. But I'm not sure what you're getting at? What has all this got to do with Donovan? You're not trying to tell me that you fancy him? Her? That you've got a thing for cross-dressing women?"

"Clive, I'm trying to tell you that Donovan *is* Mutt. It's her! I recognized her this morning and she's confirmed it."

"My Lord, Bianca!"

"Yes, I know, it's incredible. I can hardly believe it myself. But it is her. There's no doubt. I want her to stay here until she's well enough to go back to work if that's all right with you."

Mutt's hearing was so keenly on edge waiting for Clive's response that she heard ice cubes clinking together in his glass.

"I understand, darling. Of course she can stay. I have no objection."

"Oh, Clive!"

Mutt heard Annie's footsteps race across the room. She must be hugging and kissing him for being so generous. Mutt agreed. It was generous. More than she would have expected since he knew about the romantic feelings they'd once shared. But that was a long time ago and so much had happened in the interim... to both of them.

She moved carefully back to the bed and crawled into it. For old times' sake, Annie wanted to be charitable. At the moment, Mutt was grateful. She wanted nothing more than to sleep. Tomorrow was another story, the details of which she couldn't imagine.

A major turning point had just been reached. She tried not to think about what it meant. Something was about to change in her life. She was both afraid and relieved that it might mean the end of her position on the sidelines of Annie's life.

Despite many nights lying in her room trying to imagine leaving Annie and LA behind, she was now struck with the thought that the time may have come. Now that Annie knew about her, how could she possibly continue as the doorman at this hotel?

She curled up in the bed, saddened by the thought that this chapter of her life, one of the few in which Annie had appeared, was now over.

# CHAPTER TWENTY-ONE

When Mutt woke after a long and deep sleep, she was alone in Annie's room, surprised that she had been able to sleep through the night after having slept through most of the previous day. According to the clock on the wall, it was nearly nine o'clock—in the morning, she assumed. In this windowless room, it was impossible to tell.

Except for the headache, she felt almost normal. She touched the bump on her head gingerly. It seemed to have shrunk overnight. She walked to the bathroom and washed her face, then searched the closet for her uniform, putting on her pants and shirt but leaving the jacket and tie where they were.

Barefoot, she left the bedroom and wandered through the empty front room with its console television and new claw-footed living room set. Padding silently on the thick carpet, she felt like a burglar. Hearing voices drifting in through the open balcony doors, she went onto the balcony to find Clive, Annie and Gerald sitting at the table having breakfast. All of them wore dressing gowns. A silver tray that had been brought by room service lay on a sideboard, empty. On the table was a pot of coffee, a pitcher of orange juice, plates of eggs and toast and an assortment of sweet pastries.

Beyond this scene was an unobstructed, breathtaking view of the city.

At the sight of Mutt, Annie leapt up and hugged her affectionately. "You're awake! And walking about. Are you sure you should? I'll bring you breakfast in bed."

"I'm okay," Mutt said. "I can eat here." Feeling suddenly uncomfortable, she added, "Or I can go down to the dining room and order something. I appreciate your helping me out and all. I'm feeling better. I can be on my way now."

"Nonsense," Annie declared. "Dr. Freeman said you must be careful for a few days and you shouldn't be left alone in case you pass out again. You must be observed, he said, and I am completely delighted to be observing you. Sit here."

She held a chair for Mutt, who self-consciously smiled at the men and sat. Clive wore a sly grin on his face, as if he were amused at this scene. Gerald seemed indifferent, spreading strawberry jam on a piece of toast. His manner suggested he was where he belonged, and Mutt began to wonder if he had spent the night. Who was he, anyway? She had never actually been introduced to him.

"Bianca has explained everything," Clive said. "You can stay as long as you need to. Or as long as my wife wishes it." He chuckled and glanced at Gerald, who responded with a thin smile. Turning back to Mutt, he said, "I've got to say, that disguise of yours was not bad. Not bad at all! Now that the mustache and makeup are gone, I can easily see you're a woman. But what was the point of that charade?"

"I needed a job and they won't let women do this sort of work."

"Well, then, why not do a job they will let women do? These days, women work at all sorts of things. Can you type? What about a secretarial job?"

"It doesn't suit me. I like my job here."

He leaned back and crossed his legs. "Then I see no reason why you shouldn't do it. I've never had any complaints about you. Nobody has, as far as I know. You're a damned sight better at it than Chatham was." He took a cigarette out of a silver case and Gerald snapped open his lighter to light it. "The way this country is headed with women demanding more opportunities and equal pay, it wouldn't surprise me if someday you'll be able to do all sorts of jobs traditionally reserved for men. Like drive a truck."

Gerald grunted sarcastically.

"Look, Gerald, women quite capably took over our jobs here at home while we were off fighting the war. My Aunt Mary was a pipe fitter."

"What's she doing now?" Annie asked.

"She's a housewife again."

"Everybody back where they belong," Gerald said with satisfaction.

"I'm all for women doing whatever type of work they want," Clive said. "And getting paid the same wage as men for it. It's only fair."

Annie put an egg and a piece of toast on Mutt's plate and poured her a cup of coffee, smiling serenely as if she could think of nothing better than waiting on Mutt Hopper. "How do you take your coffee, Mutt?"

"Just sugar."

Annie picked up a cube of sugar with silver tongs and let it drop into the cup.

"What did you do before you were our doorman?" Clive asked.

Mutt balked, unprepared to discuss where she'd been for the last eight years.

"She was a hobo," Annie said. "You already know that."

For once, Gerald looked interested. "A hobo?"

"She's quite the unconventional sort," said Clive. "Another occupation where she had to pretend to be a man."

"I didn't have to," Mutt said. "There are women hobos. We called them road sisters. I knew one who lived on the road for years and years. Her name was Boxcar Betts. Actually, she's still out there, living in a hobo jungle in Omaha, Nebraska."

Clive shook his head. "I had no idea."

"Why would you?" Gerald asked. "It's not like you've spent much time in the bowels of society where people like that live."

"Gerald!" Annie scolded. "Don't be horrid. It's a very interesting life. Full of adventure. I would have happily gone with her if I'd been allowed to."

"You wanted to be a hobo?" Gerald laughed.

"Well, why not? I wanted to see the world. I wanted to go to Hollywood."

"You didn't have to do it in a boxcar, though, did you?" Clive pointed out. "You got here on a bus."

Mutt put her toast down. "And you became a movie star just like you wanted to."

Gerald snorted derisively, then looked sheepish and muttered, "Sorry."

"Why did you become a hobo?" Clive asked. "Was it for the adventure?"

"No, sir. It was to get from one place to another. To get from one job to another."

"You were a seasonal worker?" Clive took a puff on his cigarette.

"Yes, sir."

"A huge seasonal labor force has been riding the freights since the Civil War, so I've read. Men, mostly men, perpetually traveling in search of work, trying to escape poverty, despair and hopelessness. No, I have not lived among these men." He glanced at Gerald. "But I've done a lot of reading about the history of labor in this country. It happens to be an interest of mine. More than an interest. I'd like to talk to you more about this when you're feeling better, Donovan. I mean, uh…I'm sorry, but Bianca hasn't told me your real name. It's all very well for her to use her pet name for you, but what do we call you? I can't call you Donovan now, can I? At least not when you're off the clock. Don't worry, though. We'll keep up the ruse for you, won't we, Gerald?"

Gerald looked up from his wristwatch at the sound of his name, looking startled.

"Mutt is what most people call me."

"Well, now," Clive said, "don't you have a proper name? I can't see myself calling you Mutt."

"My real name is Shirley," Mutt said, noting the look of surprise on Annie's face. "Shirley Hopper."

Clive smiled approvingly. "That's more like it. Well, Shirley, I'm particularly interested to know what situations you faced in the orchards of California. Sanitation, working conditions, pay rates. I've heard that some itinerant workers are little more than slaves. Their so-called wages are held back to cover room and board, and the living conditions are unspeakable." He tapped his cigarette on the edge of an ashtray of green glass, nodding thoughtfully, allowing Mutt a chance to consume most of her egg before he asked, "Did you belong to a union?"

Mutt swallowed quickly. "Yes, sir. The Wobblies."

"The Industrial Workers of the World, yes."

"All the hobos did."

"Were you involved at all in union business?"

"I just got my card and that was that. I just wanted to work."

He nodded, his eyes taking on a tender look. "Did you know that last year the IWW was put on the government's list of subversive organizations?"

Mutt shook her head.

"That's right. The once mighty IWW no longer has any power. A few years ago, labor unions with Communist affiliations were outlawed. That laid the groundwork to bust any union with balls just by claiming it's got Communist principles or Communist leaders. It doesn't have to be true, you see. The rumor, the insinuation, that's enough to bring them down." Clive was clearly getting agitated. He let out a sigh of exasperation, then pressed his lips tightly together so his thin mustache became perfectly straight.

"Do you want another egg?" Annie asked.

Mutt nodded, wishing Annie would let her serve herself. She felt awkward and confused in this company, and Annie's doting made her even more self-conscious about how out of place she felt.

"The IWW did a lot of good," Clive continued. "But now, after it's been painted red, it's dead. That's what they were after."

"Who?" asked Mutt, feeling lost.

"Congress. It's big money that talks there, not the little guy picking grapes. Not even all the little guys picking grapes. Big business is against unions, naturally, because they prevent the exploitation of workers. Unions, they say, are a threat to free enterprise. And free enterprise, by God, is the American Way! Even if it tramples ninety percent of American citizens into the ground." He ran his index finger over one side of his mustache, then the other, looking thoughtful. After another puff on his cigarette, he said, "Do you think the Wobblies was a Communist plot, Shirley?"

She opened her mouth to answer, but had no idea how.

"Stop it, Clive," Annie intervened. "Let Mutt eat her breakfast without having to have a political discussion, for God's sake. She's got a concussion." She reached over and caressed Mutt's cheek tenderly.

Clive sighed and stamped out his cigarette in the ashtray. "Very well. Sorry. I get carried away on this subject." Standing, he said, "I need to go downtown. Are you coming, Gerald?"

"Yes. I'll get dressed and join you."

The men left the room, and Mutt finished her breakfast while Annie sat beside her gazing like a mother hen at its chick.

"I'm sorry about Clive," she said. "Going on like that about unions. He's very political."

"Aren't you too?" Mutt recalled the WWLS rally they had both marched in.

"I do belong to a couple of organizations that try to help people in need. I guess I think of it as charity work more than politics. I don't really understand politics. I mean, what he was saying about your union, I don't know what it's all about."

"Neither do I," admitted Mutt.

"Clive says I should be more aware of the political implications of my activities because everything we do, on some level, is political. Even that, I don't really understand. With the WWLS, we mainly try to help people...women. Poor and uneducated women. Get them to services and into programs to improve their lives."

"I sure could have used something like that when I was younger. There's a lot of women like that in the South, and I don't think we ever had a place to go for help. If we did, I didn't know about it. If you didn't have family, you were out of luck. You had to find your own way."

"Which you did." She put her hand over Mutt's. "You're a survivor, aren't you, Mutt?"

She shrugged. "I wouldn't have minded some help."

"There are a lot of people who need help, no doubt about it."

"Even here in Los Angeles?"

"Oh, sure. There are poor people everywhere. Maybe not so many here as where you're from though. I hope they have a chapter of the WWLS down there too."

"I doubt it." Mutt ate another piece of toast and finished her coffee while Annie sat idly beside her, smiling inanely.

"I wish you'd quit staring at me," Mutt said after wiping her mouth with a napkin.

"I'm just so happy! I can't believe I'm looking at you."

Mutt turned her chair to face Annie. "So you're not sorry about what happened back then?"

"Lord no! I still wish I could have gone with you. I was so sad when you left. I couldn't eat or sleep for a week. I dreamt about you for years and years. I've never met anybody like you since. Nobody who made me feel like that, like I just wanted to drown in your eyes. That's why I'm so happy now. I don't know if you feel the same way about me. I know a lot of things must have happened to you in between."

Mutt nodded, feeling overwhelmed. "A lot of things, that's for sure."

"Do you have somebody, a special somebody?"

"I don't have anybody, no."

Annie broke into a joyful smile. "It wasn't a coincidence your working here, was it? You're here because of me!"

Mutt lowered her gaze to where their hands were clasped together. Then, fearful of all that she felt, she stood and backed away.

Annie rose to follow her. "You once said you loved me. Do you still? Do you still love me, my sweet, darling Mutt?"

Mutt swallowed hard, trying to look at anything but Annie, but she was now close in front of her and impossible to avoid. "Oh, Annie, what's the point of talking like that?"

With Annie's face close to hers, her eyes full of affection, her mouth offering itself, Mutt's mind went hazy, whether from the concussion or the nearness of Annie, she didn't know. Somehow their lips came together and they embraced one another in a long, slow and sensuous kiss that left Mutt in a trance. Annie's body in her arms felt so sweet and so true that she couldn't let go. They touched one another's faces tenderly and kissed again. Mutt kissed her mouth, her eyes, her neck, and clasped her tight in both arms like a precious parcel she couldn't afford to lose.

"I do still love you, Annie," she admitted breathlessly. "I never stopped loving you. It seems like loving you is the only thing I've done for the last nine years."

Annie kissed her again, her lips full and soft and anxious. They broke apart only when they heard Clive from the next room.

"Darling," he called, "I'm on my way."

"Just a minute," Annie said, then ran inside.

Mutt stared unseeing at congealed egg yolk and crusts of bread, her mind in a fog. She shook herself to get her feet moving, then left the balcony to see Gerald and Clive near the front door. Gerald was tying Clive's tie. Annie helped him on with his overcoat. He kissed her on the cheek, then turned and smiled at Mutt before putting on his hat.

"See you this evening, ladies."

When the men had left, Annie returned to Mutt and leaned into her, her head on her chest, her eyes closed, looking totally content. Mutt held her loosely, conflicted about her feelings. When Annie tilted her head up and looked into her eyes, she pulled her closer and kissed her sweet mouth longingly, tenderly and for several seconds. With difficulty, she willed herself to stop, then opened her eyes to see Annie gazing at her with the hot flame of desire in her eyes.

Mutt stepped back and shook her head. "We gotta stop this."

"But you said you loved me. You do love me, don't you, Mutt?"

"But you're married!"

Annie frowned. "You don't understand."

"No, I don't."

"Sorry. I've been so overjoyed with having you here, I forgot how you must see things. I'll explain everything. Then I hope you'll see there's no reason we can't be together now. No reason at all. Oh, Mutt, we're going to be so happy!"

# CHAPTER TWENTY-TWO

Mutt lay on her back with her hands behind her head, blissfully happy. The room was dark but for the light from one candle on the dresser. Hearing the sound of running water in the bathroom, she smiled just to think that Annie was nearby. Annie—her true love, her lover, her friend. Her body hummed with the memory of Annie's touch and her mind reeled, reliving the past week of their intimate life together.

When Annie returned from the bathroom, she wore nothing but a pink feather boa and an impish grin. The sash of feathers was draped over one shoulder and held tantalizingly at her right hip, hiding a crucial part of her from view. One blushing breast peeked out and the other hid beneath the boa. Mutt sat up to watch her saunter in. She strode like a model on a runway, with measured paces and a wide sashay of her hips. She approached the bed and took the end of the boa from her shoulder, teasing Mutt's cheek with it. When she leaned down for a kiss, Mutt wrapped her arms around her and pulled her to the bed. When she released her mouth, Annie laughed and swatted her with the boa, then grabbed her leg and tickled the bottom of her foot with it. Laughing, Mutt tried to pull away, tortured by the feathers, but Annie held her fast.

"Are you ticklish?" she asked.

"Yes!" Mutt was finally able to pull her leg free.

Annie balanced herself over Mutt's body on her hands and knees. "Where else are you ticklish?"

"Never you mind."

Annie fluttered her fingers over Mutt's stomach, causing her to pull back. "There too?"

Seeing that Annie was coming at her again, Mutt jumped to her feet to escape her reach. Annie slithered up Mutt's body so they were standing in the middle of the bed with their bare stomachs pressed together. Annie lifted her face and puckered her lips. As Mutt leaned her head down for a kiss, Annie tickled her at the waist on both sides at once. Mutt yelped and jumped, the top of her head brushing the ceiling, then grabbed both of Annie's arms to keep her from tickling further. They struggled, giggling and wrestling with one another until one corner of the bed collapsed with a jarring thud to the floor, stunning them into immobility. They posed mid-struggle like a freeze-frame of a bizarre combat scene: two naked young women brawling atop a lopsided bed in a tangle of sheets, a pink feather boa wrapped around their ankles.

"Oops," Annie finally said, then fell to the bed laughing with complete abandon.

Mutt lay down beside her, also laughing. They held one another until their laughter turned into sporadic giggles. The giggling was eventually subdued by kisses and a renewed ardor.

Mutt moved above Annie in the candlelight, their bodies touching in the way she'd come to crave beyond any physical need she had ever had before. Skin touched, kissed and caressed. Annie's body rose up to meet her, following its desire, straining to bring their hips closer together, to fuse their aching hunger into a single furious moment of relief.

Mutt was familiar now with the smell of Annie's skin and hair and with the cues of her body during lovemaking. She was quiet. A woman who talked at all other times with easy chattiness, in the midst of lovemaking had no words, and only occasionally produced an audible moan. Her breathing patterns revealed the clues that told Mutt to touch her more directly or softer or, after she had climaxed, not at all. When she held her breath altogether, like now, Mutt knew they were nearly there.

The candlelight illuminated Annie's beautiful naked form on the slanting bed, her head on a pillow with her hair splayed out around it, her eyes tightly closed and one arm over her head, her hand in a tight fist. The other hand clenched Mutt's forearm like a vise.

It was time. As Annie's limbs shuddered, Mutt squeezed her own eyes shut and pushed herself over the edge, matching Annie's moment almost perfectly.

After a week of frequent lovemaking, she had learned a great deal about Annie's body, but felt she had still more to learn. Annie's body was a most wonderful, complex and beautiful gift, like a present that she was still unwrapping. The joys and mysteries of it seemed endless.

Mutt lay on her side, worshipping and devouring her lover's small pale body with her gaze. Nothing had ever made her happier than pleasing Annie, feeling her body grow and come alive beneath her. It wasn't like other kinds of happiness. She had a sense of awe—something had happened, something miraculous, but she didn't know how and it didn't feel like she'd had much to do with it. She just felt privileged to be there.

In the past week, she had learned a lot about Annie's life as well as her body. Everything she had imagined about Annie watching her come and go through the entrance of the Rutherford Hotel had been a misinterpretation. Now she understood. When Annie had explained her marriage, Mutt had been stunned. Maybe she should have figured it out herself. The clues were there. But she hadn't. She had taken it all in as thoroughly as had the movie-going public.

Clive Sterling was a homosexual. Gerald was his lover. The movie studio had arranged the marriage to quiet rumors about Clive. He and Bianca Montclair were legally married, but she was his wife in name only.

When Annie had explained the situation, Mutt had asked, "Why would you agree to such a thing?"

"The fact is," Annie had admitted, "that my career as an actress was at a dead stop. Did you see my movie?"

"No, I had no chance to see it."

"We should go to Clive's house in Malibu. It has a theater room and copies of all our movies. Of *his* movies, I should say. I have only two. I had a bit part in my first movie and nobody noticed. Then I got lucky and got a real part in *Coming of the Dawn*. That's where Clive and I first met. The critics didn't like me and I guess the studio didn't either. I wasn't offered another part. They've kept me under contract, but they aren't required to give me any work. After that movie, I kept waiting for a call, but nothing came. So I was broke, really broke. I was living in a crummy apartment with two other showbiz failures, and it was all we could do to make the rent each month. I figured I'd have to go back home to Nebraska. I didn't know what else to do. One of my roommates was making money by…I couldn't do that. I could never do that."

"No, of course not!"

"Clive was such a dear. He really has a very kind nature. He took me along as his date to all the parties so I was able to circulate with the movie people and stay in the limelight. He was just being a good friend, really, but people started to think of us as a couple. We didn't discourage it. It was good for us both. Even so, there were rumors about him. The studio was getting nervous. As a romantic leading man, he would have been ruined if it got out that he was a homosexual. He wasn't happy about a sham marriage, but he knew he had no choice. That's when we came up with this idea. As his wife, I'd be able to live comfortably and stay in the game. And he would be safe. All I had to do was play a part. I was an actress, after all, so why not? It was the perfect solution to both our problems."

"So everybody was happy with the arrangement."

"I wouldn't say I was happy. It's been lonely, Mutt. I don't have any real friends. Everywhere I go, I have to pretend to be somebody I'm not. Always hiding the truth. It's exhausting and depressing."

"I know how that can be."

"You do, don't you?" She touched Mutt's face gently. "I'm so happy to have you here. You've no idea how happy I am. I feel like I've been saved. I know I shouldn't complain. My life isn't hard. I have plenty of money and everything I could want. Clive is very generous and he's a good friend. And when you get to know him, Gerald is a clever and funny fellow. He's a good match for Clive, who needs someone cynical like that to balance him out."

"But there's no place for you in their relationship, is there?"

She shook her head. "Clive tries hard to make me feel included and he plays his part of husband exceptionally well, but unless we're being seen by someone, we live quite independently of one another. Mainly I live here alone and he lives in Malibu with Gerald. We do what we can to make sure nobody knows that's our regular arrangement."

"Don't you have…other friends?"

"I dated a few men early on, mostly actors. We were all trying to make connections, get a foothold in the business. But I haven't dated anyone since Clive and I started going around together. None of them mattered to me. I can honestly tell you, Mutt, that I have never been in love with anyone but you."

With Annie's confession out of the way, it had been Mutt's turn. She knew she couldn't have a relationship with Annie without giving her a true account of her own life during the last nine years. So Mutt told the story about what had happened on the Gemgiani farm and how she had spent the last eight years in the state penitentiary. She told about her brother being killed and how she hadn't been allowed to go to the funeral. She told her about the long days and nights and the years that went by where the best thing she had through it all were her memories of Annie.

"When I got out," she said, "nobody would hire me as long as I told the truth about where I'd been. I killed a man, Annie, and that doesn't go away just because they set you free."

Tears rolled over Annie's cheeks and Mutt was sorry for making her sad.

"You've had such a hard life," Annie sobbed.

"You're still so tenderhearted."

"I never knew your real name. If I had known it, I would have found you. You don't know how many times I wished I'd asked you your real name. I would have done whatever I could to help you. I'm so sorry you had to go through that by yourself." Annie put her arms around Mutt's neck and hugged her tight.

"Now you know about me," said Mutt. "You can see how we went such different ways. A lot of doors are closed to me now and I wouldn't blame you if you closed yours too."

Annie nuzzled further into Mutt's neck. "We may have gone different ways, but here we are in the same place now. Nothing that's happened to you in the meantime makes a bit of difference to me. We were meant to be together."

Since then the hours of their blissful union were uncountable. Every day, as soon as Mutt got off work, she raced up to the fourteenth floor to be with Annie. They were together as often as they could be, sharing room service meals, having drinks on the balcony while the sun set over the vast sprawl of the Los Angeles Basin, curled together on the claw-footed love seat watching television. And, of course, they made love. Mutt adored making love with Annie and couldn't get enough.

Up till now, Mutt had always thought of sex with mixed emotions. There had been nothing gentle or loving about her early sexual experiences. Sometimes, years later, she had felt the same way, coolly separated from the act of her body. Though it was physically pleasurable, sex had always seemed to her a little like an assault. A two-way assault, using someone else's body to appease the growling monster of one's carnal desire.

Until Annie. It was completely different with her. It was soft and sweet and covered her like twilight covers the earth each evening, benignly and serenely. She marveled at how different this was from her previous experiences. There was nothing embarrassing or lewd about it. It was utterly joyful and utterly satisfying, and she found herself integrated, mind and body, in loving Annie. She was whole at last.

Just as Annie had originally brought love into her life, she had now awakened her to the happiness of physical pleasure enjoyed without guilt or shame.

Mutt's life had been dramatically changed overnight. She was living in a dream and she couldn't believe how lucky she was.

"I love you," she said, her voice echoing a little in the windowless room.

"I love you too," Annie said, stroking her face.

Mutt uttered a tense, involuntary laugh.

"Why do you laugh when I say I love you?" Annie asked.

"Because it surprises me, I guess. It's hard to get used to. To think you could feel that way about *me*."

"Mutt, you just don't know what a wonderful woman you are. You're strong and optimistic, and your heart's as wide open as the plains of Nebraska. I know you think you look funny, but I think you're cute and I could look at you all day long. You think your daddy called you Mutt because of your looks, but I think maybe you got it wrong. I think he called you that because you're scrappy and resourceful and whatever bad luck comes your way, you'll battle your way out of it. You've got determination and courage and you're smart."

"Smart?" Mutt laughed again. "You must be thinking about some other gal. I never even finished high school."

"That's got nothing to do with it."

"Brains don't run in my family. My daddy used to say my brother was as slow as molasses at Christmas."

Annie smiled crookedly. "I don't know about your brother but you aren't slow at all. You're clever and beautiful and wonderful."

"Lord, Annie, you make me feel special."

"You *are* special. You're my special someone, the most special someone in the whole world." Annie wrapped herself more tightly around Mutt. "I'm so happy I found you again. I used to daydream about you all the time when I was still at home on the farm. I dreamt that you'd come back for me. Then we'd run away and ride in a boxcar out to California together. You wouldn't believe how I used to look at the men in the train cars whenever we were in town, searching for you. I wanted to go with them. Catching a train like that, it must be quite a thrill."

"Yes, it was. Always got my heart thumping hard."

"I'm sorry I never got to do it."

"You still could. There's still trains. There's still hobos riding 'em."

Annie laughed. "That would be quite the headline, wouldn't it? Mrs. Clive Sterling seen hopping a freight train."

Mutt laughed too. "I've learned quite a bit about makeup from my friend Maggie. If you really want to, I could disguise you and we could take a ride. I haven't done it myself in years and I'm sort of itching to do it again just for old time's sake."

Annie sat up abruptly. "Do you really think we could? Oh, it's ridiculous! Could we? No, of course we can't. It's a crazy idea."

The silky luminescence of her body in wavering candlelight offered an irresistible opportunity to Mutt, who reached for her and stroked her, pressing her face into the yielding softness between her breasts.

"I think we can do anything we want to," she murmured. "Right now I think I could ride a freight to the moon and back."

Annie rested a hand on the back of her head with a light sigh.

# CHAPTER TWENTY-THREE

Having put Annie through a strict list of hows, dos and don'ts regarding riding the rails, Mutt led her along the tracks to a spot just outside the railroad property where they would wait for a freight train.

Annie looked adorable in her hobo clothes. She wore a pair of denim pants, a short jacket and a newsboy cap. She'd had the hotel kitchen prepare a picnic that she carried in a paper bag. If the staff had known where this lunch was headed, they would have been incredulous. Mutt was disguised as a man, wearing a white shirt, black tie, black jacket and a derby hat. She carried a satchel with water and a blanket. According to Annie, she looked almost exactly as she had the first time they had laid eyes on one another, and this fact delighted her, eliciting a playful amorousness from her.

"How long?" Annie asked.

Mutt glanced at the beautiful Longines watch on her wrist. The four small diamonds marking twelve, three, six and nine caught the sun with a dazzling sparkle. This was a Christmas gift from Clive and Annie, by far the most expensive thing she'd ever owned. She had casually mentioned that she kept time by the clock on the Birmingham Bank building while on duty and Clive had given her this, saying, "A doorman needs a proper watch."

It was an extravagant gift and she had immediately objected to it. "It's from both of us," Annie had told her, which didn't help because she didn't like the idea of Annie being part of "both of us."

After a month of practically living in the Sterling home, Mutt had still not relaxed about her place there. Her objection to this gift, that it was "too much," was met with reassurances that she deserved it, that she was part of the family now. Clive even suggested that he would be hurt if she refused it, that it would be a slight against his hospitality. Gerald, in his typical acerbic fashion, had sidled up to her and said, "Really? You would take his wife and not a watch?"

That remark had closed the subject. Ultimately, she didn't know what she could do but accept the gift. Though the extravagance had bothered her at first, especially since the clock on the bank building was perfectly adequate and always in view, she had grown to admire the look of the watch when she lifted her arm and bent her elbow to hitch up her sleeve.

"We should be seeing a train leave the yard in about fifteen minutes," Mutt reported. "Keep low in the brush here until it comes and do like I told you. We want to get it when it just starts moving. If it's going too fast, I won't let you go."

Annie squatted in the bushes beside Mutt. "I'm so excited! We're breaking the law, aren't we?"

Mutt loved her spirit. She had loved it from the day they met. She had seemed undaunted by anything, ready for adventure, and today that quality was apparent. Her life as Mrs. Clive Sterling had muted her true personality, but now her face glowed pink and her eyes shone like stars, just like Mutt remembered her from all those years ago. She felt like she was falling in love all over again.

A creaking and groaning from the yard signaled a locomotive on the move. Mutt spotted it between several parallel tracks with stationary strings of cars. It chugged along, moving laboriously under its long load, the smokestack puffing up a black cloud.

She squeezed Annie's hand. "Here we go. We'll get on near the front before it gets any speed up. See that open boxcar?" Mutt pointed. "That's where we're headed."

Annie nodded, looking apprehensive.

"You get on first. I'll be right behind you."

After the engine passed, they ran up to the open car of the barely-moving train. Annie walked beside it for a few paces, glancing back at Mutt.

"Go ahead," Mutt encouraged.

Annie jumped up and lay on her belly in the open doorway. Mutt put both hands on her denim-clad rump and gave her a shove. She rolled into the car, then Mutt jumped in, aided by her long legs. Glancing into the corners, she was happy to see they had the car to themselves. That hadn't happened much in the old days, but fewer and fewer people traveled this way now, ever since the war and the end of the Depression.

They sat side by side at one end of the car and kissed one another, triumphant and happy. A smudge of soot adorned Annie's cheek like war paint. Mutt rubbed at it with her sleeve.

Annie laughed and hugged her around the neck, obviously full of happiness.

Mutt was happy too. Her impossible dream had come true. She had been reunited with the woman she loved. Incredibly, Annie wanted her as much as she wanted Annie. Everything in her life was wonderful now, quite suddenly. Even her job was less stressful, as her boss now treated her with a new level of respect, understanding, if only in a hazy way, that Donovan had some mysterious special relationship with the Sterlings. There had been a subtle shift in the way the hotel manager nodded his greeting to Mutt each day. Charlie the bellboy had tried to wheedle it out of her, asking in whispered tones of collusion, "So what's the deal with you and Clive Sterling?" Mutt had always had secrets and never had any difficulty keeping them. In answer to Charlie's question, she had merely shrugged.

At her post at the front door of the hotel, she conducted herself as before. Nobody would have noticed any difference. But when Annie came by, there were delicate looks of familiarity that passed between them, unseen by anyone else.

"Donovan," Annie would say, "can you call me a cab?"

And Mutt would reply, "Yes, Mrs. Sterling," as she always had, but in that second when their eyes locked together, a silent torrent of emotion poured out.

Annie opened her bag and pulled out chicken salad sandwiches, handing one to Mutt. The empty boxcar rattled around them as the back side of the city sped past the open door with its ugly factories, smokestacks and networks of clotheslines strung among modest homes and grimy apartment buildings. These tenements apparently made Annie think of Mutt's home because she asked, "When can I see your place?"

"It's not much to see."

"But I'd like to see it. It's where you live. And that other place you told me about, the nightclub where you go dancing. I'd really like to go there. I've never been to a place like that."

Mutt ate her sandwich, thinking how much fun it would be to show Annie off to the women at Bumpers.

"Why is it called Bumpers?" Annie asked, wrinkling up her nose. "Is it something to do with cars?" She stared up innocently.

The sandwich in Mutt's hand froze halfway to her mouth at the thought of Annie's question. She felt her face grow hot with embarrassment.

Annie laughed gleefully, tickled at Mutt's discomfort, and butted her with her shoulder. "I love to make you blush. You're so cute!" She linked her arm through Mutt's and squeezed out the space between them.

Mutt considered Annie's request to see her room. It seemed out of the question. Annie didn't belong in a place like that, especially if Oliver Krantz was home yelling "Go to hell!" in the next room. Mutt herself spent almost no time there lately. She had not been back to Bumpers either, though she had spoken to Maggie on the phone to let everyone know she was okay. Clive and Gerald had graciously vacated the apartment, spending all their nights at Clive's beach house. For social occasions, Clive returned and walked out with Annie on his arm, projecting the perfect Hollywood couple, glamorous and gorgeous, successful and happy. At least now Annie really was happy, Mutt thought, and not just playacting.

"My place is nothing much," Mutt said. "It's plain and simple."

"You know, Mutt, you could just get rid of it. You can live with me at the hotel. It would save you money."

"I can't do that. I'm no moocher. I've been thinking I shouldn't spend so much time at your place anyway. Or maybe I should give Clive some money for food and things."

"That's silly. Clive doesn't mind. He's just happy that I'm happy."

"He might not mind, but I do. I want to take care of myself."

Annie frowned. "You're so proud. Why can't you just enjoy our wonderful life together?" She took an apple out of the bag and handed it to Mutt. "Dessert."

The train traveled through the towns of Pomona and Ontario, and through the oil fields of Southern California with their black drills pumping up and down like prehistoric birds pecking at the ground.

"How far do we go?" Annie asked.

"Until it stops. We can't get off until then."

"Where does it stop?"

Mutt shrugged. "I don't know." She bit into the apple and the taut skin popped.

"What? You don't know?" Annie bounced up on her knees so that they were face-to-face. "But what if it doesn't stop till we get to Chicago?"

"Then we probably didn't bring enough food."

Annie looked alarmed.

"That's the way it works," said Mutt matter-of-factly. "You get on a train and you ride till it stops. Sometimes a hobo is going to a particular place, but a lot of times he isn't. He's just riding because that's what he does. And that's what you wanted to do, right, be a hobo for the day?"

Mutt grinned as Annie relaxed, still looking troubled, but resigned.

"Fine," she said, taking Mutt's arm again. "I don't care as long as we're together. We can ride all the way to Timbuktu for all I care, and I'll be the happiest girl in the world."

Mutt planted an apple juicy kiss on her forehead. She knew Annie's adventurous good mood wouldn't last through too much discomfort, so she had planned their day precisely using maps and railroad timetables. Their ride would be a couple of hours long, just long enough to be fun. It would carry them east to the town of Victorville where they could catch another freight heading west. Annie didn't need to know that. Mutt wanted her to have the experience of uncertainty that had been so much a part of hobo life. She also wanted her to get far enough away from home to feel like she had escaped. Her life was so thoroughly confined and controlled. Today it was wide open. She was free…if just for one afternoon.

Mutt tossed the apple core through the open door. She put the blanket roll they'd brought under Annie's head and lay beside her, both of them facing the outside. Eventually, Mutt recognized the stress of a straining locomotive as they climbed into the San Gabriel Mountains, leaving the vast urban sprawl of the Los Angeles Basin behind. As they gained altitude, the air grew noticeably colder and the views more awe-inspiring. Mutt unrolled the blanket and tucked it snugly around them. They snuggled together and watched the beautiful forested mountains roll by.

"This is what I imagined it would be like," Annie said, "if I could have run away with you when I was sixteen."

"It's a good thing your daddy caught up with us. You might not even be alive today if he hadn't. I don't know if I could've protected you from all the trouble out there."

Annie snuggled closer, pressing herself against Mutt's body. "What's the worst thing you ever saw when you were a hobo?"

"Now why are you asking me that?" Mutt shook her gently. "Why don't you ask me what's the *best* thing I ever saw?"

"The worst things make better stories."

Recalling tales from the hobo circuit, Mutt had to admit that was true. Anybody who had lived that life for more than a few months had seen horrible things. Violence and death. Ugly deaths from train accidents, sadistic lawmen, freezing weather, disease, or at the hands of other desperate souls willing to kill you for the half-dollar hidden in the heel of your shoe. There were endless tales of urine-soaked jail cells, hard labor on chain gangs, hobos being drowned or shot by folks whose towns had become overrun with them, as if they were an infestation of rats. During the Depression, there were tens of thousands of nomads traveling the country on trains. Even big cities couldn't handle the load of cold and hungry wanderers who flooded the missions and Salvation Army outposts. Lots of hobos wouldn't go to a hospital, no matter how sick, due to rumors of "the black bottle." They believed that hobos in hospitals were given poison, a quick and easy way to get rid of them. Whether or not that was true, Mutt knew that the life of a hobo was generally valued lower than that of most folks.

The Depression had been an era of misery, and the hobos had been some of the most miserable people alive.

Despite Annie's request, Mutt knew she wouldn't want to hear those stories. She couldn't know how ugly they were. She thought Mutt had lived a life of romantic adventure in those days, like a pirate on the high seas or a Wild West outlaw, like something from the movies. In many ways, Annie was as naïve and innocent as she had been the day they'd met.

"There's one hobo story I wouldn't mind telling you," Mutt said.

"Is it a love story?"

"It is. I call this story 'The Farmer's Daughter.'" She held tight to Annie and spoke close to her ear. "There was this girl, just sixteen, who had a mean old daddy. He was so mean, she ran away from home and became a hobo. She wandered the land, cold, lonely and begging for food. One day she got forced off a train moving forty miles an hour by the meanest old cinder dick who ever rode the rails. Right before he put a bullet in her head, she made a mighty leap off that train and lived to tell the tale."

Annie giggled.

"Though alive, she was miles from anywhere. Lost, tired and hungry, she finally came to a friendly looking farmhouse. There on the front stoop of that farmhouse was the prettiest girl she'd ever laid eyes on."

Annie giggled again and turned her head so she could catch Mutt's eye. "I think I've heard this story before."

"Maybe so, but I don't think you ever heard it told this way. The hobo and the beautiful farmer's daughter fell in love and ran away together. They were so happy. But it wasn't to last. The girl's mean old daddy took his daughter back and banished the hobo from the land, putting a powerful curse on her."

"Oh," Annie moaned. "There are a lot of mean old daddies in this story."

"The poor, brokenhearted hobo was doomed to wander, never to see her beloved again. That used to be the end of the story, but now there's a new ending."

"Good!"

"The hobo went on to have many hardships. She was even locked in a dungeon for years. One day she wandered into a strange land and found the farmer's daughter again. Except she wasn't a farmer's daughter anymore. She was a princess living in a golden castle. She was more beautiful than ever. But the hobo had become old and ugly and had a big old lump on her head."

Annie slapped her leg playfully.

"That princess had the most pure and kind heart of anybody in the land. She took pity on that hobo and gave her a kiss. Suddenly the curse was broken and they fell in love all over again."

"Then what happened?" Annie asked through a grin.

"What do you think? They lived happily ever after."

Annie turned in Mutt's arms to give her a kiss. "I'm glad that story has a new ending."

"Me too! It's a rare thing that a hobo story has a happy ending. Hoboing is a hard life, generally speaking. Today is a fun time for us because we'll be back home in our soft bed tonight, but I wouldn't want to have to go back to living like this regular-like."

"Is there anything you miss about it?"

"Sure. There are some things. It wasn't all bad. I met some good people and learned a lot about what matters in life. There's one thing in particular I do miss." She traced the edge of Annie's ear with her forefinger. "It's silly."

"What is it? Tell me?"

"I miss it most when I'm trying to go to sleep at night. In the hobo jungles when the wind blew enough to shake the branches of the trees, there was this sound I loved. It was like a lullaby to me. All the tin cans and pots hanging in the tree branches would rattle, banging into one another. Just tin cans clanking up against one another is all it was. I could always go to sleep listening to that. It was so much better than quiet."

With the rattle of the train, Mutt couldn't hear but could only sense Annie's sigh. She relaxed against her, their bodies vibrating together in their private carriage. She felt happy and contented, her arms tight against Annie's ribs, the intoxicating floral smell of her hair teasing her nostrils.

Mutt easily sensed when the train began the descent on its way out of the mountains. As they reached the valley below, the scenery changed abruptly to high desert terrain.

"Where are we?" Annie asked.

"Mojave Desert."

"Have you been here before?"

"No." Mutt knew they were well to the southeast of Tehachapi, but the barren landscape reminded her of the view from inside the prison. Dry, dusty and discouraging. She tried not to think of that too often. She tried to live in the present as she had always done. There was no reason not to live in the present now. The present was wonderful.

The desert scenery was so exotic, Annie wanted to sit up and watch, so Mutt rolled up the blanket and they sat near the doorway side by side. Mutt estimated they had a half hour left before coming into Victorville. She consulted her watch to verify it just as the train jerked violently, flinging them both to the floor. The wheels screeched with an ear-splitting whine and a loud hiss rose from below, a sound Mutt recognized as the brakes releasing air. She held Annie protectively as the train shuddered begrudgingly to a clearly unplanned halt.

"What's happening?" Annie asked, alarmed.

"I don't know." Mutt rose and went to the open door, peering out at the barren desert. Visible waves of heat danced over the landscape. There was no sign of a building in either direction. Just bare track stretching ahead over a low hill and the long line of train cars looking peaceful behind them. A cloud of brown dust drifted away from the tracks. Other than the metallic creaking of the settling train, there was no sound.

"Have we come to a town?" Annie asked, joining Mutt in the doorway.

"I don't think so. That's not the way they usually stop at a station."

"I should hope not!" She leaned her head out to look. "Then why did we stop?"

"It could be mechanical trouble," Mutt answered doubtfully. "Or something on the track."

She desperately hoped it was not what she suspected, that some hobo had dumped the air because he wanted to get off. It didn't happen often, but every once in a while a hobo would vent the brake pipe and put the whole train into emergency stop. Mutt had heard of a legendary hobo named Dumper Dan who did it for fun. He wasn't well liked among the hobos, and you definitely didn't want to be on a train with him in case he got the urge to pull his stunt. Nothing riled up the railroad crew like an unscheduled stop.

Off in the distance, heading toward them from the back of the train, two men in coveralls walked beside the tracks, stopping to shine flashlights in and under the cars.

"Uh-oh," Mutt said under her breath. "Annie, we've got to get out of here."

"Why? What's happening?"

"They're sweeping the cars, looking for somebody to arrest. We can't let them find you here." Mutt ran to the end of the car to grab their stuff, then hopped out the door and to the ground. "Come on!" she said, holding her arms out for Annie to fall into them.

They dashed to the end of the car where Mutt helped Annie onto the coupling.

"Hey!" cried a voice in the distance.

She glanced toward the men to see one of them running their way. She leapt between the cars and followed Annie down the slope on the other side.

"You'll have to run!" Mutt hollered. "Follow me and run as fast as you can."

Mutt took off running away from the track, glancing back to make sure Annie was behind her, then scanning the landscape ahead for the nearest contour that would hide them from view. She made for a slope and was soon low enough that she could no longer see the train. Keeping it out of view, she headed west with Annie right behind her. With each yard they traveled she felt safer. She knew the railroad crew wouldn't follow them far across the desert. Huffing with exhaustion, she finally slipped behind a pile of rocks and welcomed Annie into her arms where they sat breathing hard with their heads close together.

She handed the canteen to Annie. She could hear faint voices in the distance.

"Do you think we made it?" Annie whispered.

"I hope so. They won't stay long. They won't want to slip up the schedule any worse."

She took a swallow from the canteen, then waited, her ears alert to the voices of the train crew as they searched. Finally the sound of screeching metal reached their ears.

"It's moving," Mutt said with relief.

"Now what?"

Mutt stood and watched the train pull away toward the east, steadily picking up speed. After the last car disappeared, she surveyed the landscape in all directions, looking for a sign of civilization. If a hobo had stopped the train because he wanted to get off, presumably there was something here to get off for. But she couldn't be sure that was the reason the train had stopped. She saw nothing but rolling desert broken by an occasional patch of magenta verbena in bloom. It was still winter most places but here in the desert it was coming into spring.

"We need to find a road." She walked to the top of a hill. In the distance she saw the train moving further away and felt like salvation was disappearing over the horizon. This little spree had now turned serious. She knew that rails were usually built close to towns and roads but she didn't know which direction to go. They weren't prepared to spend the night in the desert and nobody knew where they were. Mutt mentally kicked herself for taking a risk like this.

Looking for anything that resembled a line of telephone poles, a dust cloud from a vehicle on a road, the glint of metal or glass, she finally spotted a curl of smoke a half mile to the south. Reassured, she took Annie's hand and they walked toward it.

It didn't take long to find the source, an open pit fire in front of a wretched looking shack with slapdash wooden walls and a corrugated tin roof rusted to the color of dried blood. Off to the right was the body of an old car with no roof or tires, brush growing around and inside it like it was part of nature. On the other side of the shack was a pile of scrap wood and rusted tools, barrels, tarps and the like. If not for the fire, Mutt would have assumed this place was long abandoned. Simmering over the burning wood was a pot full of something unidentifiable. There was only one proper chair near the fire, a wooden folding chair with one slat missing out of the back. The other seats were split logs and rocks.

Mutt shoved a loose lock of her hair up under her hat before stepping over to the fire. Adopting her old tenor voice, she called "Hello!" in the direction of the sagging door.

A moment passed before the door opened a crack and somebody peeked out with one tired-looking eye. Then the barrel of a shotgun was shoved through the crack.

"What do you want?" asked the resident.

"We're lost," Mutt replied, feeling Annie's fingernails digging into her arm. "Hoping y'all can point us toward a main road."

The door creaked slowly open to reveal an old man with a grizzled beard, his mouth hidden in the thickness of its scruffy growth. He wore a long-sleeved shirt, dingy and discolored, and a pair of denim pants, darkened to a bluish brown color. He stood bowlegged on spindly legs and held the shotgun with both hands. From the looks of him, Mutt guessed he had hopped a few trains in his day.

"How'd you get here," he asked, sounding more curious than irritated.

"We were on the SP when somebody dumped the air. The cinder dicks were on the prowl so we had to hightail it."

The old-timer's face opened up with a smile of appreciation. He let the gun hang more loosely at his side as he stepped out of his shack. "You're hobos?"

Mutt nodded. "Now and then. I'm Mississippi Mutt. And this here's…" She hesitated, realizing she had no hobo name for Annie, but almost instantly one came to her. "Angel Annie," she said, eliciting a smile of approval from Annie.

"How do you do," the old man replied, his voice louder than necessary. "I'm Rattlesnake Sam. Nice to meet you. I used to flip freights myself when I was a young man. I don't see too many 'bos around here. Trains don't stop here."

"We know."

"I used to live over by Barstow. Lots of 'bos there. Major junction."

"Do you live out here all by yourself?" Annie asked, having recovered from her fright.

"Yes, ma'am. I prefer being on my lonesome. But when it comes to my brother hobos, never let it be said that I turned a cold shoulder. Sit down, both of ya, and I'll serve up a bowl of stew."

"Thank you," Annie said, lowering herself to a log. "Running away from the cinder dicks made me hungry."

Their host grinned. "Let me get some bowls."

Mutt leaned down to Annie's ear. "Are you sure you want to eat that? There might be a good reason why he's called Rattlesnake Sam."

Annie's eyes grew wide. She glanced at the pot over the fire then back at Mutt with an impish smile. "All the better."

Mutt sat beside her and they accepted bowls of stew. It turned out to be rabbit, not rattlesnake, and Annie seemed perfectly happy with it despite the gaminess.

"What do you do out here?" Annie asked.

"Work my claim," said Sam matter-of-factly.

"You have a mine?"

"That's right. Gold mine."

It was clear that Sam's gold mine had yet to reward him for his efforts.

"That's very interesting," Annie said with genuine enthusiasm. "How did you end up being a prospector?"

Mutt observed her eating, her clothes smeared with soot, her day filled with uncertainty, trying to read her thoughts. She talked animatedly to Rattlesnake Sam, charming him with her lovely face and congenial manner, and eliciting a few stories of his travels. Despite their earlier excitement, Annie seemed totally at ease now. Mutt reflected back on Zetta's remarks about society ladies and their halfhearted involvement with the underclasses. Whatever was true about Mrs. Riley Hampton or any of the other ladies of the WWLS did not seem to be true about Annie.

Mutt was relieved to think that Annie was comfortable with all sorts of people, that she didn't find someone like Rattlesnake Sam offensive or frightening. Despite her Longines watch and new boots, Mutt was more like Sam than she was like Annie. She felt it deeply, that she hadn't changed much over the years. She had never had aspirations like Annie. Annie moved comfortably in her luxurious surroundings. She ate easily off of silver utensils and didn't mind adorning herself in the costliest clothes and jewels. But it was gratifying to know that she was just as relaxed here, sitting on a log eating jackrabbit stew, talking to a man with nothing in his pocket but a hole.

When they had finished eating, Mutt stood and said, "We'd better be getting on. We don't want to be thumbing a ride after dark."

"No, no," agreed Sam, standing with an audible crack from his knees. "Now, what you wanna do is this." He swung around and pointed. "Head straight north two miles and you'll run right into Route 66. You'll see it down below when you get up on that second ridge. There's a filling station there with a pay phone. You can call somebody or hitch a ride from there."

"Much obliged," Mutt said with sincere gratitude. She took off her jacket and handed it to Sam. "I want you to have this. It's in good shape and looks like it's about right for you."

Sam's eyes lit up and he slipped the jacket on, tugging at the lapels with a satisfied look on his face. "This is a mighty fine garment. Thank you, Mississippi Mutt! And good luck to you and your missus."

Mutt and Annie grinned at one another.

They had no further mishaps as they followed Sam's directions and arrived at the highway within forty minutes. The filling station was there as promised and provided a good place to thumb a ride. Annie took off her cap to let her sunny hair fall loose and stuck out her thumb. Within ten minutes a red Chevy convertible driven by a middle-aged man in a suit pulled over for them. Their driver, a traveling salesman, chatted nonstop all the way back to Los Angeles, kindly dropping them off in front of the Rutherford Hotel. They were back in the apartment by seven o'clock.

Annie was positively beside herself with glee the whole way back. She had loved everything about the day and would have turned around and done it all over again if Mutt had been willing.

"I love you, Angel Annie," Mutt said to her as they slipped into bed for the night. "You're a remarkable girl."

# CHAPTER TWENTY-FOUR

The Sterlings' Cadillac pulled up in front of the hotel and out stepped Annie, dressed smartly in a black bolero jacket over a pink blouse and black pants that tapered down to a tight fit around her ankles.

"Good afternoon, Miss Montclair," Mutt pronounced.

She was startled when Annie flashed her a look of utter misery, then dropped her car keys in Mutt's gloved palm and said, "Can you take care of my car, Donovan?"

She wrenched open the door, not waiting for Mutt to open it for her, and darted through. Mutt caught the open door, watching Annie nearly run to the elevator, her whole demeanor full of distress. She struggled to resist the urge to go after her, then walked to the luggage room where Charlie sat on the cart reading a Dick Tracy comic book.

"Charlie, can you park Mrs. Sterling's car?" She handed him the keys.

What was wrong? Mutt wondered, returning to the curb and painstakingly counting the minutes for the two hours remaining in her shift. When Annie had left this morning, she had been beaming with happiness, full of confidence and hope, on her way to a television set where she would be filming a laundry soap commercial.

Annie had been both happy and embarrassed at securing a role in a commercial. She was supposed to be a movie actress, but having had no roles for quite a while, she had asked if there was anything she could do, any acting job at all. It had smacked of begging and this was the result, a commercial. But it was something—it was a job, a way to get her face on screen again.

When at last it was five o'clock, Mutt ran to the back of the hotel and took the service elevator to Annie's suite, careful as always to avoid meeting any other staff member on the way. She rang the bell and Annie opened the door, then yanked her inside by the arm. She had changed into a long aqua dressing gown edged in feathery fluff and she felt luxuriously silky in Mutt's arms. Annie buried her face in her chest, sobbing.

On the television, The Lone Ranger sat on Silver, speaking hurriedly to Tonto. The volume was turned down, so Mutt didn't know what they were so excited about. Tonto turned his horse abruptly and took off galloping across the open plain.

"Annie, honey, what's wrong?" Mutt led her to the sofa where they sat beside one another, their hands clasped together.

"I had that job today. I told you about it." She sniffed.

"Yes, of course, the commercial. How did it go?"

She shook her head. "It was a disaster. The director was horrible. He would tell me to do something one way, then he'd tell me the exact opposite, so after a while, I didn't know what to do. Finally, he threw up his hands and said, 'Sweetheart, this is a fucking laundry soap commercial, not *Gone with the Wind*! Eighteen takes? This is ridiculous!'" Her face was stern and her voice deep in imitation of the impatient director. "'I don't care who your husband is, I can't work with you.' Then he walked off the set." Done with her description, Annie's face collapsed into despair and she began to cry again.

Mutt held her, feeling helpless. She wondered if Clive had put pressure on somebody to find her a job.

"I'm a failure!" Annie moaned.

"You're not a failure. People like you. You do a lot of good. Look at your WWLS work and all the charities you support."

Annie pulled back to look Mutt in the face, her eyes red. "I came here to be an actress. It was all I wanted to do since I was a little girl."

"I'm sorry. I wish there was something I could do." Mutt stroked her hair and kissed her lightly. "I have an idea. Let's go to Bumpers tonight. You said you wanted to go and they're having a Valentine's Ball. We can dance there…together. Do you jitterbug? I'm a first-rate jitterbugger. Come on, Annie, let's go out. It will get your mind off this."

Annie brightened. "Really?"

"Yes! It'll be fun. We'll have to disguise you, to make sure nobody knows it's you. We can find you something simple to wear and do something different with your hair."

"Yes! I'll be a sweet little old farmer's daughter from Nebraska."

Mutt laughed. "That's perfect."

* * *

It was no surprise to Mutt that the women at Bumpers thought Annie was adorable and all of them wanted to dance with her. She had a marvelous time being fussed over and flirted with, and it appeared that she had completely recovered from the disappointment of the ruined laundry soap commercial. At least she had forgotten it for the time being, and Mutt was happy to see her enjoying herself.

The club was decorated in red, white and pink streamers. Red bows hung on the front of the bar and a Cupid cutout spun slowly at the end of a string under the ceiling lights. The place was packed with couples and singles alike. Zetta was behind the bar as usual, serving a fizzy pink drink with strawberries called "Forbidden Fruit."

Mutt sat with Tully while Annie danced with Baby, the hit of the party tonight in a Cupid costume consisting of a sparkly tutu that left her arms and legs bare, a set of cardboard wings, a quiver of arrows over her back and a halo perched over her head on a wire.

Annie threw back her head and laughed at something Baby said to her. Her face was flushed, naturally radiant with a mere touch of makeup and lipstick the color of a pink carnation. Her hair pulled back in a ponytail, she wore a white blouse tucked into a pink wraparound skirt, a youthful outfit that stripped her of her usual sophisticated glamour and left behind a touchingly innocent-looking girl. Mutt's heart swelled with pride, desire and gratitude every time she looked at her.

"She's a doll," Tully said. "Where'd you meet her?"

"I met her years ago. She was the first girl I ever kissed. I feel so lucky to have her in my life again."

Tully took a drag on her cigarette, then grinned. "So this is the farmer's daughter?"

Mutt nodded.

"You're cute together."

"How can you tell? I've only danced with her once since we got here."

"Maybe, but you'll have your own private party later, won't you?"

Mutt felt her ears heat up and knew she was blushing.

Tully chuckled. "I'm happy for you, Mutt. It's about time things went right for you." She took a sip of her Forbidden Fruit and frowned, setting it back on its heart-shaped coaster. "I need a real drink. This is for kids." She shook her head and pushed it away, then went to the bar.

Mutt sat back to watch her darling jitterbugging. Her ponytail bounced up and down and side to side while Baby's little wings did the same.

Tully returned and squeezed into her chair at the back of the table with her gin and tonic. Pointing at Mutt's wristwatch, she said, "Hey, that's new." She took hold of Mutt's hand to look more closely at the watch. "That's some watch! What'd you do, steal it?"

Mutt pulled her hand back, realizing she shouldn't have worn the watch here. "Uh, I...no." She struggled to think of an answer.

"I was kidding, Mutt."

"Sure, I know." She fingered the band of her watch. "It was a gift from one of the hotel residents. A Christmas gift. You know those folks are loaded. They can't find enough places to spend their money."

"That's nice. Very nice. It goes well with those fancy boots you're wearing. Those are new since I last saw you too. I guess the tips are okay for a doorman at a place like that."

"Yes." Mutt felt guilty and uncomfortable thinking about her expensive boots, another gift from Clive. "Rich folks can be generous. Mrs. Pennington, one of the residents, she feeds her little dog ground beef and chicken livers. She has the kitchen make it up fresh every day and deliver it to her apartment on a silver tray. A woman like that, well, she thinks nothing about handing me a silver dollar every time she sees me."

Tully shook her head. "Seems that things are looking up for you all ways around." She took a sip of her drink. "Now that's a real drink." She watched the dancers with a wistful expression.

"Have you ever had a girlfriend, Tully?" asked Mutt.

"Now and then."

"No. I mean someone serious, someone you wanted to be with forever."

"Not for a long time." She put her cigarette in the ashtray, regarding Mutt thoughtfully, and seemed to reconsider. "There is someone, actually. Her name is Laura. She's a nurse at the hospital."

Mutt was surprised. "Really? Why haven't you mentioned her? Why haven't you ever brought her here?"

"Because she doesn't belong to me. She doesn't even know how I feel about her."

"You should tell her."

Tully shook her head. "I can't. She's married. Happily and permanently. To her, I'm that best single friend at work. The one she'd like to fix up with the bachelor accountant in her husband's company."

"Are you sure she's happily married? Maybe her marriage is a smokescreen so folks won't suspect her husband of being a homosexual and she's secretly in love with you."

Tully laughed shortly. "Damn, you've got a strange imagination! No, I'm sure it's not like that. We talk all the time at work. She loves her husband and two kids. She loves her life. There's no doubt."

"Sorry."

Tully shrugged. "It's okay. It's just the way it is."

Mutt was saddened to think of Tully being in such a hopeless situation. "Why don't you try to find someone else? There are women here who adore you."

She smiled crookedly. "The same reason you didn't find someone else."

Mutt nodded her understanding.

"That's why I'm so happy for you," Tully said. "It's not so common to have things work out with your true love. It's a beautiful story, Mutt. You've found something rare and valuable and you have to treasure it."

"I will. I do!"

* * *

It was nearly two in the morning when Mutt and Annie snuck up to the Sterling suite using the service elevator. They were both giddy from their night on the town and Mutt was anxious to get Annie alone. Watching her dance with all those other women had left her full of desire. As soon as the elevator doors closed, she drew Annie close and kissed her passionately all the way up to the fourteenth floor. She led her by the hand to the door of the apartment where Annie fumbled with her key and giggled while Mutt nuzzled the back of her neck playfully. Annie spun around with a carefree laugh and flung her arms around Mutt. Locked together in a turbulent kiss, Mutt kept her ears alert for the ding of the elevator down the hall. Annie momentarily lost her balance and banged against the door. Mutt put an arm around her waist, deciding to carry her across the threshold. She felt like a newlywed because she was so thoroughly happy and in love.

As she bent to catch Annie behind the knees to lift her, the door opened and Clive, wearing a white tuxedo, stood in the doorway glowering at them.

"What the hell?" he said. "What's all the commotion out here?"

Mutt released Annie, who swept into the apartment ahead of her. Gerald, also in formal wear, lay sprawled on the sofa, his feet crossed at the ankle on the armrest, looking completely uninterested in the rest of them.

Clive slammed the door shut. "Where have you two been?"

"Out dancing." Annie twirled toward the center of the room.

"We didn't know you'd be here tonight," Mutt said.

"We were in town for a party and decided to stay. Gerald drank too much to drive us back to Malibu."

"Me?" Gerald objected, raising his martini glass.

"Both of us," Clive assented, then addressed Annie. "Darling, what have you done with your hair and what is that you're wearing?"

Annie lifted the hem of her skirt. "This is my girl-next-door disguise. We went to a nightclub. I danced for hours and hours. I'm exhausted." She fell into the chair across from Gerald.

"A nightclub?"

"It was so much fun!" Annie exulted. "It's all a blur now, but I've never had so much fun in all my life!"

Clive spun around to face Mutt. "Now, look here, what sort of nightclub did you take her to?"

Mutt hesitated, then decided there was no reason to be coy with him of all people. "A club for women."

His eyebrows came together and his thin mustache stretched into a perfectly straight line as he pursed his lips in disapproval. "You took my wife to a place like that?"

"We just danced."

"But she can't be seen in a place like that!" He was angry, which was frightening because Mutt had never seen him angry. He was usually so easygoing and agreeable.

"Nobody recognized her. Nobody knew her there. There was no harm in it."

"No harm in it?" He sputtered. "What if there had been a raid? That kind of place is routinely raided by the police, as you very well know. If she had been arrested, my career would have been snuffed out in an instant." He snapped his fingers. "I won't even allow myself to go to places like that. It's too dangerous. It was irresponsible of you to take her."

"Sorry," Mutt said, realizing he was right about the danger. "I just wanted her to have some fun."

He shook his head, frustrated. "I can't have this! You won't take her to such a place again. In fact, you mustn't go out in public together at all. What would people make of that, if they found out you were our doorman? It's utterly unacceptable!"

"Who could recognize me as your doorman?" Mutt objected. "Look at me." She held out her hands to her sides, inviting him to realize how impossible it was for anyone to see Donovan in the woman who stood before him.

"Nobody knows you're the doorman here?"

"Well, sure, my friends know, but they're my friends. I trust them."

"Don't be naïve, Shirley. When it comes to money, there's always someone who will sell you out. Do you have any idea how much a story like this would be worth? Bianca Montclair out on the town with her doorman? Or worse, dancing in a lesbian nightclub with her lesbian lover who's secretly her hotel doorman? Can you imagine? There are people whose job it is to ferret out every possible detail about her movements. Where she goes. Who she's with. They thrive on scandal and they're always on the lookout for it. And this, believe me, is the sort of scandal that would feed the lot of them for weeks and put an end to my career."

Mutt glanced at Gerald, who for once was paying attention, sitting up on the sofa shooting darts of disapproval in her direction. She thought guiltily of the hoboing adventure she had taken Annie on. Thankfully nobody else knew about that.

Clive turned toward Annie. "The whole point of my marrying you was to create a reputation that was beyond reproach. I can't have my wife dancing with women in a lesbian nightclub! Are you trying to ruin me?"

Annie looked repentant. "I'm sorry, Clive," she said softly. "You're right, of course. I know my responsibility and I shouldn't have gone. Mutt and I do sincerely apologize."

He visibly relaxed. "All right. I do want you to have some fun, darling, but not at the expense of my reputation. If the world finds out about you and Shirley, our lives will be destroyed. Yours and mine both. I've taken enough risk as it is allowing her to be here with you. I'd be a hypocrite if I forbade it, but I need to be able to count on your faultless discretion. From now on, you will not go out together. You can be together here, but in public you are not to fraternize. Is that clear?"

Annie nodded. "Perfectly clear, Clive."

He turned to Mutt, who nodded her understanding. She did understand, better than ever. Everything Annie had was a gift from Clive in return for her role as his wife. It was a role that had to be played everywhere outside of these rooms. Mutt began to understand that Annie did not belong to her, despite how she had felt just minutes before. Annie didn't even belong to herself. Their relationship was a sideline to the larger purpose of the arranged marriage. She was Clive Sterling's wife first, Mutt's lover second.

She began to wonder if that would be enough. For the first time she began to think about where they were headed together and what sort of future they might have. All of a sudden, everything didn't seem quite so perfect for the two of them anymore.

# CHAPTER TWENTY-FIVE

"I'm so sorry, my darling," Annie said again.

She stood in her girdle and strapless bra beside the bed where a white silk evening gown was laid out ready to be put on. She had been applying lipstick, eye shadow, eyeliner and rouge with practiced expertise, and her face was now complete.

"I understand," Mutt said. "I told you I did."

"I know, but I feel horrible. It's my first birthday since we've been together and you wanted it to be special."

"It *will* be special. It just won't be with me."

Annie looked momentarily dejected. "You're wrong. It won't be special. It will be like any other big Hollywood party with champagne and boring conversation." She touched her hand gently to Mutt's cheek. "I hope you know I'd rather be here with you, truly, just the two of us. I can't think of a better way to celebrate my birthday than to be with my Mutt." She turned to the dresser to retrieve a delicate tiara that she placed over her hair with precision. It transformed her into a princess as regal and beautiful as any fairy-tale heroine. She admired herself in the mirror. "Clive should have told me about this party. It was thoughtless of him to make a surprise out of it. Of course I wouldn't have said I'd be here with you if I'd known. I wouldn't have had to break my promise." She sat on the edge of the bed to put on her stockings.

"Annie, it's okay. It's not like I had big plans. I was just going to cook you dinner. A quiet evening at home."

"I can't wait for you to cook me dinner." She stood and clipped the stockings to her garters. "You're being such a sweetheart about this."

Annie had joked that she didn't believe Mutt could cook at all, which wasn't far from true. She had cooked for her father, simple meals of eggs, fried chicken, ham and beans, cornbread and greens. The food she knew how to cook was nothing like the meals Annie routinely ate these days. Mutt had planned to make Veal á la Mornay, a dish Annie had praised at the Brown Derby. Though Mutt had never been to the Brown Derby and had never had Veal á la Mornay, or any other thing á la Mornay, she was able to find a recipe in a cookbook at the library. Before the news of the birthday party had reached her, which was just this morning, she had studied the recipe and bought all the ingredients. The kitchen in the Sterling suite, though seldom used for actual cooking, was equipped with everything she needed to make the dish. At least she didn't have to worry about ruining it now.

She helped Annie with her gown, a hip-hugging sheath that enhanced her perfect hourglass shape and left her creamy arms and shoulders bare. After closing the zipper, Mutt put her hands on Annie's waist and kissed her neck lightly. Annie spun around, kissing her quickly on the lips.

"I have something for you," Mutt said, handing her a small gift-wrapped box.

"Oh!" Annie took it with a warm smile. "You got me a gift?"

"Of course. Open it."

Annie tore off the wrapping and opened the box to reveal a brooch, a blue and white cameo with a raised image of an angel. It opened to reveal a miniature portrait of Mutt within.

Annie's mouth fell open. "Mutt, this is so sweet!" She clutched the brooch to her chest, then looked more carefully at the photograph within. "It's an adorable photo."

"I had it done just for this. The locket's engraved too."

Annie peered in to read the message: *To my angel, Annie.*

She flung herself at Mutt and hugged her tightly, then kissed her neck. "It's beautiful! I'll treasure it." She broke away and looked into Mutt's eyes. She looked genuinely moved. "I hope it didn't cost too much."

Mutt smiled. "Never you mind about that."

The locket had cost more than anything Mutt had ever bought. She knew it was a modest purchase in comparison to the kind of jewelry Annie normally wore, but Mutt hoped the personal nature of the gift would make it seem dearer to her.

Annie hugged her again. "Oh, Mutt, I love you so much!"

They kissed one another passionately until they heard the sound of men's voices from the front room.

"There's Clive," Annie said. She led the way to the front room where Clive stood in his tails and top hat looking debonair. Gerald, dressed casually, went to the bar to get a drink.

"You look stunning, Bianca," Clive said with a broad smile. He hugged her and kissed her cheek. "Happy birthday."

"Thank you, Clive. I'm almost ready. I just have to get earrings and my wrap."

"Just a moment. Before you decide on earrings, you might want to take a look at this." He pulled a box from his breast pocket and handed it to her.

She put Mutt's locket on the side table beside the sofa and took the gift from Clive. Inside was a pair of diamond earrings. They seemed to fill the room with light when she lifted them from the box. Each of them was like a sparkling waterfall and Annie gasped at the sight of them.

Clive clipped them to her ears and they all admired their fire and brilliance. Annie turned her head first one way, then the other, catching the light at different angles. She ran into the bedroom to look at them in the mirror. Clive smiled proudly to himself as they heard Annie exclaim from the other room. Then she returned wearing gloves and her wrap and carrying a white sequined pocketbook.

She kissed Mutt, then said, "Will you wait up for me?"

"I'm staying at my place tonight. I need to check in there once in a while and I know you'll be out late."

"Yes she will," Clive said. "We'll stay to the bitter end, as Bianca is the guest of honor tonight. And listen, Shirley, I'm sorry I didn't tell you about this party. I didn't think you'd have plans since you couldn't take her out. A girl really should go out and celebrate on her birthday."

"That's as true as can be," Mutt said, forcing a smile.

Clive offered his arm and Annie took it. They moved toward the door, a dashing-looking couple, a couple anyone would have mistaken for the real thing. At that moment, even Mutt had a hard time thinking of Annie as anything but Clive Sterling's wife.

"Hey, want a drink?" Gerald asked once they were alone.

"You know I don't drink."

"I know, but I thought you might need one tonight. I could pour you a root beer double." He raised his glass to her.

She realized for the first time that they were in similar circumstances. She wondered if he ever felt anything like the resentment she felt tonight.

He sauntered toward her and picked up the cameo locket from the table. "What's this?"

She snatched it from his hand. "It's nothing."

He smiled thinly and took a sip of his drink. "You want to play cards or something?"

"No thanks. I'd like to be by myself tonight."

She returned to the bedroom and put the locket on the dresser, then quickly packed her uniform in her valise. Dressed as she was in a skirt, jacket and hat, she took the elevator to the lobby and walked directly past Bleeker at the front desk. Normally she didn't take the risk that someone on the staff might recognize her face, but tonight she felt reckless. Bleeker didn't give her a second glance.

In front of the hotel, a small crowd had assembled around the Sterlings, gawking and asking for autographs. Clive signed several while their car and driver waited at the curb. Mutt shrank toward the back of the group and watched the frozen smile on Annie's face with its underlying hint of gloom. Nobody asked for her autograph. They rarely did. Not many people even knew she was an actress. Had been an actress, Mutt reminded herself. Her fame and her success were now tied exclusively to her identity as

Mrs. Clive Sterling. And even that was an act. She was starring in the role of her life and nobody knew or could appreciate it. It was a hard position to be in, Mutt reflected. But when Clive had rescued her from penury, Annie couldn't have predicted or even cared about how distressing the deception would become. Mutt understood why she had taken the deal. It had been a good choice at the time.

Finally Clive led his wife to the car and they were whisked away. The crowd rapidly dispersed and Mutt walked to the bus stop to catch a bus home. Between the bus stop and her building was a bakery where she sometimes shopped. Tonight she bought herself a piece of chocolate cake, her way of salvaging a little of the birthday spirit.

She knew she didn't have to be alone tonight. There was always Bumpers. She hadn't been there since Valentine's Day. The whole gang was probably down there right now dancing and enjoying themselves. Annie was at some magnificent ballroom, the center of attention, dancing with men in tuxedos, being buried in compliments, having a wonderful evening. Why shouldn't Mutt go out and enjoy her Saturday night too?

Her evenings with Annie lately were less than ideal. She put so much effort into trying to entertain her night after night that she was exhausted. Their life together was relegated to five rooms on the fourteenth floor of the Rutherford Hotel. Mutt was frustrated.

They were still in love, still crazy about one another. But an unwelcome thought came more and more regularly to Mutt that this situation couldn't be endured forever. Not by either of them. But she had no idea what to do about it.

She unlocked the door of her building and stepped into the entryway to find her landlord on the phone. He was in an undershirt, gray hair sprouting from his chest and shoulders.

"Naw, I dunno where she is," he said into the phone, then turned toward the door. "Well, what do you know? Look what the cat dragged in." He thrust the receiver toward her. "This is for you."

She put her valise and bakery box on the table by the door and took the receiver.

"Hello," she answered, turning her back to Mr. Wakely to emphasize her need for privacy.

He huffed and trudged away.

"Shirley," came a faraway-sounding female voice. "Is it Shirley I'm speaking to? Shirley Hopper?"

"Yes," she said, momentarily thrown by the use of her real name. She realized it wasn't one of the girls from Bumpers as she had assumed it would be. It was a woman with a southern accent, a Mississippi accent like her own. "Yes, this is Shirley Hopper."

"Oh, thank goodness I finally got you! This is your cousin Opal."

"Opal!"

"Land sakes, child, y'all are hard to get hold of. I've been calling for the last three days." Mutt glanced at the message board on the wall. Sure enough, there were two notes there for her.

"Sorry," she said. "I've been away."

"Shirley, honey, you should have written after you got out to let me know where you were. I had to get your address and phone number from the prison."

"I meant to write," Mutt replied vaguely. "How are you, Opal?"

"Well, I'm just fine, but I've got bad news about your father. I'm just going to give it to you straight. I know you and your father had your problems, but…well, now he's passed on."

Shocked, Mutt leaned against the wall. "Passed on?"

"That's right. He was found dead at the farm three days ago. It's taken me that long to get through to you. Now that I got you, we got to talk about a few things."

Despite all the times Mutt had wished her father dead, the news left her unbelieving. Her father was like the Devil. He couldn't be killed.

"How did he die?" she asked. There was no reply, so she repeated herself. "Opal, how did he die?"

She heard a deep sigh. "He hung himself in the barn. Last I saw him was at Christmas when we paid him a visit. Things weren't good with him then. I don't think he would have lived much longer even if he'd wanted to. He was in a sorry way. I told Fred when we left for home, 'That Kirby Hopper is not long for this world.' But, you know, Shirley, this is long distance, so we don't have time for all this chitchat. What I need to know is if you're coming for the funeral. We can't postpone it no more."

"I...I guess so. Yes." She felt dazed, picturing the little farmhouse with its white wood siding and the dark green linoleum of the kitchen floor. "I wouldn't mind seeing the place again. It's been a long time."

"You're going to have to do more than see it. It's yours now. You're going to have to see about selling it. You can get a little out of it, whatever the land's worth. The rest, truth be told, ain't worth a plug nickel."

Mutt barely heard the rest, the details about the funeral. It was going to take her a while to comprehend this news. In her mind, she calculated his age as fifty-one. He'd seemed older than that even when she left ten years ago.

*Hanged himself.*

# CHAPTER TWENTY-SIX

Sitting at a table in the dining car of the Union Pacific line, surrounded by fine china and gleaming chrome, Mutt was thoroughly entertained. The rocking of the car and the muffled sound of the rails were familiar, but riding inside as a paying customer, what hobos called "riding the cushions," was a new experience for her. The only time she'd ever been on a passenger train at all was once when she rode possum belly out of Milwaukee. Riding in the deafening box under the car was worlds away from this.

The dishes rattled with the movement of the train. The water jiggled in their glasses. The passengers ate mock turtle soup out of scallop-rimmed bowls decorated with purple pansies. A matching plate, teacup and saucer completed the set and an array of utensils was spread out on either side of the plate. Three forks, three spoons, two knives. It was the most elegant dinner service Mutt had ever seen. Annie had to explain to her what utensil to use for what dish.

"Seems kinda silly," she said. "Makes a heap of dishes to wash."

"True," Annie agreed. "But then it gives some poor soul a job washing dishes, doesn't it?"

Annie wore a beautiful dress of seafoam green silk with a white cape and understated emerald earrings, her hair upswept and a beauty mark penciled onto her chin. This was the first time Mutt had been out in public with Bianca Montclair, both of them undisguised. She drew everyone's eyes. She was so clearly an extraordinary personage, so clearly somebody, even if they weren't sure exactly who she was.

Mutt was still uncertain that it was a good idea to bring Annie along, but she had insisted, saying, "I won't let you go through this alone."

"It's okay," Mutt had assured her. "We weren't close."

"But he was still your father, so it's bound to affect you."

Mutt had never told Annie the real reason she had run away from home. She had only said that her father was mean, drunk and lazy and that he had beaten her regularly. All of that was true, and it was enough of a reason, so Annie hadn't asked for any further explanation.

"I'm going with you and that's that," she had insisted.

"Will Clive let you?"

"Don't worry. I'll make sure he does."

And he did. When Mutt showed up at their suite in her navy skirt and jacket, a smart little hat on her head and her legs in stockings, Clive and Gerald couldn't stop staring. They'd never seen her in what Topeka Slim had called her "Sunday go-to-meetin' clothes."

"I can't see any reason to object," Clive said. "My wife accompanying a woman friend to her father's funeral seems perfectly acceptable. Have a good trip, darling. And Shirley, please accept my condolences and let me know if you need help with anything."

So there had been no reason to refuse Annie's offer of company, and Mutt was now enjoying the rare freedom of being out in the world with her beloved.

"What do you think of riding on a passenger train," Annie asked, "as an actual passenger? Do you prefer this or the other?"

She shrugged. "It's not as rough a ride by a longshot, but wearing nylon stockings sort of cancels out the comfort of riding the cushions."

Annie laughed.

"What about you?" Mutt asked. "What do you like best?"

Annie looked startled. "That's an interesting question. I don't know if I have an answer. It's all about comfort, as you said. I guess I've gotten used to comfort. But I had a terrific time with you hoboing that day. It was such fun!"

The waiter deposited salads in front of them before wordlessly retreating.

Annie picked the tomato quarters out of her salad one by one and ate them with deliberation while watching Mutt across the cramped table. "It was a thrill," she said, clearly still thinking about their illicit train ride. "Now this isn't thrilling at all, is it? But it's comfortable. Maybe you've got to trade one for the other."

This train ride seemed unreal to Mutt. She was going home. She had never imagined going home. She had never thought she would. Annie, looking like a genuine movie star, made it seem that much more dreamlike.

After dinner they moved to the lounge car where they had coffee and snuggled into oversized chairs, each with a private reading lamp. Mutt chose a collection of O. Henry stories from the shelf of books and Annie read a *Life* magazine. They sat side by side in their circles of light, contentedly together but independently occupied. Annie sat sideways in her chair, her legs curled up beside her, and Mutt sat with her legs on the floor, crossed at the ankles.

Annie put a small box of chocolates on the table between them. Periodically Mutt reached for one without taking her eyes off her book. They were creamy centers encased in milk chocolate. Perfect with the coffee. When Mutt did look up to observe Annie, she felt comforted by her nearness, and thought this was what it would be like if it were just the two of them. She liked it. She tried to enjoy it and not think about the imperfect situation back in Hollywood.

When the door at the end of the car opened, she automatically looked up to see a well-dressed man enter, a folded newspaper under his arm. He tipped his hat toward a woman near him, then scanned the passengers through thick-framed spectacles. Mutt was about to return to her book when the newcomer laid eyes on Annie and an expression of recognition lit up his face. Absorbed in her magazine, Annie didn't notice. The man edged his way along the aisle, closing in on them. He gazed briefly at Mutt, smiling congenially.

"Miss Montclair," he called cheerfully as he reached them. Annie looked up, blinking, as the man shoved his thick-fingered hand her way. "It is you, isn't it?"

"Sorry," Annie said, "have we met?"

"Not officially, no. I'm Lawrence Burdon of the *Hollywood Observer*."

His hand still offered, Annie shook it perfunctorily. Mutt put her book down, knowing that Annie was suspicious and wary of journalists, a reasonable position to take considering the secrets she shepherded. When she was out in public with Clive, she let him field questions from reporters, and when she was out on her own, she tried to avoid them.

Mr. Burdon took off his hat and looked pointedly at Mutt, waiting to be introduced. Annie frowned and said, "This is my friend Miss Hopper."

"How do you do?" Burdon smiled. "I'm so fortunate to encounter a pair of such lovely ladies this evening. I heard you were on the train, Miss Montclair, and was hoping to run into you." He turned to Mutt. "Miss Hopper, are you in show business too?"

Annie shook her head nearly imperceptibly, signaling Mutt to avoid giving out any information. Mutt didn't need to be warned. She had learned this lesson well.

"No," she said.

"Do you mind if I sit down?" He waved his hat toward the chair next to Annie's.

"I'd really rather you didn't," she said with a sweet smile. "We're on our way to a funeral and not in the mood for chit-chat."

"I see. I'm so sorry. Is it a family member?"

"It's my father," Mutt said.

"My condolences, Miss Hopper. Then I won't stay." He seemed to be about to move on, but a thought occurred to him. "You know, you might be interested in this, Miss Montclair." He pulled the newspaper from under his arm and opened it, commenting in hushed tones. "I was only just now reading this article about Harold Parkhurst, the screenwriter, being subpoenaed to testify before the House Un-American Activities Committee. It was rather shocking to think he might be a Communist. You do know him, don't you? He's a good friend of your husband, I believe."

Annie's expression was cool, her gaze unfriendly. "I have no idea," she replied. "Now if you'll excuse me, we'd like to be left in peace."

He folded the paper and tucked it under his arm. "Very well. It's getting positively frightening, don't you think, with all these Communists taking over Hollywood? The scary thing is, you can't tell, can you? You can't tell who's red by looking at them." He stared levelly at Annie. "They might look just like me...or you. But they won't be able to hide forever. They'll be rooted out like weeds in time."

Mutt stood and faced him, angered by his insinuations. "Will you leave now or will I call the conductor?"

Burdon put his hat back on and smiled, then turned and left the car. Mutt sat down, noting the look of dejection on Annie's face.

"What an ass!" Annie said. "I shouldn't have given your real name. What if he finds out who you are? About your prison record, I mean? Clive will be furious."

"I don't think Mr. Burdon was interested in me. He seemed to be fishing for information about Clive. You handled him well."

"Why is there so much hardness in the world?" Annie asked, sounding as if she were about to cry. "Why can't people just leave other people alone? I'm so tired of it. Hollywood is full of jealousy and spite. They're hard, cruel people out to destroy you so they can take your place. That's what success is about, Mutt, the never-ending struggle to keep from being brought down by the masses of people who resent you. These reporters are like piranhas. They won't stop until your bones are picked clean."

Mutt walked Annie to their berth, her arm around her shoulder, swaying side to side in the narrow gangway with the motion of the train. When they were alone with the curtain drawn, she spoke in whispers.

"Is Clive a Communist?"

"No. And I'm sure Harold Parkhurst isn't either. I wonder what they'll do to Harold, if he'll end up blacklisted. I can't imagine having to face that committee." She shuddered.

"If he's not a Communist, what can they do to him?"

"Clive says it doesn't matter if you're a Communist or not. If you don't cooperate, for whatever reason, they'll jail you for contempt or just make so many insinuations that your reputation will be ruined. You must know how ruthless people can be when they want to show you in a negative light."

Mutt thought briefly of the prosecutor at her own trial. He had made everybody on the jury believe that she was a whore and vicious killer motivated by greed and malice, and that she had murdered an innocent, unarmed boy in cold blood. She had learned from experience that truth is not nearly as simple as she had once thought.

"Even if Harold were a Communist," Annie whispered, "why is that a crime? Why can't people have different political views? I don't understand any of this. All I know is that this business with Harold is going to upset Clive terribly."

In the tenuous privacy of their berth, Mutt held and tried to comfort Annie, a woman who didn't seem nearly tough enough for the role she had volunteered for. But Mutt was relieved that Annie was still kindhearted and vulnerable, that the grit of Hollywood had not polished her into a cold stone. She had gained some sophistication, but her heart was still wide open and her enthusiasm for life was still completely intact.

How long could a person remain warm in a cold climate? Mutt pondered. If a person was Annie, perhaps forever. That would be enough of a reason all of its own to love her.

# CHAPTER TWENTY-SEVEN

A green 1947 Nash Suburban with wide whitewall tires dropped them off outside the sagging fence in front of the Hopper farmhouse. As soon as their luggage was out of the trunk, the car sped away, its heavy chrome bumper receding from view along the unpaved road that bordered the Hopper farm.

Mutt had been in a trance ever since arriving at the train station. Jenner Springs, with its handful of streets and landmark church steeple, looked just like it had the day she left. The movie theater where she and Ray and her father had spent their last afternoon together was still there, unchanged, its marquee advertising a science fiction double feature: *Abbott and Costello Meet the Invisible Man* and *Destination Moon*. The Rexall pharmacy still stood on Main Street, the same orange sign above the door, and the old schoolhouse with its bell tower looked just as it had during all of her years of grammar school.

It seemed like a lifetime had passed since she left, but it could have been just a few seconds for all the difference it had made to the town and the countryside around it.

The thing that struck her more than the familiarity of the buildings was the sound of people talking. The Southern drawl was thick and unrelenting. As soon as they left the train, the voices began to pour over her like a cool drink of water on a hot day. She'd forgotten what people sounded like down here. Her own accent had diminished and her speech had lost its brilliant palette of colors. These sounds struck her in some deep and fundamental place inside. Quite unexpectedly and instinctively, as soon as she had heard the voices, she felt she had come home.

She stood with her suitcase weighing down her left arm, mutely looking at the house and taking in the changes since she'd last seen it.

Most of the paint had peeled off, revealing gray wood. One of the beams supporting the porch was broken in two and the roof above it sagged dangerously. The windows were clouded by years of grime. The cherry tree that had stood in front of the house had been chopped down, its location marked by a foot-tall stump. Mutt was sorry to see it gone, remembering the deep, rich taste of the fruit.

At the side of the house, the post at one end of the clothesline had fallen over. The four lines of heavy wire were still connected, running in a tangle from the ground to the still-standing post at the other end.

The barn stood behind the house looking droopy overall, chipped red paint still giving the general impression of ruddiness. Next to it a familiar Ford pickup peeked out from a patch of dry grass. It looked like it hadn't moved in years. The fields lay fallow and the chicken houses were as derelict as the main house.

The whole place gave the impression of profound neglect, and it was hard to imagine that anybody had lived here for a long time. It was like a thing that had died and been left in the sun to slowly dry out, shrivel up and turn to dust.

Mutt gulped involuntarily and felt Annie's fingers wrap around her free hand. Annie had been unusually quiet on the ride from the train station. Observing the countryside with its sharecropper homesteads had left her thoughtful. "Look at how these people live!" she had remarked as they passed a row of tiny wooden shacks surrounded by bare dirt.

"There's a lot of poverty here," Mutt had replied.

As they passed dwelling after dwelling where families lived with only the barest of necessities, Annie had shaken her head, a look of compassionate disbelief on her face. What a contrast from glamorous Hollywood, Mutt thought. Annie had never seen true, large-scale poverty. It had apparently shaken her into silence.

Mutt was startled when the front door of the house swung open with a high-pitched squeak. A stout woman in a pale floral dress and a gingham apron came out shading her eyes with her hand. She wore a handkerchief over her colorless hair and wiped her hands on the apron. Her face, only vaguely familiar from a distant memory, broke into a smile suggesting both delight and relief. She took the porch stairs with a vigilant sideways gait, then hurried toward them and caught Mutt in a solid embrace.

"Shirley, you're home!" she cried. "It's been so long. Let me look at you, sweetheart. Y'all look so grown up! I wouldn't have recognized you if I ran into you at Woolworth's. I hope I didn't get your nice suit dirty." She faced Annie. "I haven't seen this girl since she was six years old. I can't hardly believe that." Turning back to Mutt, she said, "I've been cleaning in there. The place is filthy. Dirt and cobwebs everywhere. Land sakes, I'm sure I've got a head full of them critters." She brushed ineffectually near her hair with her hand.

"I didn't realize you'd be here," Mutt said, astonished at the disparity between her mental image of her cousin and the actual woman. She hadn't seen Opal since the day of her mother's funeral over twenty years ago. Back then, Opal had been a slender young woman with curly auburn hair and darting, lively eyes. She had moved about the house like a nervous animal, bringing people glasses of lemonade and oatmeal cookies, and periodically patting Mutt on the head with wordless grimaces of sympathy. It was that Cousin Opal who had lived in her mind all these years, so she was unprepared for this older, more matronly woman.

"I'm Annie, Mrs. Hopper." Annie extended her hand and Mutt realized she'd failed to make introductions. "I'm an old friend of Shirley's."

They shook hands warmly, Opal smiling at them both as if she couldn't get over them being here.

"I didn't want y'all to show up to an empty place. Not after such a long time gone. Besides, if you're aiming to stay here a couple of nights, you'll need fresh linens and things. This is not a fit place to stay, I told you that on the phone." She looked pointedly at Annie's dress. "Miss Annie here looks like she might be happier in a motel. Y'all are welcome to stay with us at the motor inn on the highway. It's nothing fancy, I daresay, but it's clean and comfortable."

"This will be just fine for me," Annie assured her.

"We'll stay here," Mutt agreed. "It's just a couple of days."

"Well, all right, suit yourself," Opal relented. "I got a few groceries. Breakfast things. Some eggs, bread and butter and some grits and bacon. We'll have supper out tomorrow after the funeral, then you're leaving on Friday, so that should do it."

Mutt felt dazed as she followed Opal to the porch.

"Watch that bottom step," she warned. "It's nearly rotted through. I purt near killed myself on that earlier today. If you fall through that, you'll go straight down to Hell, I'm sure of it. Ya'll want coffee? I managed to get that much ready for company. Oh, I'm so happy to see you, Shirley." Opal hugged her again.

"Coffee would be nice," Mutt said, putting her suitcase down on the porch.

"Can I help?" Annie offered. She followed Opal inside while Mutt stayed where she was and glanced around at the fences, fields and road. This view could have been a postcard from her childhood. It was timeless, just like Jenner Springs.

She was glad Opal was here. Arriving here would have been hard to take without her cheerful, fond presence. Mutt had always been glad of Opal's presence. She was the only person who had loved Mutt all her life, and it didn't matter to her what she had done or not done along the way. It didn't even matter that she had gone to prison for murder. Opal still wanted to stay connected and she still signed her birthday cards, "Love Fred and Opal." She probably didn't even care if Mutt was guilty or not or what the circumstances were. Some people would think that was important. They'd need those details so they would know how to feel about you. But regardless, Opal never wavered in how she felt. She loved Mutt because they were kin. It was a simple concept, yet too difficult for a lot of people. Opal was a simple woman, and Mutt decided there was a lot of value in that.

Her father, she reflected, had not been simple. She glanced over at the barn, thinking about him hanging himself there. Kirby Hopper had been troubled and restless, and the convolutions of his mind were endless. He was a man tormented by disappointments and regrets Mutt couldn't understand. Every day, he drank until he couldn't sit up and then he went to his bed and passed out. He would sleep hard for twelve or fourteen hours, an alcoholic sleep that gave him no rest.

When he finally woke, gradually and irritably, Mutt would give him several cups of coffee, washing away the dazed look in his pink-rimmed eyes. Then she'd feed him fried eggs and flapjacks to steady the shakiness of his hands. After a couple of hours, he would be pleasant, even industrious, getting dressed and doing a few chores, joking around with her and Ray. This was often when he would drive into town and buy the necessities of their daily life—a few pounds of meat, some cheese, vegetables and bread. And of course, another couple of bottles of whiskey. As long as Ray was around to tend to the chickens, they had a little money, enough to get by on. They never had a lot, but they were better off than many people because they owned some land. After Ray and the chickens were gone, Kirby Hopper survived on the money he got from sharecroppers. But from the looks of the fields, nobody was working this land anymore.

Sometimes in those early days Mutt would go into town with her father and he'd give her a dime. "Here you go, Mutt. Buy yourself something."

She never bought anything. She put the dimes in her piggy bank. Her brother was the opposite. He bought ten pieces of penny candy every time. He didn't even save back a penny. Then when Christmas came around their father gave Ray five dollars to buy presents with because he had no money. Mutt had to open up her piggy bank and use her own money for presents. "You're such a dope!" Ray would tell her. Maybe it was true. Certainly Ray had made the right choice for himself not saving money, considering how he ended up.

What had she been saving her money for anyway? She'd kept on doing it that way all her life, saving against the uncertain future. Even her father had disapproved. "Why don't you buy yourself something?" he'd say. "You take that money Fred and Opal sent you and buy yourself a nice dress or a doll to play with." But she never did. She put the five dollars from her birthday card in the piggy bank along with the dimes.

It seemed like nothing she had ever been or done had pleased her father, not from the first glimmers of her memory.

Ray would have considered her even more of a dope if he'd known that their father occasionally stole money from her piggy bank. Maybe he intended to replace it. It got easier for him, the more he did it, like everything he did that was wrong. Eventually she hid her money in a coffee can in the barn under a floorboard, and kept a few coins in the piggy bank so he'd have something to steal. She kept expecting him to feel sorry about it and give her money back, or at least quit taking it. But he never did. And she never confronted him. The money she'd saved in the coffee can had been what she took when she left. She remembered taking it from under the floor in the barn and counting it out. She had twenty-six dollars and thirty cents. For a crazy moment, she had considered leaving it behind on the kitchen table for him because she felt guilty for leaving.

Mutt had never known why her father was besieged by anger and despair. Ray thought it was because his wife had died young. That seemed too simple to Mutt. But she didn't know her father well enough to tease out the mystery of his troubled mind. He had been an infantry soldier in World War I and had spent time in France, but other than the way he occasionally slipped in a "beaucoup" or "parlez-vous," there was no mention of it. Maybe something happened to him during the war, she speculated, that never quit tormenting him.

Whatever the reason for his unhappiness, he had destroyed his life…literally. He had said more than once that he hoped someday he would simply not wake up, that the booze would overwhelm his heart and take him out of the world. He had apparently kept trying and kept waiting as the years went interminably on for him until he finally couldn't wait anymore and decided to be more decisive about it.

Mutt closed her eyes, wondering what he had been thinking as he put the noose around his neck. He wasn't the sort to write farewell notes, so wondering about his state of mind was all anybody could do. Was he sorry for all the pain he had caused? Did he ask God for forgiveness? Was he crying? Was he drunk? Did he think of her at all before he died? Had he ever thought of her as the years rolled by?

A soft pressure against her leg caused her to open her eyes and look down. Sitting beside her was a little dog, his white snout pointed straight up at her. She knelt and laid her palm on his head, stroking his floppy brown ears. His tail, black with a white tip, thumped on the floorboards as he pushed his wet nose between her fingers.

"Tippy?" she said, unbelieving. "Tippy, is it you?"

He responded by jumping up and placing his front paws on her, then licking her hand. She hugged him and put her face next to his, pressing him into her. It was Tippy, older and stockier, but it really was him and, incredibly, he seemed to remember her.

Her tears fell on his muzzle as she started to cry, overcome with the emotion of being in this place again with its reminders of a life she had been separated from for so long. She sat on the porch with the dog in her lap, letting him lick the teardrops from her cheeks.

She heard the squeak of the front door, then became aware of a presence behind her. Annie knelt and wrapped her arms around her from behind, saying, "What's the matter, Mutt? What's the matter? Can you tell me?"

"It's my dog," Mutt replied, her voice thick with emotion. "It's my dog, Tippy."

"Oh!" said Annie, as though she understood everything. Then she too started crying.

The three of them crouched on the porch together, a bundle of tears and tail wagging.

# CHAPTER TWENTY-EIGHT

"Parkhurst took the Fifth," Clive informed Gerald as the two men nursed their glasses of scotch in the front room.

"So he didn't give them any information. He didn't name anyone."

"He didn't, but he's done for. He'll be blacklisted like the others, you'll see." Clive stood leaning against the bar. Gerald sat on the arm of the sofa. On the other side of the room, Mutt and Annie played Old Maid at a card table, vaguely listening to the men talk about politics.

"Where is this going to end?" Gerald wondered aloud.

"I wish I knew. Parkhurst isn't a Communist. He isn't even a Communist sympathizer. He's just a union organizer. He's looking for a way to give the common man a leg up. And because of that, he won't be able to work in this town again."

"Things are getting out of hand," Gerald said. "It's gotten so that if you say your favorite kind of pie is banana cream instead of apple, you're automatically under suspicion of being a subversive."

"The studio is talking about making us sign a pledge of loyalty."

"Loyalty to what?" Gerald asked.

"Loyalty to American values. Some patriotic claptrap like that. We're supposed to promise not to make movies that criticize free enterprise and *the American way*. In other words, toe the line, rat out the Reds, the Jews and the homosexuals, or you can't work here anymore."

Annie shook her head, frowning. "This is upsetting," she said quietly. "So many people we know are being blacklisted."

Though Annie had been speaking only to Mutt, Clive turned toward them and said, "Well, darling, you won't need to worry about yourself, as it happens. Your contract is up next month and I've got some bad news. I'm afraid it's not going to be renewed."

"Not going to be renewed?"

He shook his head glumly. "I tried, but we suspected this was coming."

Mutt laid her hand over Annie's. "Oh, honey, I'm so sorry."

Annie hopped up from her chair. "Could I try with one of the other studios? Now that I'm a free agent…"

"Sure, you can try!" he said a little too cheerfully. He drew her into an embrace and stroked the back of her head, gazing at Mutt with a look of complicity, as if to say, "We'll do what we can to make her happy, but her dream of being an actress is over."

It really was over, Mutt realized. With no contract, there wouldn't even be a pretense anymore.

"Annie," Mutt said, "you promised me a long time ago that I could see your movie. When do you think we could do that?"

Annie turned and left Clive's embrace, her face pink. Before she could answer, Clive banged his fist on the bar and said, "Tonight! Let's go to the beach house, all four of us, and watch it tonight."

\* \* \*

In a darkened room with a dozen seats and a wall-high projection screen, the four of them watched a private viewing of *Coming of the Dawn*. Mutt and Annie sat beside one another in the front row, Mutt with her arm around Annie's shoulders. It was fun to see her in a movie, and Mutt enjoyed herself, trying not to be critical. After all, she was no movie critic. She had seen only a handful of movies in her life, so all of them seemed marvelous to her in some way or another.

Clive was the romantic leading man. Bianca Montclair, several years younger than the woman here tonight, was the distraction. She briefly derailed Clive's character from his true love with her youth and beauty and a devious woman's wiles that the real person had never possessed.

When the movie finished, Mutt clapped loudly and hugged Annie. Clive turned on the lights.

"That was really fun," Mutt said. "I loved watching you on the screen."

Annie smiled warmly.

"I'd like to go for a swim," Gerald said. "Anybody?"

"I'll join you," Clive said and followed him to the door. "Ladies?"

"Maybe later," Annie called with a wave of her arm. When they had gone, she sighed and held Mutt's hands between them. "I wasn't very good, was I?"

"I liked it. You were the most beautiful woman on the screen."

She laughed. "Mutt, you're so sweet. I suppose if I had gone to acting school, I might have had a chance in this business. For some reason I thought I could just walk into it fresh off the farm and be fabulous. I was naïve. I'm going to give up acting. I've decided. It's just a formality anyway. Nobody's going to cast me. In the end, it just wasn't for me. It was a child's fantasy." She seemed calmly resigned.

"What is for you, Annie? If you could do whatever you wanted, what would it be?"

Annie wriggled slightly and leaned into Mutt. "Be with you."

Mutt kissed the top of her head. "I mean for work."

"I don't know. It's the only thing I've done. Other than the charity work. I mean, I do enjoy that, especially when I can see the good it does, but it isn't a paying occupation."

"You don't have to have a paying occupation, do you? Not as long as you're married to Clive."

"That's true." She shook her head. "Oh, I have nothing to complain about. I have everything anybody could want."

Annie said that a lot, Mutt thought, that she had nothing to complain about, usually when complaining. She knew she was well off and few people would sympathize with her unfulfilled desires. But Mutt did sympathize. Annie had everything anybody could want except a sense of personal achievement.

After a few silent moments fingering a lock of Annie's hair, Mutt asked, "Do you ever think about leaving Clive?"

Annie pulled away, her eyes wide with surprise. "Leaving him?"

"Yes. To make a new life for yourself, a truer kind of life."

Annie's gaze searched Mutt's face. "What do you mean?"

*What do I mean?* Mutt wondered. There was an idea in her heart, an image of herself fleeing with Annie, the two of them running away together like that couple she had seen on a train once, the two young women with nothing to call their own but love. Were those two still alive? she wondered. Had they been able to survive on love? They had given up everything they had for it. What would Annie have to give up, what would she be willing to give up, for love?

"What do you mean leave Clive?" Annie asked again.

"You *could* leave him. I'm just saying you could if you wanted to."

"Maybe I could, but why would I? He's very good to me. He's very generous. Well, you know that. You're practically living with us. You benefit from his generosity as well as I do. We have everything. No wants at all. And best of all, you and I can be together. I don't know what you're getting at."

"I don't like living off his money. Do you?"

"It's not like he doesn't get something for it. And he has the money. He has plenty of money. In fact, I don't know why you're still working at that silly job of yours. Or why you keep that rented room. You're never there. It's just a waste of money."

"Silly job?" Mutt drew back.

"It pays almost nothing and you have to stand outside in the heat all day. What's the point? If you gave it up, we could have more time together."

"You really don't understand, do you?" She stood. "You might be okay with being a man's property, but I'm not. I don't belong to anyone and I hope I never do. Down South, that's known as slavery."

"Oh, Mutt! I'm not Clive's slave." She looked amused, as if the idea were absurd.

"Really? Can you do what you please? Can you go where you please and with whom? Do you own anything? Do you have anything at all that isn't given to you by Clive?"

"But that's the way it is for any wife. He doesn't treat me badly. And I don't even have to sleep with him. He doesn't beat me or starve me or make me work. That's what slavery is about. This is nothing like that."

"I think you're wrong, Annie. That isn't what slavery's about at all. Slavery is when one person owns another person. When she doesn't get paid a wage for the work she does and she isn't free to make decisions about her life."

Annie looked up with a cloud of doubt in her eyes. "You think you're better than me, don't you?"

"At least I belong to myself."

"That's ridiculous! You're a hotel doorman and you think you're better than every housewife in America?" Annie rose from the couch to face her, looking indignant. "Seriously, Mutt? You seem to enjoy all those steaks and imported cheeses Clive buys for you. And what about those nice boots you're wearing, Miss High and Mighty? You're not really supporting yourself, are you, despite your overblown pride about being a wage earner? The only reason you're not broke altogether is that you're living with us, fed with Clive's food, warmed with Clive's electricity, clothed with Clive's account at Bullock's."

Mutt felt herself getting hot. "Are you calling me a moocher?"

"If the boots fit…" Annie turned and stormed out of the theater, leaving Mutt stunned.

She stood where she was for a moment, trying to quiet her discontent, but the same urgent thought kept coming back to her over and over: *I can't live like this any longer.*

# CHAPTER TWENTY-NINE

Mutt awoke to the sound of screeching sea gulls and the dull roar of the surf. She could smell the ocean. She opened her eyes to see that it was morning, not the bright white of morning she was used to, but a grayish, wet-smelling kind of morning. She craned her neck to look out the window, seeing a soft gray layer of fog obscuring the sky. Beside her, Annie's breathing was deep and regular, her hand curled into a tight fist under her cheek.

After their argument of the previous night, they had made up before going to sleep, each of them apologizing to the other. Though they had let go of their anger, the source of it remained. At least it did for Mutt.

She slipped out of bed as carefully as she could and dressed quietly in the bathroom before walking through the sprawling, single-story house with its skylights and gleaming hardwood floors, following the aroma of coffee to the kitchen.

She found Clive at the kitchen table in his favorite forest green dressing gown reading a newspaper. He was clean-shaven and, as usual, every hair on his head was perfectly in place. He looked up and smiled as she entered. "Morning. Grab yourself a cup."

He folded the paper and put it aside as she sat opposite him with her coffee.

"Gerald's gone out for a walk on the beach."

"Annie's still asleep."

From the kitchen, they had a view of the coast with its rugged shoreline cliffs. Clive's property extended to the shore and behind them up into the coastal hills. The nearest neighbor was three miles away. The house itself was modern with clean lines and lots of windows unbroken by panes, giving liberal views of the ocean. Every few moments the waves hit the rocks on shore, sending up a lacework of foam and spray.

"How'd you sleep?" Clive asked.

"Not well. I had a restless night."

"The bed didn't suit you?"

"No, it wasn't the bed or the room or anything like that. This is a great place."

"You like it better than the city place?"

"Yes. I've never been comfortable with city life."

"No? Farm girl at heart?"

Mutt nodded and sipped the coffee, careful to avoid burning her mouth. "This is nothing like a farm, but still, it's natural and beautiful."

"Have you put your father's farm up for sale yet?"

"No. Not yet." She gazed into his deep-set eyes, aware that he had something on his mind.

"Why not?"

She hesitated, then glanced at the door, reassuring herself that they were alone. "I haven't decided to sell it."

His expression remained passive as he lit a cigarette. "Let's go out to the garden and talk. Bring your coffee."

He cinched up the belt on his dressing gown before leading the way out. They walked in silence over patio tile and past a fountain that wasn't running. It was white stone with a scalloped bowl. Above the bowl was a cherub balancing a pitcher on its chubby shoulder. They skirted the swimming pool and arrived at a wrought iron gazebo where a glass café table offered them a secluded place to sit. A light coat of dew dampened the surface of the table. Clive wiped it off with his handkerchief and held a chair for Mutt.

"You and I haven't had a serious talk," he said, taking his seat. "It's about time, don't you think?"

"Yes, I do."

"What are your plans, Shirley?" He leaned back in the chair and puffed on his cigarette.

She appreciated his directness and wondered why Annie had never asked her this question. She apparently thought they could go on like this indefinitely, even after last night's argument. Before bed she had said, "Mutt, I'm so sorry for suggesting you're a moocher. Of course it isn't true. I know you could be on your own if you wanted to, that the only reason you're living under Clive's roof is because I want you to, because that's the only way we can be together."

It wasn't the only way they could be together, but Mutt had said nothing because she didn't want to set off a new argument. Besides, she hadn't yet formed her plan fully in her mind. But during the night, as she lay in the dark with her thoughts, she had pieced together the random ideas she'd been having into a coherent scheme. It was just as well Clive wanted to talk because it would help her clarify her thoughts.

"I want to go home," she said.

"Home to Mississippi?"

"Yes. I've been all over this country, but no other place has ever felt like home to me. Being back there again for my daddy's funeral, I just felt it. That's where I belong. So I'm not going to sell the farm after all. I'm going to live there."

"Have you told Bianca?"

She shook her head. "Not yet. It's taken me a while to make up my mind."

"Are you sure you want to do that?" He put his cigarette in the ashtray, his expression one of concern.

"I'm sure. I've been here almost a year and I still don't feel comfortable. I appreciate everything you've done for me, but I have to go."

He took hold of one of her hands. "Please don't go, Shirley. What if I found you another job? Something more rewarding. I know people. Tell me what you'd like to do." His look was earnest, convincing Mutt that he really didn't want her to go. "Give me a little time and I'm sure I can arrange something."

"That's a kind offer, Clive, but I don't want you to arrange something. I want to be on my own. It's not just about a job or money. It's about self-sufficiency."

"I do understand that, really I do. But we're just talking about a little help to get you started in some trade. Then you'll carry on completely on your own and be very successful, I'm sure."

Mutt shook her head, frustrated. "That won't fix things for me. I don't think I can ever be happy unless I'm getting my hands dirty. I'm still a simple farmer's daughter in my heart. Besides, this whole situation isn't working. I can't go on with it, being Annie's secret lover, not being able to be open and honest. It's getting harder and harder for me to watch her pretending to be Mrs. Clive Sterling."

"Pretending?" He released her hand and looked at her levelly. "Legally, she *is* my wife."

Mutt wondered if he was suggesting that he could interfere with Annie's freedom. How far would he go to protect his carefully-constructed illusion?

"Look," he said gently, "it'll break her heart if you go. You don't want to do that."

"No, I don't want to hurt her. That's why I'm going to ask her to come with me."

He reeled back in his chair, looking startled. "You're what?"

"We're in love and we belong together."

"I've no doubt you're in love. But you must realize there's more to life than that. Even the deepest love can't make up for every kind of hardship, especially for someone unaccustomed to any kind of hardship."

"I know that." She felt like she was appealing to Annie's father. "But I'd work really hard to make her comfortable."

He shook his head. "From what she told me about this farm of yours, it would be completely out of the question for her to live there. It's a dump. It should be condemned. If it weren't in the poor, rural South, it would be condemned. It's not fit for human habitation, least of all by somebody like Bianca. The idea is utterly absurd."

Stricken by his harsh words, she wondered if Annie had felt such revulsion toward the farm. She was reminded of their conversation on the train when Annie had been unable to say which she liked best, the hobo style of riding or the first-class cushions. "I've gotten used to comfort," she had said. Had she told Clive the farm was "a dump"?

"It would obviously be a different kind of life," she admitted. "But she's not happy here."

"I agree. Frankly, she was happier before you arrived. At first, obviously, she was ecstatic. But now that the novelty has worn off, she's just as frustrated with the situation as you are. Your being here is a tremendous complication. Even if she doesn't know it consciously, she knows, like you and I do, that it can't endure. I've been wondering how much longer you'd stick it out."

"I don't want to leave Annie. But I can't stay."

"And you can't take her with you. You can't ask that of her, to give up everything for love. You know she'll go with you if you ask her. She'll let her heart cloud her judgment. You mustn't ask her. It's too much to ask. What you're proposing would tear her apart."

Mutt lowered her gaze to her coffee cup, feeling ambivalent. She recalled Annie's alarm at the suggestion that she could leave Clive.

"She has friends here," he continued. "She has her charity work. She has the comfort and stability of her legal standing as my wife. That protects her from a great deal of ugliness that I'm sure you understand. You may be oversimplifying the choice you would offer her. Would she trade in her furs and diamonds for love? No doubt she would. She's never really cared for those things. But it's not that simple. It's not just material things you'd be taking from her if you took her away to live in a miserable shack thousands of miles from everything she knows. What about the community? What about friends? One person isn't enough for anybody. Especially if the rest of the world turns its back on you. Or worse. You know what I'm talking about, don't you? Even here in liberal Hollywood, things can be rough for people like us. In the conservative, illiterate, lynch-happy South, what can the two of you expect?"

"Sometimes people who have nothing are more accepting."

"Well, that's just wishful thinking." He frowned and picked up his cigarette. "Not realistic at all. In some ways, Shirley, you're incredibly naïve and idealistic. I know you care about her. I know you want her to be happy. So do I. Before you force her to make such a devastating decision, consider whose interests you honestly have at heart. Consider what would be best for Bianca."

The puff of smoke he blew out of the side of his mouth was immediately whisked away by the sea breeze.

Mutt made a deliberate effort to choke back the sensation of doom rising in her throat. "I don't know what I can do," she said, mainly to herself.

"Considering what you've said, I don't think there's any question about that. If you feel you must leave, then you must leave...alone. It's the only honorable thing to do, and I know you're an honorable woman."

# CHAPTER THIRTY

A bead of sweat ran down Mutt's left temple. She wiped it off with the back of her hand, tamping down the loose earth at the base of the new tree she'd planted in the front yard. It was just a sapling, a foot taller than she was, with a few thin branches adorned with slender leaves. This was a Southern Belle peach, pale fleshed and sweet. Spring was the wrong time of year to plant a peach tree, but she didn't care. She wanted to get it started as soon as possible and not wait until bare-root season.

The stump of the old cherry tree lay nearby on the grass. Though it was a cool day, the hard labor of digging out the stump had left her hot and thirsty. The sky was a solid blanket of soggy gray clouds. It might rain, she thought hopefully. That would muddy in the new tree really well.

Once next spring rolled around and she could see new life sprouting under her careful husbandry, then she would truly feel rooted here. She felt a few raindrops on her head and ran for the porch where she stood under the shelter of the roof. Tippy tore across the yard gleefully, unafraid of the rain. He had always had a cheerful disposition. Whatever had happened to him in the many years of her absence, he was still happy to be alive. And so am I, she thought with satisfaction. Tippy rolled over on the wet grass, wriggling into it and letting the rain fall on his spotted white tummy.

She sat down on the smooth new steps to take off her muddy boots. The broken post had been replaced so the roof wouldn't fall in. She'd gotten rid of the old rocking chair with its faded fabric cushions and hoped to replace it come summer with a porch swing. When she could afford it. She hadn't bought much yet. She couldn't buy much yet. For now, her life was all about divestiture.

Little by little, task by task, she'd return the house to a livable condition like it was when she was little, not new, but clean and functional and decorated with homey touches that told you something about its occupant. In three weeks, she had made visible progress, though there was still a mountain of things to do.

So far she'd cleaned everything inside that Opal hadn't already gotten to. She'd thrown out rugs and curtains, getting everything dingy out of the house. New ivory-colored paint had done wonders to freshen up the rooms. One of the workmen who had come in to work on the electricity had admired her paint job and said, "A fresh coat of paint can erase a world of sin."

So it can, she thought.

After making the decision to live here, she'd worried that she might feel oppressed by her more unhappy memories of this house. Although she did sometimes think of them, she found she thought of them less being here than she had when she had lived elsewhere. She had at times been haunted by those memories, lying under a blanket on the damp ground with the open sky above, or later in her prison cell where there was so much time to ponder one's past. But here she tended to remember happier times from her childhood. She had even managed to recall a few memories of her mother, jarred loose from some dim region of her brain by the familiar surroundings. She had found a box of photos in the attic and had rescued several with yellowed edges, framing them and making a wall of faces to keep her company, relatives with benevolent smiles whom she imagined having the same concerns for her that Cousin Opal did. She liked to think they were invested in her happiness and her welfare because their blood ran through her veins.

The fact was that she finally felt at home and at peace in these surroundings, more benign now than they had ever been for her in the past. It had been the right decision to come back. She was excited about her future here, and for the first time in her life the future wasn't just a hazy fog in her mind. She could project herself ahead to a time when there would be corn growing in the fields, chickens clucking in the henhouses and a vegetable garden in back with big red beefsteak tomatoes hanging heavy on the vines in August. The only thing she couldn't picture was who she would share it with. She tried not to think about how empty her heart was or if it would ever be possible to fill it again. She would not let her heartache defeat her and take the joy out of living. She wasn't like her father. She was an optimist and a survivor. Time, she thought, would bring her comfort. And time would eventually allow her to smile when she remembered her Annie.

She'd gotten as far as untying one boot when she heard a vehicle approaching on the narrow dirt road. Tippy heard it too and ran to the gate, waiting expectantly for her to open it. She hurriedly retied the boot and arrived at the gate at the same time as the postman.

Walter Mitchell had been delivering mail on this route for thirty-five years, longer than Mutt had been alive. Recently his wife had died and his sixth grandchild had been born, two events that had happened almost simultaneously. One of his daughters, the youngest, was living with him temporarily to lessen the brutal shock of sudden loss.

Likewise, he knew a thing or two about her life, though she'd never been an open book in the way many people were.

"Hi, there, Mutt," he said cheerfully, his wrinkles deepening with his greeting. A few wisps of smoky gray hair peeked out from under his official post office cap. "I've got a card for you." He fished a blue pastel envelope from his bag and handed it over. "From your cousin Opal. Happy birthday!"

"Thanks." She glanced at the envelope to verify its sender, noting the familiar handwriting. A stray raindrop landed on it, darkening the blue paper. She looked up to meet Walter's eyes.

"Nothing else?"

He shook his head. "You expecting something else?"

"Not necessarily."

She had been hoping that Annie might send her a birthday card. She hadn't heard from her at all since she left Los Angeles three weeks ago. She hadn't really expected to. She and Clive had both agreed on the need for a clean break and he had no doubt advised Annie likewise.

"It would be best if you have no contact, at least for a while, until you can both move on and overcome the worst of it. I'll explain everything to her for you."

So Mutt had left a card on her dresser that said simply, "I love you with all my heart, but I have to live my own kind of life. Goodbye, my angel. Mutt."

"It seems like every day I stop by here," Walter said, "you've done something to spruce this place up. I see you fixed the gate."

"Yes. There's plenty to do. It's my full-time job now."

"It's wonderful to see it being cared for again. It reminds me of when your mama was alive. She was a lovely woman, your mama. So sad that she passed away so young." He shook his head. "You was just a young-un when she passed."

Mutt turned the envelope over in her hand, not knowing what to say.

"Oh!" he said suddenly, his wild gray eyebrows bouncing up on his forehead. "I've got a bag full of fresh baked bread in here to hand out. You want a loaf?"

"Sure!"

He dug in the back and produced a foot-long loaf of crusty bread. "Here you go."

"Are you selling it?"

"No, no. I'm giving it away. To tell you the truth, I think that daughter of mine is losing her mind. Maybe it's just simple grief. She spends hours in her mother's kitchen baking. Yessir, hours and hours. Maybe it gives her some comfort. I don't know. But we've been throwing cakes and pies and cookies to the hogs and chickens regular. I said, 'Carol, I can't eat all these baked goods. They're just going stale and I can't even give 'em away to folks if they're stale.' So she says, 'Then why not give them away as soon as I make them? That way, they won't go stale.' So that's what I'm doing. This batch was baked yesterday afternoon. I guess there's no harm in it, if it makes her feel better."

"It's good that you've got her there so you're not alone, even if she is feeding the whole county."

"That's true enough. Speaking of not being alone, people sort of expected you to bring a fella when we heard you was coming back here to live. Just speculation, mind you. Your daddy had nothing to say about you all those years. Not that he talked much at all. I almost never saw him. He wasn't what you'd call a sociable fella. But after being gone so long, folks figured you'd be married by now."

"No, Walter," she replied, avoiding his eyes. "I'm not the marrying kind."

He shuffled his feet. "Well, now, Mutt, that's no big surprise to me. People aren't all the same and that's the way God wants it."

Tippy jumped up and planted his front paws on Walter's trouser leg.

"Tippy," Mutt called, "get down!"

"Tippy?" Walter looked confused. "Isn't that the same dog your daddy had all these years?"

"That's right. Tippy's thirteen years old. He's been here since before I ran off."

"Your daddy didn't call him Tippy."

"What'd he call him?"

"He called him Mutt."

"He did?"

"Sure did. Just like that dog he had way back when. Way back before you were born when they first came to live here. That Mutt was a hound of some kind. A true mutt, he was." He shook his head, remembering. "They had that dog for quite a few years. I remember your mama having a hissy fit one day because your daddy started calling you Mutt too. You was about three years old then."

"I've never heard about this."

"No?" His eyebrows bounced up. "You mean you don't know how you got that nickname?"

She shook her head, realizing she didn't.

"Let me tell you, then! I came by to deliver the mail that day and your mama was fit to be tied. I could hear your daddy in the house hollering, 'Hey, Mutt! Come here, Mutt!' He just kept on like that, hollering and laughing to beat the band. Your mama comes out to get the mail and says, 'He thinks that's funny, calling our little Shirley Mutt like a good-for-nothing hound dog.' So I asked, 'Why's he calling her that?' She says, 'Because whenever he calls the dog, she comes too. He says she thinks her name's Mutt, so he may as well call her that.'"

Mutt was astonished. "Why didn't he ever tell me this story?"

"Maybe he thought he had. Or he told you when you were too young to remember. Your mama never called you Mutt, but once she was gone, that just became your name to folks around here. There's a lot of folks never even knew your name was Shirley."

"I don't remember that dog at all."

"He got hit by a car when you were still little. That's something, ain't it? This here dog's been Mutt to me the last ten years. I suppose your daddy called him that because he missed you, most likely. Still wanted to have a Mutt around the place."

Raindrops started falling in earnest, prompting Walter to say, "You get inside now so that bread don't get wet."

She retreated to the porch and sat on the top step out of the rain, pondering the story she had just heard as well as Walter's belief that her father had missed her. She supposed he had.

Eventually she opened the birthday card from Cousin Opal. As usual it contained a sentimental verse and was signed, "Love, Fred and Opal." Included inside the card was a crisp five-dollar bill. Mutt laughed. She wondered how old she would have to be before Opal quit putting a five-dollar bill in her birthday card. Maybe she would never stop. It was just what she did. She sent a card every year, and every year she put in a five-dollar bill. The rate of inflation over the last twenty-seven years did not seem to impress her. More likely, she just didn't consider changing anything. She didn't think of it at all. Mutt really liked that about Opal. You could count on everything always being the way it had been, and it was nice to be able to count on something.

# PART THREE

*Spring, 1951*

# CHAPTER THIRTY-ONE

Annie heard the door of her bedroom swing open. Through her closed and swollen eyelids, she detected the light that came in with it. She pushed her face deeper into her pillow, refusing to acknowledge the intruder. She assumed it was Clive arriving with another offer of comfort or sustenance as he had been doing for the last three weeks.

"Bianca, darling," he said softly, "it's nearly noon and lunch will be arriving shortly. Suppose you get up and join us."

She didn't answer, but he didn't leave. Instead, she felt the mattress sag as he sat down.

"Mrs. Hampton called this morning," he said. "Wondering why you haven't been to the meetings. She asked if you were ill. I told her you were and she sent her regrets." A moment of silence was followed by, "You haven't been out of the apartment for three weeks. Don't you think it's time you made an effort?"

The last time she had gone out was the day she found the goodbye card on her dresser from Mutt. As soon as she understood the ominous meaning there, she had made a desperate trip to

Mutt's building, hoping to catch her before she left, to beg her to stay or, if she couldn't be persuaded to stay, to beg her to take her along.

The note in the card held no explanation. Why did she have to leave? Why did she go so suddenly and without giving Annie a chance to talk to her?

Mutt's landlord, a sour middle-aged man named Wakely, had muttered, "She moved out."

"Where did she go?" Annie had asked frantically. "Did she give a forwarding address?"

Wakely had mutely shaken his head and shrugged.

Then, to make everything much worse, she had discovered that Clive had known about it. Mutt had confided in him that she would be leaving and neither of them had told her a thing.

"Where did she go?" she had demanded. "I have to go after her."

"Calm down," he had responded. "She didn't want you to go with her."

"What do you mean? Of course she wants me with her."

"No, she doesn't. If she had, why would she have left like this, making sure you couldn't follow?"

"Tell me where she is!"

"I don't know where she is. She sold the farm and planned to leave as soon as the money came through. After that, she said, she would start a new life…somewhere. She didn't say where."

Annie hadn't even known Mutt had found a buyer. She hadn't even known the property had been put up for sale. Mutt had done all of these things without telling her. Why? She was frantic, angry and hurt.

"She has relatives," she had realized, remembering Cousin Opal. "I can find out where she is from them."

"Bianca!" Clive had said sternly, "can't you see that she doesn't want you coming after her? Can't you see that she planned it this way?"

As despair seeped in to crowd out confusion, she began to realize he was right. Mutt had planned it this way, to flee and leave no trail to follow.

Annie had known that Mutt wasn't happy with their unusual situation, but this sudden and radical solution had been completely unexpected. For the three weeks since, she had been knocked down by her emotions, alternating between sorrow and anger, and unfit for any purpose. One day, overcome with rage, she had burned Mutt's card with its obviously false claim of love and the following day she mourned its loss in a torrent of tears. She had so little of Mutt to cling to. One of the few things, the cameo locket, had remained in her constant possession. Right now, it was tucked in the palm of her hand.

Her mind whirled with ideas about how to track Mutt down and romantic fantasies about her return. But she didn't return. And the ideas for tracking her down, like hiring a private detective, were discouraged by the knowledge that she didn't want to be tracked down. What would Annie do when the private eye found her? What would it feel like to call her up and hear her reluctant and unwelcoming small talk?

Her mind was muddled and tormented. She hadn't given up the idea of the private detective. If nothing else, she could demand an explanation from Mutt. "If you loved me, why did you leave me?"

Today she had resolved not to get out of bed at all. Today was Mutt's twenty-seventh birthday. She was somewhere out in the world, alone with no one to celebrate it with her.

"Darling," Clive said, laying a hand on the blanket covering her leg, "get up now and get dressed. Let's go shopping. It's time you got on with your life."

She rolled over and sat up, facing him. "What kind of life do I have without the woman I love?"

Clive looked at her indulgently. "The same kind you had before she arrived. Pretty damned good. She's gone now and you have to face that fact."

"Why did she go?" Annie groaned, slumping over herself.

"Because she didn't like it here. Fish out of water. And she didn't like our arrangement. We've been over this."

Yes, they'd been over it. Annie, too, had been over it in her mind many times. Mutt had told her that much, that she didn't like "our arrangement." But surely they could have found a better solution than this.

"She could have taken me with her. She could have at least asked. Why didn't she ask me?"

He tugged distractedly on the belt of his smoking jacket. He looked and sounded like he was bored. "Because she's realistic. She had nothing to offer you. Nothing compared to what you have here. She did it for you. She's a kind and sensible woman. She wants you to be happy."

"How could she possibly think I'd be happy without her?"

"You're so naïve, Bianca. Do you really think love is enough to make a person happy?" He sounded irritated. He stood and narrowed his eyes at her. "I've had enough of your self-indulgence. You're behaving like a spoiled child. It's time for you to get hold of yourself and get on with your life. With *our* life. Tomorrow night I expect you to be in top form for the Actors' Guild dinner. No more tears."

He turned and left the room, leaving Annie to consider what sort of life she could have had with Mutt, just the two of them, far away from this city and the regal pampering of her life.

"Am I nothing but a spoiled child?" she wondered. Given the choice Mutt had made, she had apparently seen her that way, the same way Clive did, naïve and immature, ill-equipped for life in the real world.

For the first time in three weeks, she began to consider that Mutt may have had valid reasons for leaving her behind.

Annie suddenly had a lot of questions about herself and no certain answers. All that was certain was that she was miserable.

# CHAPTER THIRTY-TWO

"I'm sorry, Mrs. Sterling," said Bennett Jepson on the phone, his British accent softening the edges of his consonants. "I've got nothing new to report."

"I don't understand," Annie replied, walking with the phone out to the balcony. "You've been on this case for three months and you've found absolutely nothing."

"When a person doesn't want to be found, it can be difficult."

"If she wanted to be found, I wouldn't have hired you."

"To be precise, madam, your husband hired me."

Annie gritted her teeth. After several arguments and much cajoling, she had finally persuaded Clive to hire a private detective to find Mutt. But this fellow, who Clive assured her was one of the best in the business, had so far turned up nothing.

"What about her cousin Opal Hopper?" asked Annie. "Did you talk to her again?"

"Yes. I rang her last week. She still doesn't know where Miss Hopper is. They have had no communication since the Hopper farm was sold. I assure you that if I learn anything, anything at all, I'll call you immediately."

Annie hung up in frustration and returned inside, trailing the phone cord behind her. Clive poured himself a martini at the bar and asked, "Do you want a drink?"

"No."

"Look, darling, what's the point of all this? Wouldn't you be happier if you just gave it up? If she wanted to see you, you'd have heard from her. She obviously doesn't want to be found. Jepson would have turned up something by now."

"I don't think he's trying." She slammed the phone down on the side table.

Clive sighed and dropped an olive in his glass.

Annie spun around to face him. "Maybe we should hire someone else."

"No! I've had enough of this. I'm going to tell Jepson he's done with it. I've been very indulgent with you for the last few months, but this whole business is over. There will be no more time and no more money spent on your Mutt."

His voice had an air of finality that Annie decided not to challenge. He took a sip from his glass, his pinkie finger extended. She realized that she resented him. She had never felt that way before. Money, she thought. That was the crux of it. She had no money. Everything she wanted, from taxi fare to a pair of shoes, had to be approved and procured by him. Because she had no money, he oversaw her every move and had the power to dictate what she ate, what she wore, where she went and with whom.

This fact, which Mutt had challenged her with, going so far as to call her Clive's slave, had never bothered her before. Perhaps because Clive had so much money and was so generous with it, and because he had almost never said no, she had unthinkingly accepted this fundamental truth about their relationship. She thought back to when she was destitute, sharing an apartment with other young, struggling working women, before she married Clive. She hadn't had much money then, but what she had was her own, and she decided how to spend it. She could take a dollar she had earned and buy a pair of earrings and nobody had anything to say about it. At the time, she had taken that for granted. She hadn't understood how much power and self-respect was conferred by a dollar bill one had earned oneself.

Mutt had understood that. She hadn't wanted to live off Clive's money, though Clive had no qualms about it himself. He made it effortless to take his money. It was freely given. That's what Annie had thought. But it wasn't really free. There was always a price. If you take something from someone, you owe something in return. It's implicit in the bargain. Maybe all you owe is gratitude, but that's not a small thing. It's enough to take away your freedom. Mutt had wanted her freedom. That's why she had to leave. It wasn't Annie she had left after all. It was Clive.

She recalled that evening at the beach house when Mutt had hedged mysteriously around the subject of their future. "You could leave Clive." What had she been suggesting? Was that some sort of proposal that Annie had failed to understand? If she had been willing and able to leave the security of Clive's patronage, could she and Mutt have had a life together?

The phone ringing shook her from her thoughts.

"Is this Mrs. Sterling?" asked a man's voice.

"Yes."

"Mrs. Sterling, I'm so happy to speak to you. This is Lawrence Burdon of the *Hollywood Observer*. You remember me, I hope. We met on a train several months ago."

Annie recalled the unpleasant encounter with irritation. "What do you want, Mr. Burdon?"

"I just wondered if you'd like to make a statement regarding the subpoena that was issued today calling you to testify."

"What? What are you talking about?"

"HUAC has subpoenaed you. Didn't you know?"

"HUAC?" Taken off guard, Annie stuttered.

Clive, alerted by the one word that could send him into a fury, dashed over and took the phone from her. "Who is this and what do you want?"

Annie lowered herself into a chair while Clive cursed at the reporter and slammed the phone down on him. Then he walked rapidly across the room, running a hand through his hair, staring at the floor, then walked back the other way before stopping and addressing her. "It's a damned lie! He's just trying to get my goat. Of all the nerve! I'm going to file a complaint about this. Imagine *you* being called before the Committee. It's absurd! How can he expect us to believe such an asinine lie? Why, you haven't got a political bone in your body. Ha! Could you even define Communism? My God, what would they do with your testimony, I have to wonder."

Again Annie felt the unfamiliar assault of resentment toward Clive. It was strong enough to chase away her alarm and confusion over the phone call.

"You really think I'm an idiot, don't you?" she asked flatly.

He stopped pacing and looked at her, his mouth agape. "What? Uh, well, no, I don't think you're an idiot. Not at all. What a thing to say. I think you're uninformed, that's all. You haven't shown much interest in politics." He chuckled uncomfortably. "I always got kind of a kick out of your WWLS work, for instance, because you've marched in a couple of demonstrations, chanting slogans like, 'Equal Rights for Women.' But whenever I've tried to talk to you about it, you haven't much to say. It seems as if you've been going through the motions rather vaguely. You just do it, but you don't think about it much. I'm sure that if you were really interested, you'd have no trouble bringing an intelligence to bear on the issues."

Annie had always respected Clive and she could see that he was sincere. Perhaps his assessment was accurate, she reflected with disappointment. Had she been simply not paying attention?

"The thing is," Clive continued, "I've been immersed in this whole business with HUAC for a long time, so if you ever were asked to testify, say in regard to me or my associates, I'd be able to coach you. You'd be prepared. I actually do expect to be called in eventually. I mean, they're hitting points all around me, aren't they? So it's not completely out of the question that you'd be questioned too. But this thing with the *Observer*, it's just a ruse. There's no possibility in the world that you would be subpoenaed before me. You're just not politically active. You have to admit that. I'm not saying you're stupid. I'm just saying you aren't involved."

"Yes, that's probably true. Perhaps I should pay more attention. Because you have a point. If you're called in, I should be prepared to support you."

"They probably wouldn't call you, though, even then. I don't want you to worry about it." He took her hand and smiled reassuringly. "This idiot Burdon is just trying to stir up trouble. He thinks he can trip you up and get you to say something about me or my friends."

Annie smiled to let him know she wasn't worried. As he gave her hand a final pat, the door burst open and Gerald surged into the room, out of breath, his eyes wild in a way Annie had never seen.

"Clive, my God!" he said. "Bianca's been subpoenaed!"

They both stared at him, unbelieving.

He nodded emphatically, trying to catch his breath. "Her women's group, the WWLS, has been listed as a Communist-run organization. All of its members have been called in for questioning."

Clive turned slowly to face Annie, his face suddenly drained of color.

# CHAPTER THIRTY-THREE

The crowd, the cameras, the intimidating-looking, dour-faced old men assembled to interrogate her, all made Annie feel small and frightened. For years she had yearned to be on television and now she would be. But this was a role she could not have anticipated. The headline on the front page of the newspaper this morning read, "Mrs. Clive Sterling Testifies before HUAC." She noticed that they didn't use her name as they did for other actresses. As an actress, she was nobody. She hadn't worked in a long time and most people had forgotten that she ever had. Apart from her identity as Mrs. Clive Sterling, she had no relevance. She was beginning to realize how powerless that made her.

The Chief Investigator, Raymond Crick, was an ebony-haired man with rounded shoulders. He wore thick-framed glasses that he continually put on and took off. He had a way of smiling reassurances before each question, perhaps as a device to disarm her and make her feel that it was just the two of them having a casual conversation. But she had been watching these proceedings all morning and had seen him at work, so she remained keenly aware. So far he had merely asked her how she felt, what her name was, where she lived and what sort of work she did. To the last question, she had replied, "Actress," but it left her feeling uncomfortable to say it here in this public forum with so many people from the movie industry in attendance.

Clive sat on the left, easily within her view. He was clearly anxious. She assumed that he was worried she would make a fool of herself or, worse, implicate him somehow. He had grilled her for hours on what was appropriate to say and what was not. He had insisted that she say nothing without consulting her attorney, Denton Tanager, a sharp-looking young man in an even sharper-looking gray suit. He sat beside her, his serious, beady black eyes darting back and forth between the participants. Annie had just met Tanager this morning. He had mimicked Clive by reminding her, "Whenever you're asked a question, Mrs. Sterling, let me give you the answer before you speak."

"Does that apply to my name and address as well?" she had asked resentfully. "Or the color of my eyes or my dress size?"

He had stared at her unamused. But she wasn't trying to be funny. She was angry. She was angry a lot these days. Her anger seemed to be aimed in all directions, even inwardly, and she didn't understand it. All she knew was that she could trace its beginnings back to the day Mutt had left her four months earlier.

Though Clive had paid off the private detective and taken him off the case, Annie had not abandoned her desire to find Mutt. She didn't know how she would do it, but she knew she would try again. And when she finally did find her, she would never leave her. She would do anything, give up anything, do whatever it took to keep them together.

She was angry at Mutt too. For doubting her. As Clive had explained it, Mutt had given up Annie to spare her the hardship of a life without luxury. *As if I would choose diamonds over the woman I love!* She was angry that Mutt didn't give her a chance to make her own choice. She was angry that Mutt and Clive had discussed the situation and made decisions without her. About her life. About what was *best* for her. What right did they have, either of them, to be so presumptuous? Why did they think she couldn't make important decisions or reason like an adult?

In her less angry moments, she could forgive them both because she had allowed herself to slide lazily into a life where decisions were made for her about practically everything. She hadn't taken responsibility for herself for a long time. So why shouldn't they bypass her input on this decision? Why shouldn't they consider her too passive, weak and self-indulgent to be able to make a monumental decision about her future?

She had once been a strong, spirited young woman with a passionate zest for life. But something had happened to her. Mutt had noticed it. She had said, "It seems this soft way of living has sucked some of the fight out of you."

Her mind kept returning to that night at the beach house when Mutt had asked her if she could leave Clive. In a roundabout way, her answer must have sounded like "No." She hadn't taken the question literally or seriously. She hadn't understood the real meaning behind it. What she had since reasoned out was that Mutt had wanted her to leave Clive and go away with her.

Annie had begun to understand that there were ways in which she had disappointed Mutt. She understood that things could have turned out differently if she had been stronger and braver. She was full of regret over her part in losing Mutt, and she lived for the opportunity to have another chance with her.

"Mrs. Sterling," Crick asked, "are you now or have you ever been a member of the Communist Party?"

"No, sir." Her voice echoed slightly with the amplification of the microphone.

It seemed that Clive and Mr. Tanager both nodded their heads in unison, punctuating her answer. She was their marionette, she mused, her every move and every word carefully scripted, to include what clothes she wore. Gerald had been her dresser today, choosing a sedate blue suit, understated white hat and white gloves with rows of three pearl-like buttons that she nervously fingered whenever she folded her hands on the table. On her jacket she wore the cameo brooch Mutt had given her, comforted by the idea that a tiny bit of Mutt was here with her on this trying occasion.

"Are you a member of the Women's Welfare and Literacy Society, hereafter known as the WWLS?" Crick removed his glasses and scrutinized her.

"Yes, I am."

"How long have you been a member of that organization?"

"One year."

"Can you describe for us, Mrs. Sterling, what sort of work the WWLS does? What is its purpose?"

Tanager leaned closer to her to say, "It's a charitable group that raises money for women's relief programs."

Annie said, "It's a charitable group that raises money for women's relief programs."

"How many members does the WWLS have?" Crick asked.

"I have no idea."

"But you attend meetings, do you not?" He deposited his glasses on his nose.

"Meetings?"

"We have heard testimony from others that weekly meetings are held at the home of Mrs. Riley Hampton."

Tanager leaned in to say, "Just say yes."

Annie frowned at him, then addressed Mr. Crick. "You mean our Wednesday tea parties?"

"If that's what you prefer to call them."

"That's what they are. We have tea and chat about this and that."

"Well, then, Mrs. Sterling, can you tell us what you chat about at these…tea parties?"

Tanager leaned over to offer some advice, but Annie proceeded without giving him a chance. "I'm sure you wouldn't be interested in that, Mr. Crick. Ladies' gossip. You don't look the type to appreciate that sort of thing."

There was an audible titter among the audience.

Mr. Crick stiffened, then smiled benignly. "I assure you, I *am* interested. Please tell us what you talk about."

"All right. Hair styles is a favorite topic, as you might imagine. And makeup. And we've often spent hours discussing hem lines." She glanced at Clive to see his face askew with perplexity.

"Do you ever discuss politics?" Crick asked.

"Politics? Oh, yes, of course."

"Just tell the truth," Tanager said without moving his lips, as if he were a ventriloquist.

"We've been known to talk about the president," Annie said. "Most of the ladies think that Mr. Truman is exceptionally handsome. We do enjoy seeing him on television. And Bess Truman, what a lovely woman. Don't you think she's lovely, Mr. Crick?"

He cleared his throat. "That's not exactly what I had in mind. Are you aware, Mrs. Sterling, that Congress has cited the WWLS as a Communist-led organization?"

"I have heard that recently."

"Do you know Mrs. Riley Hampton?"

"I dare say I must know her, mustn't I, since I go to her house for tea every Wednesday?" Annie smiled at the audience as scattered laughter arose from the room. She let go of the buttons on her glove, feeling more relaxed.

Crick pulled his glasses off. "How long have you known her?"

"Two years."

"In those two years, have you ever heard her say anything anti-American?"

"Anti-American? Could you explain that, Mr. Crick? Could you give me an example?"

"Anti-American, Mrs. Sterling, would be anything against the United States government, its president or its system of values."

"Its system of values? What exactly do you mean by that, sir?"

"Mrs. Sterling, have you ever heard Mrs. Hampton or any of the women of the WWLS say anything negative about the United States or any of its actions?"

Annie laughed lightly. "Do you mean have I ever heard them voice an opinion? A difference of opinion with American policies?"

"Yes, that's what I mean."

"Mr. Crick," Tanager said, raising his hand like a traffic cop. "Mr. Chairman, can I have a moment with my client?"

The chairman nodded.

"What are you doing?" Tanager whispered with his hand over the microphone. "Just answer the question."

Between her teeth, making sure her smile remained intact, Annie said, "Do you really expect me to tell them anything that might implicate any of my friends? Or anybody, for that matter?"

"You've sworn to tell the truth, so tell the truth. The sooner you answer their questions, the sooner you'll be out of here. They don't want you. They want the ringleaders."

Annie stared at him but said nothing. He turned to the front of the room and said, "Thank you, Mr. Chairman. We're ready to proceed."

"Answer the question, Mrs. Sterling," the chairman directed.

"As I understand the question, you want to know if anybody at our tea parties ever expressed an opinion."

"No, that is not the question," Mr. Crick said. "The question is, did anyone express any subversive opinions. What we are trying to get at, Mrs. Sterling, is the nature of propaganda put forth in the meetings of the WWLS and who was responsible for it. Are you aware that Mrs. Hampton is a member of the Communist Party?"

"I have no knowledge of that."

"Did you ever suspect it?"

"No, sir."

"Did nothing ever come up in your association with the WWLS that would lead you to suspect Communist sympathies."

"No, sir."

"Not even during the planning of your rallies? I have a photograph here of you marching in such a rally. Can you please verify that this is you?"

The photograph was handed to Annie.

"Is that you, Mrs. Sterling?" the chairman asked.

Annie handed the photo back to Crick. "That's me, yes."

Crick waved the photo over his head. "I offer this document in evidence as exhibit Sterling number one. Let it be known that the protest sign Mrs. Sterling is carrying reads, 'United We Will Win.'" He turned back to Annie. "What does that mean, in your opinion? United how? Win what?"

"Well, now that you ask, I'm sure I don't know. Anyone you talk to will tell you I'm completely ignorant when it comes to politics." She flashed a smile toward Clive.

"You were carrying the sign. You must have had some thoughts about what it meant."

Tanager leaned toward her and she elbowed him away. "No, no, not really. Someone gave it to me to carry, so I carried it."

"Who made the sign? Who gave it to you to carry?"

"I don't recall."

"Who planned this rally?"

"I don't recall."

"It wasn't that long ago, Mrs. Sterling. Surely you can remember…"

"I'm sorry. I can't."

"Well, then, can you tell me who else normally came to your tea parties?"

"No, sir."

Mr. Crick yanked off his glasses. "You went to these meetings every Wednesday for the last year and you can't tell me who was there?"

"I'm not very good with names."

The audience laughed unreservedly this time.

"We're not here to play games," Mr. Crick said. "Mr. Chairman, can I have a direction to answer?"

"I direct you to answer the question," the chairman said.

"I have answered. I've answered all of your questions."

"But you've answered them evasively," Crick pointed out. "You do want to cooperate with us and take these proceedings seriously. Failure to do so could result in a charge of contempt and a jail sentence."

Annie glanced at Clive, who looked horrified. She couldn't help but smile. She didn't want to implicate him in anything and she knew she couldn't disassociate herself from him. She couldn't suddenly be seen as an independent agent, however much she suddenly felt like one.

"I *am* cooperating, Mr. Crick," she said. "I've answered all of your questions. I'm sorry if my lack of understanding is frustrating you. I've never had any interest in politics. My only exposure to anything of this nature has been here this morning, and none of it has made any sense to me. The WWLS is a charitable organization that works for better living conditions for women and children. At Christmas time, we deliver food and toys to poor families. We fund programs to teach adults to read. We help fund shelters to care for people who have no place to go. That's my experience of the WWLS. If that's what you consider subversive Communist activity, then I am apparently a Communist myself."

A collective gasp rose up in the audience. Clive leapt to his feet and shouted, "No!"

"Sit down, Mr. Sterling," ordered the chairman.

Tanager grabbed her arm and said, "Take it back!"

"Are you saying you're a member of the Communist Party?" asked Crick.

"No," Annie answered calmly. "I'm saying that I don't understand what the WWLS is doing that you consider subversive. I've never heard or seen anything in this group that I would describe that way."

Crick slid his glasses up on his nose. "It may well be true that you and other members of the WWLS participated in these good works, but the true purpose of the WWLS is to raise money for the Communist Party. Let's go back to the question of who organized the protest rallies."

"I don't recall."

"Was it Mrs. Hampton?"

"I don't recall."

"Who normally took charge in your group?"

"Nobody comes to mind."

"Do you want to be found in contempt of this committee, Mrs. Sterling?"

Clive shook his head vigorously back and forth, looking thoroughly alarmed.

"No, sir," Annie said.

She could imagine the angry tirade she would face later when Clive would demand why she had deviated so dangerously from the script he had given her. Had she followed his script, the gist of which was to tell the truth as clearly and briefly as possible, she would have betrayed the women of her group, many of whom routinely expressed opinions criticizing government figures and policies, as everyone sometimes does. But perhaps even more importantly, she would have colluded with a process she found abhorrent. It had become clear to her as she sat in the audience all morning that this was a witch hunt, driven by fear and malice. Prior to today she had only vaguely understood what these hearings were about, half-listening to discussions between Clive and Gerald over morning coffee. It had always seemed to have nothing to do with her. Politics in general had always seemed impersonal and boring. But now she realized what Clive had been trying to tell her all along, that everything one does is political. Even doing nothing. Maybe especially that. She wondered how much he would object to her using his own words here today.

"From what I've heard this morning," she continued directly into the microphone, "the only requirement for being labeled subversive is to have an opinion. How is that anti-American? We're all different kinds of people, a fact that should be celebrated, not feared and punished. There's no single American mind. Everyone is entitled to his or her varying beliefs and opinions, and these are private matters, not crimes. It seems to me that the crime being committed here is your attempt to invade the privacy of American citizens with these inappropriate questions."

A round of applause burst forth from the audience. Annie caught Clive's eye. He looked stunned, then very slowly, a thin smile appeared on his face.

The chairman banged his gavel to silence the crowd.

"This speech is irrelevant," Crick objected, "and a distraction from the purpose of this investigation."

"Resume your line of questioning," the chairman instructed.

Though she was doing her best to confound the hearing, there were certain things Annie had said that were the absolute truth. For instance, she had carried a sign in a rally that said "United We Will Win" because someone had handed it to her. She really didn't know what was behind it. She didn't know what they were trying to win. She had chanted fervently along with the others. "Equal Pay for All!" "Free Women Now!" Yet she hadn't fully understood what they were protesting or what they were fighting for. She was like a dog in a pack, excited by being in the pack, but just a follower. She had managed to sidestep real involvement and deeper understanding, and now she was ashamed. Now she was like a woman who has just gotten her first pair of glasses and could suddenly see individual leaves on the trees. She didn't even know she had been missing anything before.

*From now on*, she thought, *I won't miss a thing*.

# CHAPTER THIRTY-FOUR

"Bianca, darling," Clive called from the hallway, "your diamond earrings aren't in the safe." He emerged into the living room wearing his trousers, socks and undershirt. "You know, the ones I gave you for your birthday."

She looked up from the book she was reading. "I know. I sold them."

"Sold them?"

"Yes, sold them. I also sold my furs and most of the other jewelry. I did not sell my phony wedding ring." She held up her left hand to display it.

"Phony—" he sputtered. "There's nothing phony about that ring. It's worth a fortune."

She shrugged and resumed her reading.

"What's the idea," he demanded, "selling all this stuff?"

"I need money."

"But all you have to do is ask. I'll buy you anything you want."

She closed the book in her lap. "No, not anything. I'm going to hire my own private detective to look for Mutt."

He rolled his eyes. "Not that again! Will you never get over that woman?"

"No. I never will. Never!"

He dropped onto the arm of the sofa. "This makes no sense. You sold all your valuables to hire a private detective, then you'll turn right around and expect me to buy you more furs and jewels. So it's not really your money, is it?"

"I don't want any more furs and jewels."

"Whether you want them or not, you have to have them. How would it look if my wife went about dressed in rags?"

She sighed in exasperation. "I don't know, Clive. How would it look? What kind of shock would the world go into if your wife were an ordinary woman instead of this doll you dress up?"

"You're in a bitchy mood today."

"Look. The things I sold were mine, even if you did buy them. But I'll pay you back if you want."

"Pay me back?" He laughed derisively. "With what?"

"I'm going to work."

"Work! Doing what?"

"I'm going to work in the cannery. They're hiring and there's no experience necessary."

He sprang off the couch. "No, you are not! My wife is not going to work in a cannery!" His look of outrage faded, replaced with a grin. "You're joking. You're pulling my leg. You would never survive a job like that. So dirty and exhausting."

"I'll manage."

His smile disappeared as he regarded her serious demeanor. "I don't understand. What has happened to you?"

"I want something of my own. I don't want to rely on you for everything. I need to do something useful."

He looked dumbfounded, returning to the arm of the sofa. He sat mutely for a moment, then noticed the book in her lap and asked, "What are you reading?"

"It's an autobiography of a man named Richard Wright. It's called *Black Boy*. It's about his life growing up in Mississippi."

"Your reading list lately is quite surprising. It used to be nothing but dime-store mystery novels. Is it for that class you're taking?"

"Yes. The books Professor Rios has us reading are eye-opening. I had no idea people wrote books like this. Books that can make you think things you never thought before and can change you, change you on some deep level way down inside." She turned the book up on its spine. "You know, Clive, we're so isolated from the real world."

"Bianca, this is the real world too. It's not the poor South or the punishing lines at the cannery, but it's real."

"It doesn't feel real to me." She gripped his arm. "Clive, I want to get my hands dirty!"

He glanced at her hand on his sleeve. "How's that supposed to work with that expensive manicure of yours?"

"Symbolically, Clive, for God's sake!"

"Really, Bianca? I've never heard you talk symbolically before. Is that something you've gotten from Professor Rios and those thought-provoking books?"

"Maybe so."

"Funny...your Mutt said the same thing to me, that she wanted to get her hands dirty. But I'm sure she meant it literally."

"Yes, she would have. And maybe I do too. I don't really know what I want to do, but I know it's not this. It probably never was. That dream I had as a girl, to be a glamorous actress, it was just my plan for escaping the conventional life that my mother and grandmother and all those women before me got trapped in. I didn't want to be like them, that's all. I didn't know who else I could be. I didn't have anyone to show me anything different. Just actresses in the movies. The characters they played were all strong-willed and full of passion. I wanted to be like them, but I couldn't separate the characters from the actresses themselves. I don't want to be Bianca Montclair anymore. That was just a childish fantasy. I want to be Annie Callahan again. Don't you ever want to be somebody else, Clive?"

He slid off the arm into the cushion beside her. "Actually, I've been thinking seriously about a change. HUAC is heating up again with a whole new round of Hollywood hearings. It's very unlikely that I'll escape being called this time."

"You might not be called."

"I might not, but I'm on edge all the time about it. Besides, the way things are going, it's no fun making movies here anymore. Some of the others have gone to Europe to make films. A whole little Hollywood is assembling over there with people who can't work here anymore. Good and talented people. I want to go there too."

"For how long?"

"Indefinitely."

"Oh, Clive!" Annie panicked. "I can't go to Europe. I don't want to go. I need to stay here and find Mutt."

"Yes, I know. I wasn't asking you to come with me. I've been thinking about this for a while now. Our arrangement isn't really working anymore. I know you're unhappy. Things are different. You've changed. You're not suited for the position anymore, really. As you said, you want something else. The woman posing as my wife needs to be content with that. Like you were in the beginning."

"You're firing me?"

He smiled. "You're going to divorce me. We'll trump up a story to give you grounds. I'm having an affair with some cute little blond, for instance. In a way, the scandal will solidify my reputation as a ladies' man, won't it?" He took hold of her hands between them. "There was a time it wouldn't have occurred to me to send you out into the world to fend for yourself. But I think you'll do fine. You seem such a capable woman now. I'm sure you can find something fascinating to do with yourself."

"I suppose," she said quietly.

"Is this idea all right with you? That we get a divorce and part ways?"

She nodded. "Yes. I do believe I've played this role out."

"And you should have gotten an Academy Award for it, darling!" He smiled fondly. "Okay, then. We'll get the ball rolling with the cute little blond story. We can keep this place as long as you need it. When the divorce is final, there will be alimony, of course."

"Oh, you don't need to—"

"It's okay. It'll help you get started in whatever new enterprise you fancy. Besides, you've been more than a wonderful wife to me.

You've been a great friend." His eyes watered with sentimental feeling.

She gave his hand a squeeze. "All right. That will be very helpful in the beginning."

"So it's settled. There will never have been a more amicable divorce than ours in the history of mankind."

"We should try to show a little bitterness, at least for the press."

"They'll eat it up. They do so love a scandal!" His mustache twitched with mischievous excitement. "Now, darling, before you hire that private eye, there's something else. I intended to tell you this if you agreed to the divorce. You're going to hate me. But, believe me, I did it because I thought it was best for you. I was trying to protect you from rushing headlong into a disaster. And yes, I admit it, I was selfish. I wanted to keep you here for obvious reasons." He glanced down at their clasped hands, avoiding her eyes. "Well, we both thought it was best for you to stay here with me."

"Both? What are you talking about?"

"Your Mutt and I." He looked up and seemed to steel himself. "I've misled you. I know where she is."

# CHAPTER THIRTY-FIVE

Mutt sat in the porch swing, Tippy curled up beside her, as the sun dipped lower in the west, turning the sky lavender. She wore shorts and a short-sleeved shirt, a glass of lemonade on the table beside her. In her lap was a book about World War I. This era had taken on added meaning because of her father's role in it. She had found some papers and memorabilia in a box in the attic, things packed away after the war and left untouched for decades, including letters he had written home to his new wife, Grace. They were love letters with sentiments any young man far from home would express for his bride. It was hard for Mutt to believe that Kirby Hopper had ever written such sweet and tender words, or that he had ever written letters at all.

Having discovered the sentimental side of him, she yearned to understand what had changed him from that loving young husband into a bitter, angry man bent on destroying himself.

The answers were most likely not in this book she was reading, but she reasoned that everything she found that went into making him was part of the answer, including a detailed description of the Battle of Soissons, fought in July, 1918. On the accompanying page was an artist's illustration of the Allied troops, including American infantrymen hunkered down in earth bunkers in a French wheat field. She didn't know if her father had fought in this battle, but he may have. So she tried to imagine him lying there on his belly in the sweltering heat of summer, hugging the ground as bullets flew over his head, thinking about the day when he would walk back into the arms of his bride.

She was distracted from her book by Joshua, her sixteen-year-old farmhand. He walked up slapping his gloves on his overalls to shake off the dust. He was a slight boy with uncommonly pretty features. He exceled in school and, despite the huge difficulties for a black boy from a poor family, hoped to somehow attend college. Mutt believed he would find a way to do it, as it seemed to be the only thing he cared to do. As summer had turned to fall, she had grown fond of Joshua, identifying as she often did with runts and underdogs. He had few friends and his father was hard on him, trying to bully him into manhood. He was a quiet young man who liked books, and his father had never learned to read. That was just the beginning of how wide the gap between them stretched.

"All done, Miss Hopper," he said, planting a dusty boot on the bottom step of the porch.

"That's fine, Josh. If you're thirsty, there's a pitcher of lemonade inside."

"I am thirsty!" He craned his neck to look at her book. "What are you reading?"

"A history book about World War One. I'll loan it to you when I'm finished."

"Thanks. I guess I've read all your other books already."

"That's true. Your appetite for books is even bigger than your appetite for apple pie."

His eyes widened. "Is there apple pie?"

"Not today, but tomorrow there might be a blackberry cobbler. Miss Ruta next door, you know her, don't you? She brought over half a dozen jars of berries she put up this summer. I'll tell you what, I haven't had a blackberry cobbler in a good long while, and I've got a mighty big hankering for it. When I told her that, she said she'd bake one for me tomorrow. And then she aims to show me how to do it myself. Truth be told, Josh, I'm not much of a cook."

"I know that, ma'am," he said in a mock serious tone, trying to suppress a grin. But it won out on him and he went into a full-fledged giggle to boot. When he recovered, he asked, "Is that a library book?"

"Yes."

"I've got a library card, but I hardly ever get to go to the library."

"Why's that?"

"Too far to ride a bicycle."

"That's true. Your daddy won't take you when he goes to town?"

"He thinks I read too much. He says it'll ruin my eyes and he can't afford to get me glasses. He says I should play baseball instead. But I don't want to play baseball. I'm no good at it. All the other fellas make fun of me. You won't believe this, but my daddy thinks books are evil. All except the Bible. But I've read the Bible so many times I can tell you what the apostle Matthew had for breakfast on this day in the year aught two."

Mutt laughed.

"When I'm older and have my own place," Joshua declared, "I'm going to build bookshelves all up and down every single wall in my house and fill them up with books. All kinds of books. I don't care what they're about. I like every kind of book there is and I don't believe any kind of book is evil."

"I gotta agree with you on that, Josh. It makes no sense to call a book evil. Or good either for that matter. But don't you tell anybody I said that."

He looked at her quizzically. "You're a mighty unusual woman, Miss Hopper."

"Am I?" She chuckled lightly. "If you only knew the half of it, young man…" She hooked a thumb toward the sad-looking vehicle by the barn. "If we ever get that old truck running again, we can both go to the library any time we want. Meanwhile, I'll have to rely on Miss Ruta and her boy Sam to get me back and forth."

"You have always depended on the kindness of strangers," he said with an odd formality. Apparently seeing her confusion, he said, "That's from a play by Tennessee Williams. *A Streetcar Named Desire*. Tennessee Williams is my hero."

"I've heard of Tennessee Williams, but I've never seen a play of any kind."

"Neither have I. But I've read them. Lots of them. I never told anybody this, Miss Hopper, but it's my particular dream to go to New York and see a Broadway play." He shook his head with the sheer magnitude of the thought. "*A Streetcar Named Desire* is one of my favorites. They've made it into a movie with Marlon Brando and Vivien Leigh. She plays Blanche DuBois, the one who says that line."

"Vivien Leigh?" One of Annie's original favorites, Mutt recalled. "Isn't that something?"

"I'd sell my teeth to see that movie."

Mutt smiled at Josh's melodramatic pronouncement. In some ways, he reminded her of Annie, which made her all the more fond of him.

"I'd like to see it too. Maybe we can figure out a way. Meanwhile, I'll get you some books at the library when I get back to town. Just let me know what kind you want."

"Really? Oh, Miss Hopper, you're a kind and fine lady! You are the kindest, finest lady in all of Mississippi."

She chuckled. "Okay, Josh."

"I'm gonna get me some of that lemonade now." He stepped past her on the way into the house, then stopped to ask, "Have you ever been married, Miss Hopper? I was just wondering."

Puzzled, she glanced up at his earnest brown eyes. "No, Josh. Never."

"Do you have a beau?"

She shook her head, wondering what was behind this line of questioning.

"Don't you want to get married?"

"No! I'm almost certain I never will be married."

"A person doesn't have to be married," he stated, then smiled as if he had discovered something new. "That's okay, isn't it?"

"Yes, it's okay. If there's nobody you want to marry, you don't have to get married."

He nodded. "Then I'm sure I will never be married too."

"There's no need to decide that today. You'd better get on home now if you're going to get there before dark."

"You know, I've been thinking." He ran his hand through his curly black hair, looking at the ground. "Since it's getting late and tomorrow's Saturday and I've got to be back here again first thing in the morning, would you mind too much if I slept in the barn tonight? I'm kinda tired and it's a sensible thing, don't you think?"

Mutt knew that he and his father had been arguing a lot lately. From their conversations, she understood that Josh and his father agreed on absolutely nothing, including Josh's future. There was no mystery as to why he might want a respite from his family.

"You don't think that old barn will fall down on you in the night?"

"Oh, no! It's as sound as a bell. The timber's strong. There's nothing wrong with that old barn that a paintbrush and broom can't fix. Maybe I can work on that after the henhouses."

"Okay. Go inside and call your folks. If they say so, I'll find a sheet and pillow and we'll make you a comfortable place out there. It's going to be a warm night, so I'm sort of tempted to sleep outside myself."

"When you were a hobo, Miss Hopper, I bet you slept outside plenty." His eyes brightened with the thought.

"I surely did. But not because I wanted to. Too much of the time it was cold and wet. I almost never had a nice place like that fine old barn to sleep in."

Mutt had been doing her best to dampen his flights of fancy regarding hoboing. She was afraid he was getting it in his head to run away. Early on she had told him stories, embellished for the sake of entertainment, about life on the road. But once she saw the spark of longing in his eyes, she'd put her efforts into discouraging him.

"Much obliged, Miss Hopper." He ran into the house to make the call.

She wondered why Joshua was so set against marriage and why he was thinking about such a thing at his age. Surely there was nobody pressuring him to get married. One unforeseen day his eyes would land on somebody and he'd fall in love, and then he'd want nothing more than to bind himself as irrevocably as possible to that person for the rest of his life. That kind of feeling is impossible to imagine when it hasn't yet happened to you.

It had been six months since she'd left Los Angeles and Annie, yet she thought of her and mourned the loss of her every day. Annie still lived in her blood and her brain as powerfully as ever. She had hoped the separation would allow her to find some peace eventually, and maybe it still would, but so far the ache inside felt as keen as it had the day she had written her farewell note and walked away from the Rutherford Hotel for the last time. There were many days that she fantasized about hopping on a train and heading west just to walk into Annie's arms again, if she'd have her. Then she started thinking about the kind of life she'd have there and had to talk herself out of it. This was where she belonged.

She hoped that Annie had fared better in moving forward with her life. She shut the book in her lap and laid it on the table beside her.

Looking out across the bare fields, she saw a cloud of dun-colored dust and knew a vehicle was on the road. Tippy ran barking for the gate as the car approached and slowed. Mutt didn't expect it to stop in front of her house, but it did, pulling a few feet past her gate. She stood, eying the car with amazement. It was a beautiful new Cadillac Sixty Special, candy apple red with gleaming chrome bumpers and a sleek, long body punctuated at the back with two short fins holding perky, gumdrop-shaped taillights that flickered as the driver turned off the engine. It was the kind of car never seen in this part of the world. Mutt had seen cars like this gliding past the Rutherford Hotel in Hollywood where there was no shortage of wealth. But such a car parked in front of her house in Jenner Springs, Mississippi was almost too much to believe.

She blinked hard, but the magnificent Cadillac was still there. She walked across the yard to the road just as the driver's side door opened and a small, slender woman with a blond ponytail stepped onto the gravel. She ripped off her sunglasses with the flair of someone unveiling a statue.

Mutt was struck dumb. She stood on her side of the fence, staring immobile for such a length of time that Annie finally put her hands on her hips and frowned.

"Aren't you gonna say howdy?" she asked. "Where's all that Southern hospitality I've heard about? A girl drives halfway across the country to see you and all she gets is a blinking idiot."

Mutt put her hands to her face in astonishment. Tears stung her eyes. Annie's face also dissolved into emotion as Mutt opened the gate and flew into her arms.

They clung to one another in a long and vigorous embrace. Mutt was overwhelmed with the smell and touch of her. It was Annie. It was really Annie.

"How did you get here?" Mutt asked, pulling away so she could look into Annie's face.

Annie laughed. "I drove, silly. All the way from Los Angeles."

"By yourself?"

Annie nodded. "Clive offered to come with me, but I wanted to do it on my own, as a symbolic gesture of independence. It was quite an adventure! I'll tell you all about it later." She spun around to face the house. "Why, look at this place! It's so inviting, all brightened up and cheerful. It doesn't look like the same place at all. You've done wonders with it!"

"Why didn't you call or write? Why didn't you tell me you were coming to visit?"

"I wanted to surprise you."

"You did! I thought I'd never see you again. I've been missing you like crazy. I can't believe you're really here. So you drove yourself all alone?" Mutt ran her palm across the smooth, cool surface of the car. "What a beauty!"

"It was a gift from Clive. He wanted to be sure I had a reliable car to make the trip." She opened the trunk to reveal three large suitcases. Tippy jumped up on his hind legs, peering into the trunk.

Mutt had concluded a thousand times that visiting Annie was a bad idea, but that didn't dampen her happiness at this moment one little bit. "How long are you staying? You brought enough luggage for three months."

"That depends." She turned to face Mutt. "How long would you like me to stay?"

"Oh, Good Lord, Annie, what a question! There's no sense asking me. I'd like you to stay forever!"

Annie's eyes were alive with joy and mischief. "That's what I was hoping. So the rest of my stuff will be delivered next week. Oh, don't worry, Mutt. I'm not bringing everything, just a couple of pieces of furniture. I sold most of it, just like I'm going to sell this car and get something more practical." She breathed deeply, glancing around at the house, the barn and the rolling fields beyond. "I'm so excited about living in a place like this, doing good, honest work among good, honest people!" She dove into Mutt, clinging to her. "I've been somebody else for so long. I just want to be myself now, Mutt, and have people know me, the real me, little Annie Callahan. Nobody knew who I was in Hollywood. I nearly forgot who I was myself."

Mutt was stunned, still unable to get her mind around this development. She was sure it wasn't real. How did this happen? She had so many questions.

"You're going to stay here, Annie? You're going to live here... with me?"

"Yes!" Her smile softened with uncertainty. "That is, if you want me."

"Are you crazy? There's nothing I want more."

Mutt clung to her warm, familiar body, and quickly found her lips with her own. With her hand on the small of Annie's back, she pressed her in close and kissed her passionately until they were both breathless and filled with wanting for one another.

When Mutt opened her eyes, she caught sight of Joshua over Annie's shoulder. He stood twenty feet away in the yard, his mouth hanging open in amazement. She had forgotten about him completely. She didn't know how long he'd been standing there, but he had seen all anybody needed to see to understand. She let her arms fall slack around Annie's waist and searched Joshua's eyes for a hint of his thoughts.

The stunned expression on his face abruptly changed into an unexpected smile, one of the biggest smiles she had ever seen on him. He was grinning, as the old folks say, like a possum eating a sweet tater.

*Oh, Lord!* she thought. *What a fool I've been!* She smiled back at him in relief and understanding.

"What did your mama say?" she asked him.

"She said yes," he announced triumphantly. "She said I could stay here anytime I felt like it, so long as I didn't bother you. She said you should take out of my wages for anything I eat. I know I only asked for tonight, but it's a long way back and forth, and as long as school's closer to here and all, there's no sense in me making the trip home every night." He held his hat in both hands in front of him. "I won't be any trouble, Miss Hopper. I promise."

"Who's this?" Annie asked.

"This is my hired hand, Joshua Brown. He's been a godsend, helping me get the henhouses back in operation. We only have a few chickens so far, but this'll soon be an egg farm again, Annie." She turned back to Joshua, who stepped over to the fence. "Josh, this is a dear old friend of mine, Annie Callahan. From now on she's going to be staying here too, so it looks like all of a sudden we've got ourselves a little family of sorts."

"How do you do, Miss Callahan," he said with a big, toothy smile. "I'm pleased as can be to meet you!"

Mutt grinned at them both and couldn't help feeling that every step she had taken in the twenty-seven years of her life had been leading her to this one moment and this one spot, that finally everything was about to fall into place for her. From now on, she would be living the life she was always meant to live.

"Josh," she said excitedly, "there's still a few apples on that tree out back. Go fetch them, will you? I'm going to make your mama's apple cake to celebrate."

His eyes brightened before he tore off around the side of the house.

"You think I don't know how to cook, don't you, Annie? Well, I was never much of a cook but I can make a mulligan stew and fry a chicken. And you're going to be happy enough with my eggs tomorrow morning. You won't find eggs like this in Hollywood, no, sir. Fresh as fresh gets. No silver trays, no. It won't be like room service at the Rutherford Hotel. There won't be any fancy French cheeses or somebody to change your sheets for you." She paused to take a breath, looking into Annie's fond blue eyes. "But we'll make do."

Annie looked amused. Mutt realized she'd been talking unusually fast.

"We'll make do just fine, my love." Annie slipped her arms around Mutt's waist. "Finer than a frog's hair."

# EPILOGUE

## *Present Day*

Covered with an even layer of sweat beads, the iced tea pitcher sat on the table next to the porch glider. Mutt poured herself a glass, then drank half of it down. She opened another birthday card, squinting into the setting sun. This one was from Joshua Brown in New York City. Finding a printed letter inside, she unfolded it and slipped on her reading glasses.

"Remembering you on your special day, my dear Miss Hopper. Happy birthday! I trust you will be happy to know that I'm about to be married. Can you believe it? I'll never forget the day I decided I would never marry all those years ago. Do you remember that? It was such a sense of relief to think I could make that choice for myself. It seemed such a radical choice at the time, but you'd done it, hadn't you? So I decided I could do it too. I could make choices that other people wouldn't understand and wouldn't approve of. Of course, it never occurred to either of us back then in the fifties that we would ever be able to make this choice, to marry the person we loved. Jeremy and I have been together thirty-five years, and we are just now getting married. This must be the longest courtship in history! Maybe not. I know a lesbian couple going on fifty years. They're getting married too. New York, you crazy, gay old town with all your senior newlyweds! What a heady time for us all!

"If you want to come for the wedding, you would be most warmly received, but I know it's hard for you to travel these days. We're planning to come out for the holidays to visit my sister. You know, the 'good' one. Jeremy and I will come by to see you then, for sure.

"In other news, I should probably retire and make way for playwrights with younger ideas, but I can't seem to stop writing. I'm working on a new play that has a character based on you. Loosely, I promise. It's partly autobiographical, partly allegorical, about a boy lost in despairing darkness until he meets a woman who seems like an ordinary woman, but turns out to be magical. Among other things, she teaches him to fly. Thank you, as always, for saving my life. All my love. Josh."

Mutt smiled to herself and slid the card back in the envelope. That boy was still fond of exaggeration. He was technically not a boy anymore, she realized. He had to be nearly seventy! She shook her head, unbelieving, and set the cards aside, saving the rest for later.

No card from Cousin Opal this year, she reminded herself. Even in times when there was no shortage of birthday greetings, she had always treasured Cousin Opal's card. True to expectations, it had never varied, always addressed to "Miss Shirley Hopper" and always containing a crisp five-dollar bill. And always, until Fred died, signed, "Love, Fred and Opal." Then Opal had become too sick to live alone and Mutt had brought her here during her final illness. She'd been gone several years now and Mutt missed her terribly. The Hopper family had worn mighty thin. Mutt was the last.

She shook off the sad thought of Opal's passing.

It had been a hot day with no wind. As evening approached, a small sip of relief moved in on a southerly breeze. It wasn't much, enough only to stir the daintiest of the dozens of wind chimes surrounding her. The one made of seashells, made by that sweet little Charmaine, jostled with delicate clinking. The one above the stairs made of tin cans, rusted top to bottom now, made a sound that took her back so far, back to cool nights on the ground with blankets of damp newspapers, her stomach full of mulligan stew, listening to the snapping of a campfire and cans rattling in the tree branches, sending her to sleep with their lullaby.

The sound took her back also to the day Annie had given the mobile to her. She had made it herself, tearing off labels and punching holes in the bottoms of the cans. Campbell's Pork and Beans. Del Monte Pears in Syrup. Maxwell Brothers Coffee. She had strung them together with wire and hung them from a hook between the two columns on the front porch. When she'd first seen and heard it, Mutt had been delighted and tremendously moved by the gift. The cans had been shiny then.

Beginning with Diana, the unwed mother Annie had rescued from the street, the young people had been inspired by Annie's creation to hang their own wind chimes here, a reminder of their stay. Over the years, one after another, the objects had multiplied so that the porch was now overrun with them.

She peered through the chimes to locate Diana's, geometric pieces of colored glass made from pop bottles and Mason jars. It made a pleasant tinkling sound, drowned out now by all the others. But when it was originally hung, it had been a charming companion to Annie's tin cans.

That was a long time ago, Mutt thought, thinking back to the day Annie had first mentioned Diana, about three months after her own arrival in that big, fancy candy apple red Cadillac.

"There's this girl I met the other day." Annie's voice had been serious and intense. "She's fifteen and pregnant. Her parents kicked her out when they found out about the baby and told her to go live with her baby's father."

"And she can't do that?" Mutt asked.

"No. She was raped by her uncle."

Mutt stiffened. "Did she tell her parents?"

"She tried to, but they don't believe her and her uncle has threatened to kill her. Right now, she's living in an alley behind a restaurant. She gets her food out of their trash. Mutt, I just can't bear it!" Annie's eyes welled up with tears. "I thought if we cleaned out your brother's old room and put a bed in there…"

"Yes!"

"Just until the baby comes," Annie pleaded. "By then I'll be able to get her some help. There's a place in Jackson for unwed mothers, but they're full up right now. I can get her on a waiting list."

"I said yes," Mutt replied gently.

Annie threw her arms around Mutt's neck, kissing her face. "I love you, Mutt," she had murmured gratefully.

That was the beginning of how things were here for decades. It hadn't been planned. It had just happened. First there was Josh living in the barn. Then there was Diana nursing her baby in Ray's old room. What a surprise it had been to Mutt to end up with a baby crying in this house. And that wasn't the only time it had happened either. Annie came across them in her travels around the county, children and young adults with no options and no resources. She made it her business to find them help, to take them where they needed to be, to reconcile them with family members, to get them into social service programs. When she couldn't find any other way to help them, they came here. The barn had become a dormitory. It wasn't always easy and it wasn't all fun, but it was gratifying, especially gratifying to Mutt to think that this place, a place where she had been hurt so badly, had become a refuge for these other children in need.

At times Mutt had been overwhelmed by the depth of their neediness, but Annie never seemed daunted. She had so much of herself to give. She wanted to be tired at the end of every day. From the very beginning, her energy had amazed Mutt. Somehow she just knew what needed to be done and she did it. She hadn't been here more than a week before she had sold her fancy car and bought a clunky-looking van.

"What're you going to do with that?" Mutt had asked, surprised by the choice.

"I'm going to start a bookmobile."

"A bookmobile? Why on earth do you want to do that?"

"I want to change the world!"

Then Mutt had watched with wonder as Annie outfitted her van with books and started touring the countryside dispensing literature…and much more.

"I went to Compton today," she said one evening about a month after starting her bookmobile. "Those people have never had a library before, traveling or otherwise. Women came in with half a dozen little ones looking for picture books for them. They didn't know how to read themselves, but their children will. And if I have anything to do with it, so will some of them!" She had waved her fork defiantly across the table at Mutt. "I told them about the adult literacy program at the county library, how they can take lessons for free. All they have to do is get themselves there, and if they can't manage that on their own, I'll take them."

Mutt smiled. "After you teach them how to read, then what?"

"That's up to them. Reading is the first step. It doesn't matter what they read, just that they do read. That's when they'll start thinking about possibilities. That's when they'll think beyond their own front doors. You were right about Hollywood, Mutt. Here is where we have to plant the seeds of change, here where there is the greatest need. I see so many people in this county with nothing. It's so sad. They have no hope. They know nobody cares about them and they have no future."

"You care about them."

"You're right. And I think they can see that. The looks on those women's faces today was exciting. You could just see them waking up to the idea that they could change their lives. I even registered four women to vote. Women got the vote more than thirty years ago, but this country is full of women who've never exercised that right. How do they expect things to get better? How do they expect government officials to represent their interests when they don't vote? Those white men in Washington will never care about the problems facing poor Negroes in the South if they don't apply pressure. A lot of pressure. It's all about who's going to vote for them…or against them. So that's what I tell them. If you want medicine for your sick kids, you have to vote. If you want your husbands to have jobs, you have to vote. If you want to control your own destiny, you have to vote. Because nobody's going to give you anything unless you ask for it."

"You really are a subversive, aren't you?"

"If it's subversive to want change, then yes I am."

"That's exactly what subversion is, honey. I'm mighty proud of you."

Annie had smiled thankfully, her mouth full of potatoes. Mutt really was proud of her. Thinking back to what she'd been like when they had reunited in Los Angeles, she was amazed. But this Annie was the Annie she had met in Nebraska. This was the Annie she had fallen in love with.

Oh, Annie! she thought, remembering many such evenings. Tireless, tireless Annie, with her endless crusades through the ages. Civil rights, women's liberation, gay rights. Their icebox, with its collection of magnets, read like a history of twentieth-century America.

She lifted the glass of iced tea and touched it against her cheek, letting the cold invade her skin. Annie never did regret coming here. Mutt was sure of that. They had been happy, truly happy.

In the distance, from the direction of the barn, she heard a girl squeal and a dog bark. They still called it the barn, but it was now "The Barn" with capital letters. One of the kids had painted those words on a plaque over the door.

Suddenly a dog appeared, running full speed across the front yard with something in his mouth. A second later, a teenage girl ran past, her smooth limbs bare and her long dark hair flying free. This was Lina, Mutt reminded herself, but wasn't convinced she had it right. The boys and girls blurred together after a while.

"Hey there," Mutt called.

The girl stopped abruptly and faced her. "Hi, Miss Hopper. I didn't see you there."

"What're y'all running after?"

"Tippy stole one of my headbands." The girl walked over and sat on the top step, eyeing the pile of mail on the table. "Wow! Are those all birthday cards?"

Mutt nodded. "It'll take me a week and a Sunday to get through all these. But this isn't even the half of it. I got a whole slew of e-cards on the computer this morning."

She shook her head, thinking about e-mail and all the changes computers had brought into people's lives. Poor Annie had never gotten the hang of computers, but Mutt had taken to them. She supposed she'd had a leg up just knowing how to touch type. She could thank the Tehachapi women's prison for that.

"The kids are making you something," said Lina, her smooth brown face lighting up with a sweet smile.

Mutt glanced around at the dozens of mobiles above her. "It wouldn't be something that hangs from a hook, would it?"

"I'm not gonna say. It's a secret. How old are you, Miss Hopper?"

"Oh, honey! I'm a genuine antique. I was born in the year of our Lord nineteen hundred and twenty-four, so you figure it out."

Lina squeezed one eye shut as she did the math, then grinned with her new understanding.

Figuring out that nobody was chasing him, the dog reappeared around the corner of the house, standing off a distance from the porch eyeing Lina, her purple headband in his mouth.

"Tippy!" she called, in a sweet, inviting voice. "Come here, boy."

He didn't move. Clearly, he was hoping to be chased some more.

Lina turned back to Mutt. "Why do you call all your dogs Tippy?"

"Same reason I call all you young'uns Honey. So I don't call you by the wrong name."

Lina gave her a cross-eyed look of skepticism.

"My first dog was named Tippy," Mutt explained, "and he lived to a proper old age before he caught the Westbound. When I got my second dog, I named her Duchess, but I kept forgetting and calling her Tippy. Pretty soon she thought that was her name, so we changed it. I've done had so many dogs named Tippy, I wouldn't be able to call them anything else. So that Tippy there, the one with your headband, is Short Tippy. And the one in the house is Slim Tippy. And then there's Gimpy Tippy, the three-legged one. They do have their own names, but it's just easier for this old brain to think Tippy. And that's why I call them all Tippy…Honey."

"Oh, Miss Hopper, you know my name!" Lina frowned in mock disapproval. Short Tippy shook his head rapidly back and forth, trying to interest her in their game.

"What kind of dog is Short Tippy?"

"He's a beagle mix. I don't know what he's mixed with. He's a mutt like all of them. Mutts and runts, that's what we got here. All rescued from some sad situation. I always figured that a poor mutt or runt that had a rough beginning deserved a better chance later on. It's how life balances out." Tippy barked, trying to get their attention.

"Are we having cake and ice cream?" Lina asked.

"Well, of course, child. You can't have a birthday without cake and ice cream. Bailey's churning the ice cream on the back porch. As far as I'm concerned, there is nothing better than home-churned vanilla ice cream. Put a scoop of that in a mug of root beer and you've got yourself one of the best things in God's creation. As for the cake, well, we'll see about cake. Cake may or may not appear, but Joanie's making something special for supper. I don't know what it is but it smells like it's come down from Heaven."

Tippy barked again and Lina leapt off the porch and ran after him, chasing him around the side of the house.

Up the road, a battered white van came into view and slowed as it approached, turning off the road into the side yard. It was decorated with a design of hardback book covers ringing it from the front bumper to the back doors. Above the row of books was the word "Bookmobile" in faded block lettering.

Annie emerged from the van and waved toward the porch, then went around to the passenger side to pull out a long pink box. She walked over, balancing the box across both arms with a cloth grocery bag swinging from one wrist. She wore a pair of brown hopsack pants and a blue, short-sleeved shirt, her white hair piled up and pinned in place. A few strands had come loose and hung across her cheek. She looked adorable, her cheeks flushed and her forehead shining with a thin layer of perspiration.

At the bottom of the steps, she handed the box up to Mutt, then climbed up, pulling herself along with a firm grip on the railing.

"Happy birthday, my love!" she beamed. "You thought I'd forget to pick up the cake, didn't you?"

"No, of course not! You left that big note to yourself on the board in the kitchen, so I knew you'd remember. *Pick up the cake*, it said with twenty exclamation points after it."

"But I might have forgotten since this morning. It happens... frequently. And honestly, I almost did forget the cake, but here it is and it's a masterpiece!" She pulled open the lid of the box to show it off.

The white surface of the cake was dominated with the head of a comical long-eared dog wearing an old-fashioned hat with a hole in it. "Happy Birthday, Mutt!" was written in red icing beside it.

Mutt chuckled and kissed Annie's cheek. "It's perfect."

"I thought so too."

"What's in the bag?"

"I picked you up some root beer. I had to go clear over to the Hickory Grove Co-op to get the kind you like, but you're worth a little trouble now and then, especially on your birthday."

The screen door opened behind them and Joanie appeared in a white apron, wiping her hands on a dish towel. With aspirations of being a professional chef, this girl had taken over all the cooking for the farm. Next year she'd graduate high school and Mutt was not looking forward to the day she left them to go to culinary school.

"I thought I heard you, Annie," she said. "Is that the cake?"

Mutt handed it over. "Can you put it inside for later?"

Joanie nodded. "Supper'll be ready in half an hour."

"Whatever you're making in there," Annie said, "it smells wonderful. I'll bet it's something we can't even pronounce."

Joanie smiled slyly, but did not reveal her surprise. She retreated into the house and Mutt returned to her seat, handing her iced tea glass to Annie. "Have some sweet tea, sweetie."

She took a swallow, then collapsed onto the porch swing. "I'm beat!"

"You were gone for hours."

"Yeah. Everything takes longer than it used to." Her face perked up with a thought. "While I was in town, I ran into that old coot Henry and finally talked him into that Main Street mural. He said, okay, okay, Annie Callahan. I can see you're not going to give up on this idea until you're dead. And maybe not even then."

*That old coot Henry* was Annie's way of referring to Henry Williams, the mayor of Jenner Springs.

Mutt patted her arm. "That'll make the kids at the high school happy."

"Absolutely. Henry thinks it's going to look sinister or, at best, pathetic. He doesn't know these kids. Some of them are extremely talented. You know, they're going to draw on the buildings anyway, so why not channel that impulse in a positive direction? Okay, so it'll be a little edgy. That's better than stodgy, isn't it?"

"I couldn't agree more." She took the tea glass back from Annie and refilled it. "I picked a peach off that tree today. First one."

"By all rights, that tree shouldn't have lived this long. You've got a magical thumb when it comes to plants."

"You treat 'em right and they'll hang around long past time."

Annie gave her a sideways glance. "That explains a lot of things, doesn't it?" She leaned all the way back in the glider, her legs splayed out in front of her. "I forgot to mention that I got an e-mail from Clive yesterday."

"Oh? How's old Clive?"

"Well, you know, he's old!" Annie laughed. "But he still likes to keep his hands in the business, if only as investor. His latest project is a documentary series about…" She grinned. "You'll never guess."

"What?"

"The Depression," Annie announced. "There will be a whole episode about the masses of homeless men and women traveling the country in search of work."

"Hobos."

"Right. Hobos. He wants them to interview you for the film. I think it'll be a hoot. You'll do it, won't you?"

Mutt shrugged. "Why not? But I'm not going to Hollywood. I'm too old to travel."

"That's okay. They'll send a film crew out here. He might even come himself. He's been talking about coming out for another visit for years. It'd be nice to see him again."

Annie sighed and laid her head back on the cushion. A fine series of wrinkles adorned her upper lip and deep creases lined her mouth. Her eyelids drooped low into the outer edges of her eyes.

*She is the most beautiful woman I have ever known*, Mutt marveled. Annie smiled fondly at her as if she had heard her thought. In her lively blue eyes, Mutt saw a sixteen-year-old girl with splendid dreams twirling in a makeshift cape in the dim interior of a horse barn and pronouncing, importantly, "How do you do? I'm Bianca Montclair."

Mutt reached over and took her hand, wrapping her fingers snugly around it. They silently watched the sun sink into rows of green cornstalks while a symphony of wind chimes escorted it into twilight.

Bella Books, Inc.

*Women. Books. Even Better Together.*

P.O. Box 10543
Tallahassee, FL 32302

Phone: 800-729-4992
**www.bellabooks.com**